JENNIFER JOYCE is a writer of romantic comedies who lives in Manchester with her two daughters and their Jack Russell, Luna. She's been scribbling down bits of stories for as long as she can remember, graduating from a pen to a typewriter and then an electronic typewriter. And she felt like the bee's knees typing on THAT. She now writes her books on a laptop (which has a proper delete button and everything).

Also by Jennifer Joyce

The Mince Pie Mix-Up
The Wedding Date
The Little Teashop of Broken Hearts
The Little Bed & Breakfast by the Sea
The Wedding That Changed Everything
The Single Mums' Picnic Club
The Accidental Life Swap
The Christmas Cupid

Our Last Summer

JENNIFER JOYCE

ONE PLACE. MANY STORIES

HQ
An imprint of HarperCollins*Publishers* Ltd
1 London Bridge Street
London SE1 9GF

www.harpercollins.co.uk

HarperCollins*Publishers*
Macken House, 39/40 Mayor Street Upper,
Dublin 1 D01 C9W8

This paperback edition 2023

1
First published in Great Britain by
HQ, an imprint of HarperCollins*Publishers* Ltd 2023

Copyright © Jennifer Joyce 2023

Jennifer Joyce asserts the moral right to be
identified as the author of this work.
A catalogue record for this book is
available from the British Library.

ISBN: 9780008581244

As always, for my amazing girls, Rianne and Isobel

Chapter 1

'Sorry, darling, the queue is horrendous. They've only got one person on the till and the line's nearly to the door.' The woman on the phone next to me places a finger to her lips and winks. We're not standing in a queue. We're not standing at all. We're perched on high stools at the airport bar. She has a glass of wine in front of her while I'm yet to be served. 'But I have managed to grab the perfume for your mum. I'll be as quick as I can.' She ends the call before taking a long sip of her wine.

'The hubby.' She jiggles the phone in her hand. 'I've left him at the play area with the kids while I grab some last-minute gifts.' She looks down by her feet, where there's a bag resting against her stool. 'Thought I'd give myself a five-minute wine break before I have to face nine hours in the air with a teething toddler and a lovesick pre-teen who's devastated at leaving her "true love" behind in LA.' She places her phone down on the bar so she can do the air quotes one-handed. 'The hubby does this sort of stuff all the time. I'm just popping to the shed for five minutes to fix this or that, he says – usually when his sister turns up with her demon kids – so this—' she holds up her glass '—is my shed.' She takes a sip of her wine. 'Are you travelling on your own or have you escaped for a breather too?'

'I'm on my own.'

The woman raises her wine glass again. 'Lucky you.'

'I don't feel so lucky. I'm on my way back home for my little sister's wedding without a plus-one.'

The woman tilts her head to one side. 'Ouch. But still not as bad as dealing with a screaming kid while your husband pretends to be asleep. Want to swap places? I'll go to your sister's wedding and get very, very drunk and you can administer Calpol to a toddler and offer heartfelt advice to a dejected eleven-year-old who will "never love again" after saying goodbye to her "holiday romance".' She does the single-handed air quotes again.

'I'd quite like to get very, very drunk actually.' Starting now. I haven't been home for four years and I'm not looking forward to it – and not just because Heather's getting married. I shoot a hopeful glance at the barman but he's still serving the massive group of lads at the other end of the bar.

'Me too, but I can't leave Phil and the kids much longer. We're due to board in twenty minutes.'

There's almost an hour until my flight and I'm not sure whether this is a good thing or bad. On the one hand, I have a bit of a reprieve before I have to board, but on the other it's simply prolonging the agony. It feels like I'm in the dentist's waiting room instead of an airport bar, my anxiety wanting me to stay forever on the plastic seat but the throbbing, excruciating pain wanting the tooth yanked, asap. My stomach is a jumble of nerves and I can feel my armpits prickling as I tap my nails against the bar.

I really need a drink.

'You look like you need this more than I do.' She offers me her glass of wine but, tempting as it is to down it, I'd rather wait for something a bit more potent than the dregs of a stranger's glass of wine. I've been feeling a sense of foreboding over this trip from the start, but it isn't as though I have a choice in the matter. I can't say thank you very much for the invitation but I'd rather stay in LA if you don't mind. As desperate as I am to stay

2

in California, I can't. Believe me, I've tried to think of excuses not to return to the UK, but none would have been sufficient to get me out of this journey back home. I'm going back to England, to Little Heaton, whether I like it or not.

I really, *really* need that drink.

I crane my neck to try to see past the group of lads, so that I can shoot such a heart-rendingly pleading look at the barman that he takes pity on me and throws a drink my way, but the gathering at the bar is far too big and I can't even see the member of staff I glimpsed on my way inside. There must be at least fifteen guys and they're all pretty beefy, with broad shoulders and what appears to be a couple of boulders tucked under the sleeves of their T-shirts. My best friend Yvonne would *love* to be here right now, surrounded by a pack of all-American guys who are buzzing about whatever adventure they're about to embark on.

They're showing off their super-white teeth as they laugh and joke, slapping each other on the back and play-punching each other on the arm. High on life, it seems, but then I bet *they're* not heading to a boring, sleepy little village where everybody knows your business before you do. I bet they're going somewhere exciting. Somewhere fun and wondrous and life-affirming – trekking the Inca Trail to Machu Picchu, a walking safari in Kenya, snorkelling with sharks in the Galapagos or climbing Mount Kilimanjaro in . . . the place where Mount Kilimanjaro is.

These men are jetting off for a fun-filled time and I'm being dumped on the set of *Emmerdale*, but without the murders, stalking and affairs to liven the place up. If I sound jaded, it's because I am; I'm thirty-two, very much single, and I'm about to travel thousands of miles to attend the wedding of *my little sister*. I mean, she's twenty-six for goodness' sake. What business does she have living happily ever after with the man of her dreams while some of us go home to an empty apartment every night to eat sad little meals-for-one in front of the telly? And it isn't even good telly because your viewing is interrupted with adverts for erectile disfunction medication every thirty seconds. Kim Wilde never mentioned *that* when she was bragging about being a kid in America, did she?

Maybe I will have the dregs of that wine after all. Except my new friend has just polished it off and is slipping off her stool.

'Better go and rescue Phil. I hope you have a nice time at the wedding.' She stoops down to pick up her shopping bag. 'And you never know, you might meet somebody.' She winks before turning to rejoin her family and I could weep with relief when I see the all-Americans finally move away from the bar with jugs of beer. The barman heads towards me, a slightly smug smile on his face as he closes the small gap between us with a confident swagger, and I fight the urge to yell at him to hurry up. I'm in desperate need of a drink to steady my nerves about the fact that I'm going to see everyone back home in Little Heaton for the first time in four years. Mum, Dad and Heather. Yvonne. *Tomasz.*

My stomach lurches and I have to clutch onto the bar for support. I can't do this. I can't get on this plane and go back home where I'll have to face up to what I did. What I lost.

'Anything, ma'am?'

The barman is resting his forearms on the bar and leaning towards me, his smile less self-assured than it was a moment ago, his eyebrows pulled down low. I guess he's asked me what I want to drink at least once before and he's wondering why I'm gazing at him like an idiot. Or maybe he thinks I fancy him. He probably gets that a lot. His shirtsleeves are rolled up, showing off tanned, toned forearms, and he's got the sort of messy hairstyle that looks like he's just rolled out of bed when really he'll have been perfecting the look at the mirror for ages. He reminds me of Ed: the height, the hair, the smile that makes his whole face light up. He doesn't have Ed's tattoo, though. His inner wrist is free of Butters from South Park, which had seemed a ludicrous image to brand yourself with at the time, but now I miss seeing it. I can't watch *South Park* anymore

4

because it brings back memories of Ed that are too painful to revisit. I'd take the adverts for erectile dysfunction meds over those recollections any day.

'A clementine Bellini. Please.' I only just remember to tack the 'please' on at the end. It isn't the barman's fault that he reminds me of Ed, that seeing him on the other side of the bar is dredging up memories of that night in Little Heaton. I can practically feel the roar of the motorbike as it sped off into the distance, can taste the fear as it disappeared from view, the roar diminishing to a rumble. It has been four years since the accident but still the grief rises all over again as I think of that night and I remember the hysteria as the news travelled around the village. I want to press my hands to my ears to drown out the wail as Ed's mum thrashed in her husband's arms as she tried to break free so she could run to her baby and save him. But it was already too late. Ed was dead. None of us would ever see him again.

Where's that drink?

'Thank you.' I manage to pull my lips into something that vaguely resembles a smile as the barman places the glass down in front of me. It's served in a champagne flute with an orange slice sitting on the rim while a twist of peel bobs on the surface.

'Nice accent.' He tilts his head to one side and narrows his eyes. He doesn't sound like Ed, which is a relief. 'You're British?'

'Yes.' I take a demure sip of the cocktail. I want to down the whole lot in one go but manage to hold back so I don't come across as a drunk. Plus, I don't want to choke on the orange peel. As much as I'd like a man to wrap his arms around me, I don't think performing the Heimlich manoeuvre counts as a romantic move, not even after four years of being single.

'London, right?' The barman points his finger at me, grinning as though he's hit the jackpot.

'Cheshire.'

'Chesh-uh?' He shakes his head. 'I haven't heard of that place. Is that near Edinburgh?'

'Closer to Manchester. Excuse me, but I need to make a call.' I slip off my stool and grab my drink, placing the money for the drink down on the bar, including a generous tip to make up for my flakiness, and head for a table in the corner. Yvonne should be home from work by now, so I FaceTime her, hoping she'll pick up and take my mind off the fact I'm about to stuff myself into a tin can that will somehow travel through the air at mind-blowing speed before dropping me off to the place where I lived through an actual nightmare. I'll have to wander the streets suffused with memories of Ed – and of Tomasz. Because I lost one of my best friends the night of the accident but I also lost the love of my life too. Tomasz is alive and well but what we had is gone forever.

'Elodie!' My best friend's face appears on my screen, her cheeks all puffed up as she grins at me. 'Are you at the airport?' Her grin falters and there's a hint of suspicion in her voice. 'Please tell me you're at the airport.'

'I am. I promise. I'm in the airport bar. See?' I turn my phone and pan around before turning the screen towards me again. The barman is faffing about with a cocktail shaker but he's too far away for Yvonne to see how much he looks like Ed. I'd show her the group of all-American guys but she'd probably drool all over the screen.

'Good, because I can't wait to see you.'

'You're seeing me now.' I wave at the screen with my free hand. 'Hello. It's me – Elodie.'

Yvonne raises her eyebrows while the rest of her face remains blank. 'Yeah, because this is the same as seeing you right in front of me. The same as hugging you. Man, I miss our hugs. I can't believe it's been four years since we last had a squish.'

I remember that last squish. It was at a different airport, in a different country. A different *life*.

'I miss our squishes too.'

'I'm going to give you the *biggest* squish when you get here.' Yvonne bounces up and down and clasps her hands together. 'I'm so excited. When do you board?'

My stomach churns. 'About forty-five minutes.' I take a sip of my drink to try to settle the nerves.

'Is that a cocktail?' Yvonne leans forward to get a better look. 'What time is it there?'

I press my lips together as I place the glass back down on the table. When I speak, my voice is small. 'Ten a.m.'

'*Nice.*'

'I thought it might take the edge off. I'm really not looking forward to being back home.' I look down at the table, focusing on a deep scratch in the dark wood. 'I'm not sure I can do it.'

'Elodie Parker.' I can't bring myself to look up at the screen of my phone, but I can guess what my friend's expression is like from the stern tone of her voice. 'Stop being a scaredy-cat and get your arse on that plane.'

Yvonne has always been on hand with her encouragement over the years: *Elodie, stop being a scaredy-cat and say yes. You'd be perfect for this promotion. Elodie, stop being a scaredy-cat and go over and talk to him. Ask if you can have a ride. Elodie Parker, stop being a scaredy-cat and tell him you're sorry, before it's too late.*

'You cannot miss your sister's *wedding.*'

'Can't I? Please?'

Yvonne gives a wry smile. 'It won't be that bad. And it could be worse – you could be a bridesmaid. I bet she's making them wear something hideous, just so she looks even more amazing.'

'That would be such a Heather thing to do.' I nod before dropping my gaze back to the scratch on the tabletop. 'It's just . . .'

Tomasz. What if I bump into him after all this time? Little Heaton is a pretty small place. Suffocatingly tiny. What if he looks happy? Happier than he was with me, if that's even possible? Because I don't want to sound arrogant but we were blissfully happy before the accident. We had plans for the future. Big, exciting plans.

But also, what if I *don't* see him? Because as much as I'm filled with dread at the thought of seeing him after all this time, after everything that happened, the things I said, I'm also scared that I won't see him. Ever again. And that makes me ache. I never allow myself to think about him usually, which is much easier here in California with thousands of miles between us, but back home it'll be different, because even if I do manage to avoid him, there will be reminders of him, of us, everywhere.

'Do you ever . . .' I brave a peek at my friend. She's sitting forward, her face filling up the screen, wating for me to elaborate. 'Do you ever . . .'

Yvonne tilts her head to one side as I falter again. 'Do I ever what?'

I suck in a breath and hold it for a second or two before I puff it out. 'Do you ever wish you could go back and do things differently?'

Because I do. I wish, with all my heart, that I could go back and change it all. Grabbing my cocktail, I fish out the orange peel twist and dump it on the table so I can drain the glass in one go, hoping that the alcohol will help to numb the pain of going back to the place where it all went so horribly wrong.

Chapter 2

After another cocktail and with encouragement from Yvonne (which included threats of violence if I failed to show up) I'm now crammed into my seat on the plane, too hot and stuffy, with a too-chatty neighbour on one side and someone already snoring on the other. Boarding had caused a welcome distraction from the fact I'm on my way home, but the nerves kick up another gear as I buckle my seatbelt. The safety video is being played while the cabin crew demonstrate what to do with oxygen masks and life jackets in case of emergency, but I need an oxygen mask right now as I struggle to gulp down enough air. We're actually moving along the tarmac and any minute now we'll pick up speed and bump up into the air, up into the clouds, and I'll be racing towards Little Heaton.

'You okay there, honey?'

The woman sitting next to me leans her head towards me to check on me as I clutch at both armrests, my breathing coming in panicked little puffs.

'Do you think it's too late to get off?'

She gives the rattly laugh of a heavy smoker. 'Probably a teensy bit too late, I'm afraid. But you'll be fine, I promise. There's really nothing to worry about. You're more likely to get hit crossing the street than the plane going down in flames.'

'It's not the flying bit I'm afraid of.' It's what comes after. The Tomasz bit.

'You're British.'

Before the safety demonstration, my neighbour had been chattering on since she plonked herself into the aisle seat next to me, but I realise now that this is the first time I've actually spoken myself. I've been far too busy trying to not freak out to form words. Perhaps the alcohol is starting to work after all if I'm managing to communicate by means other than panicked, rapid eye blinks.

'You going home?'

I nod, squeezing the armrests again when I realise my grip has loosened ever so slightly. 'Only for a visit. My sister's getting married.'

The woman beams at me – a proper mega-watt, Hollywood smile. 'Oh, how lovely.' I smile back but I can't match my neighbour's enthusiasm. I have nothing major against my little sister or her groom, but the thought of flying back to England, of rocking up in the village we grew up in . . . My neighbour rattles out another laugh. 'Not so lovely then?'

'No, no. It is lovely. It's just . . .' I look at the woman sitting next to me. I'm sure she introduced herself, back at the beginning, before we'd started to taxi out, but it was while I was checking there was definitely a sick bag in the little pocket in the back of the seat in front of me and I didn't quite catch her name. Dolly? Polly? Not important. The important thing is this woman looks like she's *lived*. She's tried to mask the passage of time; there's definitely some filler in those lips and Botox to the forehead and around the eyes and mouth, and her hair is bleached almost as blindingly white as her teeth, but there's the raspy laugh and the hint of a fading tattoo just peeping out from the collar of her shirt. I don't have any tattoos. I was always too much of a wuss. I almost got one once, when Ed got Butters tattooed on his wrist, but I was too scared to go through with it. But this woman wasn't.

10

She's brave. Much braver than I've ever been. I wonder if her heart was ever so broken, she didn't think she'd ever be able to crawl out of bed again?

'What is it, honey?'

I take in a deep breath, filling my chest right up as I think about telling this woman everything. Going right back to the beginning, where it all started. I've never spoken about it, not even to Yvonne. Never relived those days, not even the happy ones. But I could talk about it now. My neighbour looks kind and thoughtful. A giver of honest advice. And we have several hours stretching out in front of us, so why not? I can pull out the thoughts I keep pushed down, examine them, test them out, unburden myself without risk, because I will never see this woman again once we leave the plane.

'Oh, look.' The woman's eyes have flicked past me, past the next row of passengers, towards the window. 'We're up!'

I turn towards the window. She's right – we are up in the air. I've been so distracted, I hadn't noticed. I've even loosened my grip on the armrests so I'm barely holding on at all. I am very hot, though, and my fingers are jittery as I start to unbutton my cardigan.

'Worst bit's out of the way now.' She pats my hand and smiles at me, but she's wrong. This is the easy bit. The worst bit is to come, when I arrive in the village and the memories hit me full pelt. I feel queasy just thinking about it.

'You look like you need a drink.' She sits up straighter and pats me on the knee. 'Let's get you some wine and you can sit back and tell your Aunt Doll all about it.' Reaching up, Dolly presses the assistance button – *bong!* – before aiming a mega-watt beam at me.

'I think they'll be coming round with the troll—'

My words are snuffed out as we're hit with a sudden bout of turbulence. It's so forceful, I'm dragged backwards and pinned back against my seat. My hands are back on the armrests, gripping with all my might as I squeeze my eyes shut. I'm going to need the sick bag if my seat rocks side to side any more vigorously. But the rocking stops, which is a massive relief until I'm pulled backwards again, as though the headrest of my seat has been wrenched downwards and I'd be staring up at the ceiling if I was brave enough to open my eyes.

This isn't turbulence, I realise as a roar starts to build up in my ears. There's something very wrong with the plane. The roar intensifies, and it reminds me of the motorbike seconds before Sacha sped away out of the village with Ed on the back, helmetless and vulnerable. I never saw Ed again after that and I push that final image of him away as the roar surges. The sound is deafening and it feels as though my ears or my brain will pop with the pressure, and then I'm falling, the air rushing by at incredible speed. I'd cry out, scream, but I can't open my mouth.

The plane has broken, depositing me into the sky and I'm falling. I'm going to die, right now, without ever seeing Tomasz again. Without telling him that I'm sorry and that I've never stopped loving him. That I haven't moved on, no matter how hard I've tried. I've dated – disastrously – for the past four years and nobody has ever come close to him.

'Elodie!'

I hear my name through the roar in my ears. It isn't Dolly – I'm certain I didn't get around to introducing myself and we're currently falling to our deaths from a broken plane so it isn't the time for small talk.

'Elodie!'

I can feel the air on the back of my neck now, lifting my hair. I feel oddly free, despite the knot of fear tight in my stomach and the way I'm clinging on to my seatbelt so tightly I can feel the rough material cutting into my skin.

'Elodie! Let go!'

It can't be Dolly, so it must be someone from the other side, encouraging me to pass as peacefully as I can under the circumstances. But I don't want to let go. I want to cling on to life, thank you very much. I don't want to die. Not like this. I'm only thirty-two. Far too young to die. It would be a tragedy, and it'd definitely put a dampener on Heather's big day. I'm not saying she wouldn't go through with it – this is my sister we're talking about here – but it'd be a more subdued celebration than she's been planning, with the mother-of-the-bride howling into a tissue as the vows are exchanged rather than demurely dabbing at her eyes.

I wonder if the reverend would give them a two-for-one deal. Buy a wedding, get a funeral free . . .

'Elodie! *Let go.*'

The voice is insistent and much louder now. And it sounds familiar, which makes sense, actually. Because aren't you supposed to be welcomed into the afterlife by a loved one? So it's comforting and death feels a bit less shit?

But who do I know who's passed? It can't be either of my grandfathers as the voice is clearly female, and it can't be my grandmothers either. My grandma on my dad's side used to speak like Queen Elizabeth even though she grew up in a rat-infested two-up two-down with an outside bog – and I very much doubt she'd drop the charade even in death – and my other granny is still going strong according to Mum's emails.

The voice is definitely northern. It screams 'home', and not the tiny apartment I've been renting for the past few years. It screams England. Little Heaton. My childhood bedroom overlooking the cricket grounds. Listening to Kim Wilde and wishing with all my might that I was brave enough to spread my wings and fly the hell away from the stifling village. It screams visits to my grandparents' house on a Sunday. Screams sitting in the back of the car with Heather during hot summer trips, or riding my bike through the village with Yvonne and Ed, pedalling as fast as we could, whizzing down the dusty track to the woods and . . . wait a minute. *Yvonne*. No, it couldn't be. Yvonne hasn't passed. She was very much present earlier, when she was giving me a pep talk to get me on the plane.

'Elodie! Stop being a scaredy-cat and *let go.*'

That was definitely Yvonne with her trademark encouragement. How many times had she talked me into doing something by calling me a scaredy-cat? I'd shoved sand down Ryan Pilkington's underpants to prove I wasn't a scaredy-cat when we were in reception class. I'd snogged Jack O'Leary on the coach to Chester Zoo, swiped bubble gum from the minimarket, crept out of the house to go to parties and made prank phone calls, all to prove myself over the years. *I'd even boarded a plane and ended up falling through the sky to my death.*

'Elodie Parker! Let. *Go.*'

There she is again, clear as day. But the ghostly voice cannot belong to my best friend because she's alive. Isn't she? Oh God. What if something terrible has happened to Yvonne too? A traffic accident (more common than a plane falling to pieces in the sky, according to Dolly) or sudden illness – a heart attack, or a stroke, something like that. Because although Yvonne is only in her early thirties, it happens, doesn't it? *It's so tragic. She was no age at all.* They'll say the same thing about me and all the other poor souls who were on the ill-fated flight to Manchester airport: Dolly, the man who'd been snoring next to me, the pilots and cabin crew. Perhaps not the obnoxious bloke sitting behind me, who'd rhythmically drummed on the back of my seat while we'd taxied to the runway, distracting me as I'd tried to concentrate on not throwing up. I hope that when my seat had been flung backwards, it had smacked him in the face.

'Elodie! For God's sake! Tell her, Ed!'

My eyes fly open. *Ed?*

I see blue sky first, broken up by the wispiest of clouds. As I suspected, I'm no longer on the plane. I'm no longer in my *seat*. I'm falling through the air, backwards, my feet tilting up towards the . . . trees? Yes, those are definitely trees surrounding me, and the sky I spotted is only a tiny patch, a little window in the canopy of leaves, but how did I fall so quickly? How am I so close to the ground that I'm below tree level? I don't have much time then. Any second now I'm going to splat onto the ground. On a scale of one to Jesus-fucking-Christ, how much do you think it's going to hurt?

'For God's sake, Elodie!'

This voice doesn't belong to Yvonne. It belongs to my sister, who I also thought was very much alive. She'll be gutted if she's kicked the bucket before saying I do.

'How old are you? You're *twenty-four*. Get a grip, you loser.'

Twenty-four? I wish. Life was much simpler when I was twenty-four. Back when I still had hopes and dreams instead of crushing disappointment.

I know you're not supposed to, but I look down. I'm soaring above a body of water, but it isn't a vast ocean where I'm about to plunge to my death. It's a river – and not a particularly wide one at that.

'You promised you'd help clear out the loft. It's a mess. Mum's kept *everything*. It's all been shoved up there. Paintings from when we were in nursery, old toys, certificates, those matching dresses she made us wear for Aunty Laura's wedding. They were minging. Do you remember? White with blue flowers. We looked like the teacups from Gran's wedding set. Hold on a sec. *Are you wearing my new shirt dress?*'

Heather's rattling on but I can't take it in. I'm too focused on the fact that I've somehow ended up on a swing, with my sister and my two best friends somewhere close by. My feet tilt downwards and then I pause in the air for the briefest of moments before I swing back out again.

'You're going to have to let go, Elodie.'

Despite Yvonne's words, my grip tightens on the rope between my fingers. It wasn't the seatbelt I was gripping onto after all, but I still don't want to let go. Of the rope or of life. I'm not ready to die. There's so much I haven't done. So many regrets. I can't pass to the other side yet.

'Don't you dare drop into that filthy water.' Heather's tone has risen to near-hysteria. 'You'll ruin my dress.'

'Don't worry. I'll catch her when she swings back over.'

I start at the sound of Ed's voice. A voice I haven't heard for so long. My sweet, beautiful Ed *is* here. I twist to catch a glimpse of him, which sends the smooth trajectory of the swing off kilter. I twist again, to face forwards, but that only makes the swing wobble further and in the panic, I slip from the thick branch seat of the swing. The palms of my hands burn from the friction of the rope as I cling on with all my might, but then I'm falling. *Again*.

It all happens so fast; one second I'm sitting on the branch seat, the next I'm in the icy water, the skirt of my dress billowing around me. The shock of the fall and the chill of the water is enough to keep my attention away from the trio standing on the river bank for a few seconds, but then I spot them. Heather, covering her mouth with both hands, Yvonne jumping up and down while whooping with joy, and lovely Ed, beckoning for me to join them. The jolt of déjà vu when I spot them is so intense it makes my stomach turn. I haven't seen them for years, not in the flesh, and yet here are they, standing in front of me.

'Look at the state of you.' Heather's eyes are wide and her nostrils flared as she looks across the river. She must be having a lazy day because her usually sleek hair is mad frizzy, the curls growing upwards instead of down. I quite like it like this. It's more natural and makes her look younger. 'You can buy me a new dress. I'm not wearing that one after it's been in that gross water. It's probably full of river slime and fish poo.'

'I think we have more important stuff to worry about than a stupid dress.' My feet are bare – I've lost not only my seat and *an entire plane* but my socks and shoes as well – so the riverbed is slushy underfoot. I step on a sharp rock and almost stumble.

'That *stupid* dress cost me forty quid. I want a new one or I'm telling Mum it was you who broke the cat teapot.' I snort as I continue to wade across the water. That was *years* ago, and it wasn't even me who broke it. 'That's up in the loft as well, by the way. Minus the ear, obviously. I think Mum's got a problem.'

I'd say so. Both her daughters are dead. I'd hardly say she's feeling her best right now.

'Anyway, I'm off. I need to chuck all that crap Mum's kept hold of before she hides it somewhere else. Like my bedroom.' She pulls a face, her lips stretching out to reveal her teeth, and there's a glint as the sun catches the braces on her teeth. 'Don't be long. If you make me clear everything by myself, I'm definitely grassing on you about the teapot.'

Heather has gone by the time I make it to the river bank. Yvonne jumps up and down as I drag my feet the last few steps.

'You did it! I can't believe you finally let go.' She covers a giggle with her hand. 'Shame about the dress, though.'

Ed reaches out a hand to help drag me up onto the bank. 'I thought Heather was going to stick around and kill you.'

Yvonne snorts. 'And miss out on clearing the loft for twenty quid? Are you mad? That's half a dress.'

I'm back on solid ground but my hand is still clutching onto Ed's. I don't ever want to let go, just in case he leaves me again.

'What's all this about clearing out a loft?' Is it metaphorical? Like some sort of baggage-shedding ritual I have to go through before I'm allowed to pass through to the other side? And can I say no thanks, I'd rather go back to living if that's okay?

'Are *you* mad?' Yvonne stoops to pick up a pair of white trainers. 'It's *your* loft. You're clearing it out for the conversion.'

'Conversion?' I frown as Yvonne shoves the shoes towards me. 'What am I converting to?' An angel? With wings and a halo and a flowing white nightie-like dress?

Yvonne looks from me to Ed and back again. She tilts her head to one side. 'Are you trying to be funny? Because that was worse than one of Ed's attempts at humour.'

'Oi.' Ed pokes his foot out, nudging the toe of his trainer into Yvonne's calf. 'I am *hilarious*. You think I'm funny, don't you, Elodie?'

'See.' Yvonne juts her chin up in the air when I fail to answer. 'Even Elodie thinks you're as funny as thrush.'

There's a weird sensation murmuring in my stomach, and not just because Yvonne has brought up a yeast infection. I'm starting to piece bits of this encounter together and none of it makes sense: the rope swing, Heather's hair and the braces she had removed during her second year of uni, the broken teapot and a loft conversion. And then Heather's assertion that I was twenty-four. I look closely at Yvonne. Her eyebrows are slightly bushier than usual, as though she hasn't had them threaded for a while, and she hasn't worn her hair with a wet, slicked-back look for years, because she realised it made her look like she hadn't washed her hair for a week. And Ed – my lovely, beautiful Ed – doesn't have the Butters tattoo on his left wrist.

I take the shoes and lower myself to the ground as I try to process what's happening to me. *Am* I dead – or have I somehow travelled back eight years in time?

Chapter 3

I'm glad Yvonne's taken the lead because although I used to know these woods like the back of my hand, it's been years since I navigated the worn tracks in the woodland floor that will lead us out onto the lane. Some of it looks familiar: the huge tree across the river with a girth so wide Ed, Yvonne and I couldn't make our fingers touch as we stretched our arms around it, the bend in the river up ahead where Ed would build campfires, the clearing to the right where we'd play cricket or lay about under the shade of the trees when it was too hot. We spent our childhoods in these woods. Laughing, sharing secrets, daring each other to climb higher up the trees, competing to see who could swing and drop furthest out into the river. I'd never been brave enough to let go of the rope. Until now, I guess. My dress – *Heather's* dress – is sopping wet and clinging to my thighs as evidence of my accidental courage.

'You all right?' Ed slips his hand into mine as we veer away from the river, swerving right and picking our way over the dirt and broken branches as we head into the trees. There's no worn path here but we know the way. *Knew* the way. As familiar as the scenery is, I'm not sure I could find my way back to the lane unaided these days.

I shrug in response to Ed's query. I'm not sure if I am all right or not. On the one hand, I may not be dead as I'd feared, but on the other hand I've somehow hopped back in time to become my twenty-four-year-old self again. *Can* you be all right in that situation? It's odd to say the least. Unsettling. A complete head fuck, actually.

'Heather won't really kill you.' Ed gives my hand a squeeze. I'd forgotten what it was like to have my hand in his. It's comforting, despite the weird situation I've found myself in. 'Maybe just rough you up a bit.' He grins at me, and it's a full-on goofy, toothy grin, and at that moment in time, I don't care why I'm here because Ed's here too and it makes my heart feel full. I'll go with it, soak up every Ed-filled second, and deal with the details later.

'It's quite nice though, isn't it?' Yvonne steps across an exposed tree root, shuffling immediately to the right to avoid a prickly bush. Ed and I wait for her to elaborate, to fill us in on the conversation she's started partway through. 'Your gran moving in. Most people shove their wrinklies in nursing homes and begrudgingly visit once a month these days.'

My stomach flips and I squeeze Ed's hand tighter. Gran. The loft conversion. I do some quick calculations in my head and yes, that *did* happen eight years ago, not long after her fall that resulted in a hip replacement.

'Yvonne, who's the prime minister?'

Yvonne turns her head to look at me over her shoulder. Her non-threaded eyebrows are pressing towards each other and her top lip is raised on one side like a bad Elvis impersonator. 'You what?'

'Who's the prime minister?'

Yvonne turns her head back so she's facing forward again. She side-steps the narrow ditch that she twisted her ankle in, aged seven. 'What is this? An episode of *The Chase*?'

'No, I'd just like to know who the prime minister is.' Because if she says who I suspect it is, I may have to freak out. Perhaps

I should be freaking out already, because time travel or not, I'm currently walking through the woods in Little Heaton with Yvonne and Ed instead of sitting up in the sky in a plane. Yes, I *definitely* should be freaking out but I'm oddly calm. Perhaps it's the soothing ripple of the river behind us, or the fact that Ed is here, holding my hand? I never in a million years thought that would happen again and whatever the reason I'm here is – death, time travel or lack of oxygen during the plane malfunction causing hallucinations – I'm grateful for this time with Ed again.

'Did you take in dirty river water?' Ed pauses, our entwined hands meaning I'm halted too. 'Did you hit your head on a rock?'

'No, I just want to know who the prime minister is.' I set off again, quickening my step so Yvonne doesn't leave us behind.

'She's taking the piss.' Yvonne glares at me over her shoulder. 'But the joke's on you because I *do* know who the prime minister is. It isn't as though I could have missed them – they've been all over the bloody telly lately.'

'Then who is it?'

Yvonne's quiet for a moment. The only sounds are the trickling water in the background and the snapping of twigs underfoot.

'It's that guy. You know the one. Posh git with the smug-looking face.'

Ed snorts. 'That narrows it down a bit.'

'You know who I mean.' Yvonne wafts a hand about. 'I know who it is. I do. But his name's gone.' She turns, so she's walking backwards while facing us. 'Do *you* know who the prime minister is?' She aims the question at me, eyes narrowed in challenge.

I know who the prime minister is in the present day, because even though I've been living in the US for the past four years, I still keep up to date with UK current affairs. Not entirely by choice, I might add. Dad's rants are frequent, and Mum often has to snatch the phone off him to rescue me if he gets into a particularly heated stride.

But is this the present day? Or are we back in a post-coalition,

21

pre-referendum world, before they added a revolving door to Number 10 to make it easier to switch the leader of the country after the latest scandal? A world where Dad's rants were even more frequent and there wasn't a phone to be snatched away as a form of rescue?

'See? She doesn't know either.' Yvonne flashes a satisfied grin before she turns back around, hopping over a low bush that leads onto a dirt track.

'I do know.' Ed and I follow Yvonne over the bush. She's waited on the dirt track and falls into step with us as we make our way along the dusty path so I'm now sandwiched between my best friends, which is a glorious place to be. If this is death, I welcome it with open arms. 'It's . . .' I pause for a moment, because if I get this wrong, I'll never live it down ('Hey, Elodie, remember when you thought you'd travelled back in time? Ha ha ha.') '. . . David Cameron.'

'That's the guy!' Yvonne nudges me with her shoulder. 'I told you I knew who the prime minister was.'

'But you didn't though.'

Yvonne juts forward, so she can look around me and shoot daggers at Ed. 'Er, yeah, I did. I just couldn't think of his name.'

We're about to step off the dirt track and onto the lane that will take us into the village when there's a deafening roar, a bit like the din I heard earlier, when I thought the plane was in trouble. Maybe this is it. Maybe death is catching up with me, tardy but now fully ready to cart me off to the afterlife. But I'm not ready to let go of Ed all over again. Not when I've only just found him again. I squeeze Ed's hand, as though I can ward off death and keep Ed if I hold on tight enough. He pulls me backwards as the roar intensifies, and I shut my eyes, shutting out death, real life, anything that means I'll lose Ed. The noise is almost breathtaking in its ferocity, but then it starts to recede and I'm still standing on the dirt track, still clinging on to both Ed and to life.

'Dickhead.' Ed's insult is audible now the roar has tailed off. I open my eyes and see the motorbike disappearing around the bend up ahead in the lane.

Sacha. Of course. The day we cleared out the loft to enable its conversion into usable rooms was the day the Nowaks arrived in the village. It didn't seem significant at the time but our lives would be shaped by the arrival of this new family in Little Heaton. Ed and Yvonne don't know it and I almost envy their blissful ignorance of what is to come.

Ed pulls on my hand as he and Yvonne step out onto the lane, but my feet are planted firmly on the dirt track. 'It's okay. The road's clear now.' He gives my hand a gentle tug but I refuse to move. I don't want to go any further into the village because I know who will be there once we go around that bend. I can't bring myself to look at my friends so I study the thorny bush running the length of the lane instead.

'I don't want to go home.' There's a knot of dread in my stomach that's loosening into nausea. I want to lean over and expel the cocktails I drank in the airport bar all over the gravelly lane.

'I know clearing out the loft is a pain in the arse but at least you're getting paid for it. And we'll help, won't we, Yvonne?'

'We will?' I still can't look at my friends, but I hear Yvonne yelp. I'm guessing a sharp elbow from Ed. 'Yeah, yeah, course we'll help. Come on then. Let's get it over with.'

I don't want to move, but it'll make no difference whether I stay or go. The events following the arrival of the Nowak family happened in the past and this weird little trip down memory lane won't change that.

Little Heaton is much prettier than I remember it. While I'd found it closed in and smothering, it's actually clear and open, with oceans of green beyond the quaint, higgledy-piggledy buildings. Black-and-white Tudor-style houses sit alongside thatch-roofed cottages, Edwardian terraces and semi-detached bungalows with

23

dormer windows, their neat gardens bursting with colour: red and pink roses, sunshine-yellow peonies, zingy orange zinnia.

We turn left once we've crossed the footbridge over the canal and the bright yellow railings of our old primary school are like a beacon in the distance. I yearn to rush over to the school, to remember those blissful years of hopscotch in the playground with Ed and Yvonne, of slightly warm milk after playtime and stories on the carpet, all of them with happy endings. I don't want to remember boring assemblies or lessons practising handwriting skills or Mr Hinchcliff's bad breath, but the happy memories are a salve. I didn't think I missed Little Heaton, didn't think my move to California was anything but the escape I'd been planning for years, yet the sight of it – of my childhood home, being with the friends who knew me inside out – makes me feel mournful of those four years away.

I want to run through the village. To see it all, to drink it all in and remind myself that it wasn't all bad, but Ed and Yvonne are striding on, following the path to the heart of the village, and I go with them, afraid they'll vanish if I take my eyes off them. We pass the butcher's and greengrocer and the minimarket, and I smile, despite myself, picturing Mrs Gacey standing behind the counter in her tabard, eyes watchful for 'thieving little swines' filling their pockets with sweets. There are flowers everywhere on the high street, filling window boxes and hanging baskets and the three-tiered planters either side of the war memorial.

'Sacha. There you are. *At last.*'

The name pulls me out of my reverie, and I look across the road to the Royal Oak. The doors to the pub are wide open and a woman with waist-length strawberry blonde hair tied back in a low ponytail strides out. My heart is pounding as I watch her stop in front of the motorbike that had roared past us on the lane. I feel a sense of déjà vu so strong it almost takes my breath away, because she's exactly how I remember her the first time I saw her. She's wearing the bubble-gum-pink shorts with a white lacy vest top and gladiator sandals, and the stance – hands on hips and head tilted to one side – is absolutely spot on as she stands in front of the motorbike.

'Looks like the new owners are finally moving in.' Ed nods at the white van parked up outside the pub. I tug on his hand to keep him moving but he remains in place.

'Wow.' Yvonne stops too, placing a hand up to her forehead to shield the blazing sun. Both motorbike and owner are leaning against the pub wall, the owner cupping his hand around the cigarette in his mouth as he lights it. He looks up, taking a drag before exhaling a slow cloud of smoke in the air. He doesn't see us. His eyes are on the woman in front of him.

'Where've you been?' She's still standing with her hands on her hips, her head still tilted. 'You should have got here before us on that.' She points at the motorbike before resuming the hands-on-hip stance.

Sacha runs a hand through his mop of dirty blond curls. 'I had to say goodbye to Ronnie, didn't I?'

'And he probably thought he'd get out of unpacking.' A new voice emerges from the van parked in front of the pub.

Sacha smirks as he places the cigarette between his lips. He shrugs. 'Did it work?'

'Nope.' Somebody jumps out of the back of the van onto the road. I pull on Ed's hand again but he doesn't budge. 'There's still loads to do. Me, Dad and Grandpa have taken the big stuff in but there's tons of bags and boxes and stuff.' He turns and lugs a huge cardboard box from the van. He lists to the left, overcompensates and lists to the right, and then he's off, pretty much steady as he heads into the pub.

'You heard your brother. Lots to do. Chop chop.' The woman claps her hands before she grabs a box of her own from the van and heads into the pub. Micha Nowak, the new landlady of the Royal Oak. I'd been in awe of Micha the first time I'd seen her. She was so much cooler than my own mum, and she lit up

Little Heaton with her pink shorts and made it feel a slightly less bland place to live.

Her son remains in place, smoking his cigarette as he leans against the wall, seemingly in no hurry to help his family. I pull on Ed's hand, more urgently this time. I need to get away, to put as much distance between myself and the Nowaks as I can. I barely glimpsed Tomasz behind the huge box and it feels like luck was on my side, because I don't want him to see me like this, soaked through with grubby water.

Yvonne leans towards me, her voice hushed when she speaks, even though we're across the road from the pub and have yet to catch the attention of the motorbike rider.

'He. Is. Gorgeous. Go and talk to him.'

I shake my head. I will not go and talk to Sacha Nowak. I don't even want to look at him. I may have unfairly heaped the blame for Ed's death on Tomasz, but Sacha was definitely at fault. If it wasn't for him and his stupid, reckless riding, Ed would still be alive.

'Who do you think Ronnie is?' Ed, too, is talking in hushed tones.

'Who?' Yvonne is talking to Ed but she's still watching Sacha. If she were a cartoon, her eyes would be heart-shaped. I can't judge her, though. I was as mesmerised as she is the first time I clapped eyes on Sacha. When I didn't know any better.

'Ronnie. He said he had to go and say goodbye to him.'

Yvonne shrugs, eyes still trained across the road. 'A mate, obviously.'

Ronnie. How had I forgotten? I wonder where Ronnie is now, in the present, non-weird world.

'Go on, Elodie.' Yvonne wafts a hand in a shooing motion. 'Go and talk to him.'

I shake my head. I can't. I won't.

Yvonne sighs. 'Stop being a scaredy-cat and go over and talk to him. Ask if you can have a ride.' She winks, her lips spreading into a grin.

'Why don't *you* go and talk to him?' Ed turns to Yvonne to raise his eyebrows in challenge before he turns back to Sacha. He's lifted one of his knees so his foot is resting against the wall now and his head is tilted up to the sky as he puffs lazily on his cigarette. He looks as though he doesn't have a care in the world and I can feel my hands start to tremble with anger. With the injustice. My beautiful best friend died and he's standing there, at the scene of the crime almost, because this is where it all began, here outside the pub. The argument. Sacha and Ed on the bike. Me begging Tomasz to stop them. And later, those words that I could never take back. The words that changed everything.

It's your fault Ed died.

'*I* can't go over there and talk to him. Look at me!' Yvonne points at her chest. 'I'm wearing a Mickey Mouse T-shirt.' She leans over and pokes me on the arm. 'Go and talk to him. Please. Big me up. I'll go home and get changed into something less loser-ish.'

'I can't.' I lift the skirt of my dress. 'I'm soaking wet.'

I didn't have that excuse the last time. Ed had caught me when I swung towards him and pulled me onto the river bank so I didn't end up in the water. I'd gone over to talk to Sacha while Yvonne pelted it home to ditch the T-shirt. If only I hadn't. If only we had never met Sacha Nowak. Everything would have been different.

'Fine.' Yvonne swipes the palms of her hands down the thighs of her jeans. '*I'll* do it.' With her hands clasped behind her back to give off a casual air, she wanders across the road to the pub to introduce herself to Sacha. I know what will happen next: Micha will return, followed by her younger son, and she'll tell the story of why they've relocated to Little Heaton, which is rather a sweet story involving her in-laws and the castle up on the hill. But I can't bear to hear it now. I could shout out to Yvonne, call her back over – she isn't quite across the road yet – but what would be the point? Yvonne would laugh in my face if I told her the truth. If I told her that meeting the Nowak family will

27

lead to heartbreak and devastation. And it isn't as though this is real. I can imagine the past – so vividly it feels genuine – but I can't change it. We did meet the Nowak family that day. And Ed died as a result.

Chapter 4

I can't do it. I can't stand here and watch my world unravel all over again. As much as it pains me to leave him, I can't hang around, knowing that Ed is going to die.

'I have to go. Heather's waiting.'

'Wait. We'll come with you. Help with the loft.' Ed takes a step, but I press a hand to his chest to stop him. It's too much. Ed. Sacha Nowak. Being back in the village. The bizarre time-hop thing. And Tomasz will be back any minute now. I can't see him. Speak to him. I'm scared. Scared that he won't remember what we had. Scared that he will and he won't forgive me for what I did.

'No. Don't. I don't want your help.' I start to run, ignoring the cries of my friends as I fly through the village. Muscle memory takes me away from the Royal Oak and back towards the canal. My thighs burn as I sprint across the iron bridge, turning on autopilot as I reach the cricket grounds and barrel into my child-hood street. The street is lined with stone houses with red-tiled roofs, their front doors leading straight out onto the pavement. My house is the fourth one on the left, the one with the pitch-roofed porch added above the door and the skip standing outside.

'There you are! Give me a hand with these.' Mum's struggling under the weight of a mountain of magazines, stepping gingerly over the threshold so she doesn't end up flat on her face on the pavement. Her hair is pulled back into a ponytail with a red velvet scrunchie that I think was mine or Heather's when we were little, and she's wearing a pair of leggings with a trailing thread at the ankle and a T-shirt with a logo so faded I couldn't take a guess at what it once was. She has a bag lady look about her but I want to throw my arms around her and squeeze the life out of her because I haven't seen my mum for four years and it hits me like a speeding bus how much I've missed her. My chest feels full, as though someone's pumped up a balloon in there, and I can feel love and happiness radiating from every pore.

Mum peers at me from behind the magazine mountain. 'What happened to you?'

I look down at Heather's soggy dress. 'I fell in the river.'

Mum's eyes flick upwards, to the bright blue cloudless sky. 'You're twenty-four, Elodie. When are you going to grow up?' She stomps towards the skip and chucks the magazines over the side.

'You should recycle those.' It's a dickhead thing to say when I haven't seen my mum for four years but I can already feel the balloon in my chest deflating and it's crabbiness seeping from my pores now.

Mum turns sharply to look at me. 'And you should be helping clear out the loft instead of messing about in the woods. Come on.' She places a hand on my damp back and guides me towards the front door. 'Get changed – *quickly* – and then go up and help your sister. I'm putting the kettle on. I'm gasping.' She fans herself with one hand while she uses the other to urge me inside and towards the staircase. But I don't want to help clear out the loft. I want to hide. To process. I tried not to look at Tomasz when he emerged from the van, but how could I not? My eyes had been drawn to him and my heart had ached even as my words from the past screamed at me inside my head. *'It's your fault Ed died. You should have tried to stop them. I wish I'd never met you and your family.'*

Had I meant those words at the time? I don't believe them now, haven't for a long time, but back then, during the immediate aftermath of the accident when Sacha got away with a few injuries while my best friend died? I don't know. I know I'd loved Tomasz. Proper head-over-heels, and-they-lived-happily-ever-after love. But Ed was gone, forever. I'd been angry, bereft, totally heart-broken, and I'd taken it out on Tomasz. Squashed up what we'd had into a little ball of fury and tossed it away.

I'd loved him. So much.

But I'd loved Ed too.

I dart up the stairs, ignoring Mum's offer of tea, and push my way into the bedroom on the right, the one next to the bathroom. I haven't been in this house for years, haven't slept in this bedroom for even longer, but it feels familiar. Comforting. The bedroom is cramped, with twin beds squeezed into the small space. Heather and I had slept in bunk beds when were younger, and we'd had to sacrifice space when we'd insisted on separate beds. There are wardrobes standing in the alcoves and a chest of drawers under the window and the overstuffed room had only added to the trapped, stifling feeling I'd been so desperate to escape from. But now this bedroom feels authentic. It's *real*. This space had once been a refuge. A place to laugh and cry. Somewhere I belonged. I fit in this room and I'm not sure I've ever fit in anywhere else in quite the same way.

'Elodie? Is that you?'

There's a frantic edge to Heather's voice but I ignore it and gently push the door shut before creeping across to my bed. The covers are crumpled, the duvet hanging half off, and I straighten it before climbing into bed and covering my head in an attempt to disappear. I don't want to be here. I want to go back, to the plane, to my real life where everything makes sense. I don't belong here. I've been here before and I'm not sure I can go through it all again without crumbling to pieces. It's so cruel to make me live through losing Ed twice without being able to change a thing.

The covers are whipped away from my face. Heather's looming over me, her face lined, lips pursed, her hands planted down on her hips.

'What the hell, Elodie? You're supposed to be helping with the loft. *And you're crumpling my dress.* What is *wrong* with you? First you mess about on the rope swing like you're still eight years old, then you lounge around in bed with wet clothes like a sloth.'

'What's wrong with me?' I laugh as I scrabble up into a sitting position. 'What is wrong with me? I'll tell you what's wrong with me.' I stand up so I'm face to face with my sister in the small space between our beds. 'I'm not supposed to be here.'

Heather drags in a deep breath. She folds her arms across her chest before she releases the breath in one big huff. 'I know you're not supposed to be here.'

'You do?' Hope blooms: if Heather knows about my misplacement, maybe she knows how to fix it. How to bring me back round to reality.

'We *all* know, Elodie.'

I lower myself slowly onto my bed. They all know? Yvonne and Ed? Mum? So why didn't they say anything? Why have they let me play this thing out as though it's real? They could have clued me in, told me what's happening. Why I'm repeating this awful day.

'You never stop going on about it.' Heather unfolds her arms, holding them out for a moment before she lets them flop against her sides. 'How you're too good for this place. How you're going to get out of here as soon as you can, but do you know what, Elodie? You're twenty-four. You can leave at any time, so why don't you?' She raises her eyebrows, waiting for me to answer but I don't say a word. 'You could have gone to uni. Done something with your life. But here you are, still living at Mum and Dad's and playing in the woods like an overgrown teenager. *I'm* getting out of here.' She jabs herself in the chest with her index finger. 'I'm not staying here to work in the stupid minimarket for the rest of my life.'

'I won't stay here working at the minimarket for the rest of my life.' I hold Heather's gaze, the backs of my eyes burning with rage. How dare she judge me and my choices? And if she thinks she's getting out of here any time fast, she's deluded. I could tell her. Wipe that smug look off her face. Tell her that in eight years' time she'll still be in Little Heaton while I'll be in California, living my dream. Sort of. Four years ago, my dream didn't involve living alone in a tiny apartment with views of a brick wall or silently raging every time an advert for limp dicks popped up (unlike the poor malfunctioning dicks) on my telly screen.

'What are you girls doing in here?' Mum's in the doorway, two mugs of tea in hand. 'We need to get on with this loft. The builders are coming first thing on Monday morning and there's so much to do.'

'Sorry.' I stand up and squeeze past Heather, heading for the wardrobe in the right-hand alcove. 'I'll get changed and I'll be right up.'

I wait until Mum and Heather have disappeared up the ladder to the loft before I close the door, leaning my back against it as I squeeze my eyes shut. Heather doesn't know why I'm here. None of them do. As far as everyone else is concerned, it's eight years ago and nothing is out of the ordinary. So it looks like I'm stuck here, forced to relive this day. I don't know what to do, how to wake myself up from this weird-ass dream, so I simply change into clean, dry clothes and climb up into the loft.

'Jeez, there's a lot of stuff up here.'

I pause on the ladder, so only my head is poking up into the loft. There's no natural light up here and while there are a couple of lamps providing some light, it's still pretty gloomy. Despite the lack of light, I can see the piles of crap that have accumulated over the years. It hasn't even been stored neatly, simply shoved haphazardly wherever it could fit so there are bulky computer monitors stacked on top of wonky-looking chairs and dusty black bags. There are three monitors that I can see from here, but there could be more tucked away in Crap Mountain, and there's at least two tellies and a VHS player stacked up among a plastic baby bath, half a Christmas tree and a threadbare deck chair.

'It's your mother.' Dad's head pops up from behind a ginormous stack of newspapers and I feel the balloon in my chest reinflate. I thought seeing my parents on a screen or hearing their voices over the phone was enough, but it really wasn't and I feel the pressure of tears building up. I've missed out on so much by pushing my old life away and the balloon bursts as a pain as sharp as a knife slices through me because I can't snatch back those lost years. Dreaming about the past won't change a thing.

'She can't throw anything away.' Dad's eyes slide towards Mum. 'I just found a bag of plastic tubs with no lids.'

'You never know when they'll come in handy.' Mum pulls a Kwik Save carrier bag closer, her hand resting protectively on top of it.

'I do know when they'll come in handy. Never.' Dad jabs a finger at the carrier bag of tubs. 'Elodie, love, stick that in the skip before she gets too attached. And take that bloody teapot down as well.'

Mum's eyes widen. Forgetting the tubs, she snatches the broken cat teapot from beside her and holds it to her chest. 'Not the teapot. I'm going to fix it.'

Dad puffs out a laugh. 'You've been saying that since Christmas. And how *can* you fix it? The ear's missing.'

'She could take it on *Repair Shop*.' I've never seen the TV show myself but Yvonne raves about it, even though she usually ends up a blubbering mess when she tells me about the items that were brought in to be fixed.

'Which shop?' Mum clutches the teapot closer to her chest. 'They do repairs? Is it in town?'

Heather has been shoving old teddies into a bin liner, shuddering and wriggling her fingers as each one leaves her hands, but she pauses so she can glare at me. 'Don't encourage her. This is why this place is such a mess. Just fling the teapot in the skip and get on with clearing.' She grabs a crocheted rabbit, checking it for spiders before pushing it into the bag. 'I didn't know it was this bad when I signed up to help. I'll have to have a million showers to get clean again. Ugh.' She shudders dramatically. 'I don't see why *I* should have to do it when it isn't my mess.'

'Because the builders are starting work on the conversion on Monday.' Dad disappears behind the newspapers again. 'And it's either this or your gran bunks in with you two.'

'But I won't even be here most of the time.' Heather bustles a yellow bear into the bag with more aggression than is necessary. 'I'll be away at uni in a few months. Gran can have my bed.'

'And when you come home for the holidays?' Mum carefully places the broken teapot in the bag with the lidless tubs.

Heather shrugs before continuing to throw the soft toys into the bag. 'Can't she just go in a nursing home? She'll be all right once she's got used to the smell of piss and boiled cabbage. She might like it.'

'The smell of piss and boiled cabbage?'

I catch Dad's eye and can't help smiling at his quip. Heather doesn't find it funny and rolls her eyes at him.

'She might like living in a nursing home. There'll be people her own age there, and bingo and stuff. What's she going to do here?'

'Lots.' Mum tucks the Kwik Save bag into the corner of the room and beckons me up into the loft, because I'm still just a floating head at the hatch at this point. 'She's going to help your dad in the garden and we're going to sign up for some clubs.'

'But what about during the day when you're at work?'

Mum pauses for a moment, but she juts a hand in my direction as I scramble onto my knees, finally fully in the loft. 'Elodie can pop over on her lunch break.'

Heather grins slyly at me. 'Congratulations on your new job as Gran's babysitter.'

Mum shoots Heather a dark look. 'Gran isn't a child. She doesn't need a babysitter. She just needs a bit of care and company. I hope you're not going to make her feel like she's a burden when she's living with us.'

Heather ties the bin liner. 'Like I said, I'm going to be away at uni most of the time so it won't really affect me.' She stands up and grabs the bin liner and the Christmas tree segment. There's still a foil bauble attached to one of the branches. 'I'm going down to the skip. Give me the teapot.'

Mum shakes her head. 'I'm going to take it to the repair shop in town. It's better than dumping it in landfill.'

Dad's head pops up from behind the newspapers. He runs his tongue over his teeth as he looks at me in the poor light. 'Thanks for that, Elodie. We'll be lucky to part with half of this junk now. Quick, get moving it down to the skip before she spots anything else she thinks can be fixed.'

Heather glares at me as she passes to head down the hatch. Keeping my head down, I shuffle over to Crap Mountain and start to dismantle it. There's all sorts here: dressing up outfits from when Heather and I were little, records that could probably make a few quid (but I'm afraid to point this out) and bits and pieces of bric-a-brac. I work hard, bagging it up and dragging it down to the skip and I'm sweating more than I do taking part in the spinning classes at the gym. Okay, that *one time* I took part in the spinning class at the gym.

'Right.' Mum stands up, stretching out her back. 'I need to go and put tea on.'

'Do you have to?' Strangely, I've quite enjoyed the four of us being cooped up here in the loft, gently teasing Mum about her hoarding or winding Dad up about the evidence of his short-lived hobbies: wine-making, matchstick models, computer coding, line dancing (Dad had tried to stuff the cowboy boots in a bin bag but Heather had pounced and we'd taken delight at ribbing him about it ever since). The family had felt fractured even before I'd left for California, with Heather away a lot of the time studying and me moving into the flat above the charity shop with Tomasz, so it's been nice spending this time together, even with the spiders and the humidity and the hard labour.

'The troops need feeding.' Mum ties the full bin bag by her feet and hefts it towards the hatch.

'I'll help.' Heather scrabbles up on to her feet, swiping her grimy hands down her T-shirt.

'You will not.' Mum cocks an eyebrow at Heather. My sister has never offered to help cook a meal and it's obviously a ploy to get out of clearing out the loft. 'You'll carry on up here, thank you very much.'

With a heavy sigh, Heather drops down onto her knees and drags a cardboard box of old crockery towards herself while Mum bobs down the hatch, calling out a final 'yeehaw' at Dad, which makes Heather and I snigger. Dad waits a moment after she's disappeared before he leaps across the loft towards the Kwik Save carrier bag.

'Quick. Grab that teapot while she's distracted.'

Dad and Heather pop down to the skip with the crockery, teapot and yet another batch of newspapers. We're making good progress with Crap Mountain but there's still a way to go. Shuffling forward, I grab the handles of a battered suitcase and drag it away from the pile. The top is covered in a blanket of dust and I shudder as I pinch the zip between finger and thumb and feel soft cobwebs instead of hard metal. Supressing the icky feeling, I drag the zip around the perimeter of the suitcase and throw the lid open.

'Oh my God.'

How could I have forgotten about this, the reason I ended up in California four years ago?

Chapter 5

I'd always felt smothered by Little Heaton, as though I were too big, too fast, too *everything* for the drowsy little village. The hodgepodge dwellings – Georgian mixed with Edwardian, Victorian, post-war and the new-build development at the bottom of the hill – may have seemed quaint to most, but it felt confused to me, as though Little Heaton couldn't decide what it wanted to be. I suppose the village reminded me of myself, because I didn't know what I wanted to be either, only that I wanted to be *something*, and I was never going to achieve anything in dreary Little Heaton. But did I ever do anything about it? Did I study hard to reach my potential like Heather? Did I dream of travelling the world, soaking up culture like Ed? Did I squeeze every bit of adventure from life like Yvonne?

No. I did none of those things. I whined about life in Little Heaton. Bemoaned the lack of adventure and culture. I aspired for more, was bursting to be free of the place, but I didn't do a thing to escape. Until this day. This is the day it all changed, and it started up in the dark, dusty loft one ordinary summer afternoon.

The suitcase is as stuffed to the gills as the loft itself, crammed with yet more soft toys and records, columns of cassette tapes, yellowing certificates and postcards, a bundle of knitted blankets, jumpers and cardigans, and stacks of posters. My hands delve straight for the cassette tapes, clawing through them until I find the one I'm looking for. Originally, I'd dragged the entire case down to my bedroom, poring through my mum's past, reliving her childhood as I played the cassettes, an assortment of shop-bought singles and albums and mix-tapes. But this time there is only one I need. And there she is.

I stare at the cassette for a moment before I press it to my chest, my eyes closing to savour the memories of that day. Slipping the cassette into the pocket of my jeans, my attention is back on the suitcase. The posters are at the bottom, wedged underneath the knitwear. I bypass Duran Duran, Adam & The Ants, Blondie, The Human League. There's only one poster I need too. Only one poster I tacked to my bedroom wall as though I was still a teenager, moving it up to the newly converted bedroom up in the loft a short while later. It became my inspiration. My escape. I was leaving Little Heaton, somehow, and I was going to start the life I was always supposed to.

There was a cassette player stored in the loft somewhere, because Heather and I only had a CD player in the bedroom and I listened to Mum's old music somehow. I move quickly, because Dad and Heather will be back from the skip at any moment. Leaping at Crap Mountain, I pull at grubby bin bags and falling-apart boxes until I find it. The red and black Walkman. It's old and missing its headphones and batteries, but I know it works and that I'll find replacements downstairs. I hear the front door closing and the murmur of Dad and Heather's voices drifting up the stairs so I make a dash for it, scuttling down the ladder onto the landing with the Walkman tucked under one arm and the poster clamped between my teeth. I make it to the bedroom a couple of seconds before I hear my family clambering up the ladder.

'Elodie?' Heather pokes her head through the hatch as I creep out onto the landing. 'We're not done up here.'

'I was just going to put the kettle on.' I reach up to touch my throat. 'All that dust. I'm gasping. Do you want a brew?'

Heather narrows her eyes at me, pausing for a moment before she answers. 'Go on then. I'll have a tea.'

'Coffee for me, love.' I don't see Dad, but I hear him loud and clear.

'Take this down to the skip on your way.' Heather's head disappears and the gap is filled by the suitcase. I climb up a few rungs of the ladder to take its weight as she lowers it down. 'Don't let Mum see it. It's full of her junk.'

I wonder what would have happened if it had been Heather who'd opened the suitcase eight years ago, judging the Eighties mementos to be nothing but junk to be tipped into the skip. Would I have ended up in America, or would I have stayed here in Little Heaton, idling my life away, forever coming face to face with everything I'd lost? Walking the streets filled with memories of Ed. Bumping into Tomasz in the minimarket. Passing the pub where it all kicked off that night. LA wasn't all I had hoped for but at least it wasn't *that*.

The suitcase whooshes down the side of the skip and thumps into the bottom. We've been up in the loft for a couple of hours but the skip isn't anywhere near full. I should go back up into the loft and help Dad and Heather but I head into the living room instead, opening drawers in the cabinet and rifling through until I spot the set of earphones bundled in the corner. Shoving them into my pocket, I head into the kitchen, where Mum's peeling potatoes.

'What are you looking for?' Mum's already put the peeler down and is wiping her hands on a tea towel as I start to rifle through the nearest drawer.

'Batteries. I found a Walkman up in the loft and I want to see if it still works. No point chucking it if it does.'

Mum predictably, because she'll use any excuse to cling on to things, opens the drawer next to the sink and pulls out a new pack of AAs.

'How are things going up there?' She returns to the potatoes, grabbing the peeler and the half-naked spud.

'Good. Still a lot to do though.' I back away towards the door with sluggish steps. I'm eager to feed the batteries into the Walkman – nothing would take me back to this moment in time more than listening to that song again – but I'd also quite like to wrap my arms around Mum and tell her how much I've missed her.

'You'll keep it, won't you? The Walkman? If it still works.' Mum swipes a strand of hair off her forehead with the back of her hand. 'I know you all think I'm mad, but I just don't see the point in throwing away something that still has some life in it, even if it's a little battered.'

I can't help thinking about my relationship with Tomasz. I threw it away because I'd thought it was beyond repair, but was there still hope? A little bit of life that I couldn't see because I was too blinded by grief and my need to run away? Should I have been more like Mum and clung on, just in case?

'Yes.' I twitch my lips in an attempt at a smile. 'I'll keep it if it still works.'

I turn and bolt from the kitchen. From the house. My feet batter the pavement as I run towards the woods, and I'm already tearing at the pack of batteries, my fingers clumsy and ineffective in their haste. I take a different route to the woods, so I don't have to pass the pub as I don't want to be reminded of how powerless I felt after the whirlwind that is Sacha Nowak came into our lives. I want to remember the hope, rediscover the strength I gathered on this day. The resolve to change my life. To pinpoint exactly what I wanted and to go for it. To do whatever it took to be happy.

Tomasz made me happy. For a brief time, before it all went horribly, devastatingly wrong. But I can't claw those moments back. Those days are gone. But I still have this song. The song that came before the Sacha Nowak whirlwind. The song that picked me up and spirited me away from the fallout.

With the batteries slotted into the Walkman and the earbuds plugged in, I drag the cassette from my pocket, fumbling fingers pulling the case open. I haven't yet reached the woods but I can't wait a second longer. The tape is in the Walkman. The volume is up. I pause on the pavement, my breath ragged, pulse racing, and I press play. The rapid beat begins. The slightly eerie synth sounds. And then Kim Wilde, being a kid in America.

I take in a huge lungful of air, allowing it to rest until my lungs start to burn. My eyes are closed as I take in the lyrics. Everything sounded so much better in America. It was murky, and vibrant, and buzzing with life. It was everything I wanted and needed. Everything I hadn't been able to imagine, laid out before me. I was leaving Little Heaton and moving to America and I wasn't ever going to look back.

Chapter 6

'Kids In America' plays on a loop as I make my way to the woods, my feet autopiloting their way to the clearing near the rope swing. It's peaceful here, with the grass soft underfoot and the trees creating a barrier from the real world, encircling me like a giant, woodland hug. I find a good spot to sit, with a patch of dry grass and a wide tree trunk to lean against. I set the song going again and think about what's happening to me. *Why* it's happening to me. Being flung back in time is impossible, yet here I am. It isn't a dream or an hallucination. It's all too real. Too vivid. I could feel dust in my nostrils while up in the loft, could taste it on my tongue, can feel every ridge on the bark of the tree as I run my finger along it. For whatever reason, I'm reliving this day but I need to wake up back on the plane. Or, better still, wake up back in my apartment, back in California. I can't stay here in Little Heaton, knowing what will happen but being powerless to change it.

My phone vibrates in my pocket. It's been buzzing in there on and off for the past twenty minutes but I've ignored it. I take it out now and unlock the screen. Five missed calls and now a text. All from Heather. She wants to know where I am, because I'm not at home, clearing out the loft. But her words are a lot more sweary. I play the song one last time before I set off through the trees, finding my way easily to the lane that will lead me through the village. It seems I don't need Yvonne to lead the way after all; all those years of hanging out in the woods has embedded a map of it in my brain. I even remember where to duck to avoid low-hanging branches and when to swerve to steer clear of ditches and exposed tree roots.

We used to disappear for hours in the woods when we were kids. We'd light campfires and toast marshmallows, which Ed excelled at due to his years as a Boy Scout, and there were unlimited make-believe adventures to be had. We'd grown out of hanging out in the woods years ago – around the same time Yvonne started seeing Craig Radcliffe, who was older than we were so could get served in the pub while Ed, Yvonne and I would hide away in a corner of the beer garden. The woods, fun as they'd been, simply couldn't compete with alcopops.

It's a bit weird then that we'd gone into the woods to mess about on the old rope swing when we were twenty-four, and I'm trying to recall the reasoning behind it when I hear my name being called. I turn to see Mrs Gacey standing in the doorway of the minimarket with a face like thunder.

'What are you playing at? You're late.' She taps her wrist before she disappears into the shop, the door slamming behind her as she grumbles to herself. Christine Gacey was the cranky old cow who owned the minimarket with her husband, who only seemed to emerge from the flat above the shop to go to the pub or to head into town to spend the day – and the shop's takings – in the bookies. And I had the pleasure of working for them. Looking back, I can understand why Mrs Gacey was always in a mood, but back then I simply saw her as a tyrant in a tabard.

'Five o'clock.' Mrs Gacey is standing behind the counter in front of the cigarette display, unfastening her trademark tabard, but she stops and folds her arms across her sagging bosom when I walk into the shop. 'You are supposed to start at five o'clock on the dot so I can have my break. It's now . . .' She unfolds her arms so she can consult the watch on her wrist. '*Twelve and a half minutes past.*'

'Sorry. You must be starving. There'll be a new Band Aid single released for *you* this year. "Do They Know It's Christine?"'

I don't say this, unfortunately, because even now, eight years on, I'm still not brave enough to backchat Mrs Gacey. Instead, I look down at the tiled floor and mumble an apology, promising not to be late again.

'There's stock that needs putting out – give Mr Gacey a shout if you can't manage the spuds.'

I sneak a peek up at Mrs Gacey, to see if there's a hint of amusement on her face, but she's deadly serious, as though if I *did* ask Nigel for a hand lugging the huge sacks of potatoes to the veggie display, he'd be right there, sleeves rolled up and eager to help.

'And watch out for those Radcliffe boys.' Mrs Gacey pulls the tabard over her head. 'They were in here last night, trying to fill their thieving pockets with sweets. The older one nearly got away with it but I caught the little swine red-handed and marched him home. Not that the mother or father gave a damn.' She tuts as she aggressively folds the tabard into a neat square. 'They should bring back National Service. Teach the little buggers a bit of respect. My Gary never behaved so appallingly and Dominic is the sweetest boy you'll ever meet.' She places her tabard on the shelf underneath the counter. 'Come on. Don't stand there gawping. That fruit and veg should have been out hours ago but I've been rushed off my feet.'

I glance around the shop, which is void of any customers. Unless someone's hiding behind the pocket money toys carousel?

'I'm booked in for a shampoo and set. Shaz is keeping the salon open late, especially.' She steps out from behind the counter, smoothing down her blouse at the front. 'And then Mr Gacey's taking me out for my tea so you'll need to lock up tonight. You need to find yourself a good husband, Elodie, and then you'll get taken to posh restaurants too.' Mrs Gacey sounds so smug and her lips are *almost* flickering upwards in what could be described as a smile if you'd never seen real happiness before.

'Mr Gacey win on the horses then?' Past me wouldn't have dared to be so flippant, but the question pops out before I can stop it. Mr Gacey was fond of the horses, but it wasn't very often that he backed the right one. More often than not, he could be found dipping his hand in the till rather than treating his wife to nice meals out.

The flickering at Mrs Gacey's lips ceases. The corners are now firmly down as she eyes me across the shop. 'I beg your pardon?'

I swallow hard and focus on the tiled floor. I'm not so brave after all.

'You need to watch your mouth, young lady. No man wants to marry a sassy girl, especially the grandson of a vicar. Are you still courting Edward? Perhaps I should have a word with Reverend Carter, hmm?'

I raise my head and look Mrs Gacey dead in the eye. It's on the tip of my tongue to tell her that in a few years, Reverend Carter would give anything to have his grandson courting a girl like me, sass and all. But I don't say it.

'Ed and I aren't together. We're just friends.'

Mrs Gacey puffs air out of her nostrils. 'You don't fool me, lady. I've seen you cavorting through the village together. Always giggling and holding hands. You're all over each other. Just friends, my eye.'

I could tell her that men and women can be just friends, that not everything comes down to sex. But I don't. Mrs Gacey isn't the first person to mistake me and Ed for a couple, and even I thought we'd end up together for a long time too, because I'd never loved anyone as much as I loved Ed. Until Tomasz.

Hauling the huge sack of potatoes from the storeroom to the front of the shop makes my arms and lower back burn, but I somehow manage to drag it across the shop floor. It's baffling that I never developed a hernia while working at the minimarket.

46

'Here. Let me.'

A pair of hands clutch the sack of potatoes and I recognise them. How could I not? I could map out every freckle on their wrists so when I look up, puffing a strand of hair off my sweaty forehead, I'm not surprised to see Tomasz Nowak. Despite the warning, my stomach flips when I see him and my heart starts to gallop. Where Sacha is tall and brooding with dark blond curls and long lashes framing brown eyes, his little brother is fairer, with his strawberry blond hair flopping over his ears and into his eyes. His face is largely hidden by the hair, but you can see it is more open than Sacha's. Tomasz was mellow to Sacha's brashness, kind to his disinterest, calming to his unruliness. Unlike his brother, Tomasz isn't the kind of guy who would break your heart. Which makes it even more distressing that I broke his.

I snatch my hands away from the sack and take a step backwards. Apart from the glance earlier outside the pub, this is the first time I've seen Tomasz since the day I told him I was leaving for California, alone, and that I never wanted to hear from him again. I'm unnerved by the reunion but if Tomasz senses my discomfort, he doesn't show it and simply gets on with the job of dragging the heavy sack in front of the veg display.

'Thanks.' My palms are sweaty after the exertion of moving the spuds from the stockroom so I swipe them across the back of my jeans.

'No problem.' Tomasz shrugs before he delves into the sack. I watch him for a moment as he transfers potatoes from the sack to the box lined with plasticky-looking fake grass. 'Are you just going to stand there and watch or what? You're like my brother. He thinks he can stand there looking pretty while I do all the hard work as well.' He grins at me, to show he's kidding, but I hold on to his words. *Looking pretty*. Did he really think I was pretty back then, at the beginning? Even when I was make-up-free and grubby from an afternoon in the loft? I want to ask him but I can't seem to form the words and instead distract myself by jumping into action and grabbing handfuls of potatoes to stack in the display box.

'I think I saw you earlier. Outside the pub. We've just moved in.'
He noticed us. He noticed me.

I nod, my eyes focused on the task of filling up the box with potatoes. I can't look at him and not blurt out all the words I've been holding in for four years.

'You think this is bad.' I see Tomasz, waggling a potato, out of the corner of my eye. 'Try working for your parents.'

I give a puff of contempt. I still can't look directly at him. 'You think working in a pub is bad? Trying making beds and cleaning toilets. You can tell a lot about people by how they leave their beds and bathrooms.'

'They have you making their bed and cleaning the bog?' I realise I've put my foot in it. I didn't start working at the hotel for another few months. I sneak a glance at Tomasz and see him pull a face before I snatch my eyes away again. This is what happens when you let your guard down. You forget to be careful and make mistakes.

'No, but I wouldn't put it past Mrs Gacey.' I wipe my sweaty forehead. I should be used to the heat after living in California, but it's a stuffier kind of heat here and there's no air con. 'I was just saying there are worse jobs than pulling pints.'

'I guess, but I really need to find a job out here, as soon as.' Tomasz's face cracks as a grin spreads across his face. 'What have you done to yourself? You've got a big dirty streak across your forehead.' He points at my hands, which are filthy from handling the unwashed potatoes. 'Come here.' Pulling the sleeve of his T-shirt over his hand, he wipes at my forehead with a gentle touch.

'Thanks.' My gaze drops to the potatoes as I take a step away. I knew looking at Tomasz was a mistake, because being near him is unnerving and it feels as though the past is rushing at me, bulldozing me with every thought and emotion from back then. All those feelings of love and loss and grief that I so carefully packed away as I jetted off for California are unfurling before me and I'm afraid to acknowledge them in case I break.

There are reminders of Ed all over Little Heaton: the woods where our adventures were set, the church where his grandfather preached and the adjoining hall where Ed and I met as babies as our mums bonded over tea and biscuits and a shared lack of sleep. There's the pub where we had our first legal drink and the war memorial opposite, which Ed fell off after too many legal drinks and had to have stitches across his temple, and every single pavement we ever walked along. And although I didn't know Tomasz nearly as long, Little Heaton is packed with memories of him too: the beer garden where we spent lazy summers, the flat above the charity shop that was small but ours, the canal that we would stroll along as we made plans for the future.

Recollections of my life with Tomasz and Ed are as much a part of the village as the hodgepodge buildings, but it's bittersweet being here because as much as I cherish each and every memory, they only remind me of how much I miss them. There are no more memories to be made, and it's crushing to face up to that.

Chapter 7

'I'll finish this later.' I plonk the potato I'm holding in the display box and wipe my grubby hands down the sides of my jeans as I head for the counter. I'll feel safer with the barrier between us. 'Thanks for your help.'

'No problem.' Tomasz brushes the palms of his hands together. 'I'd better grab the milk and get back to the pub. Gran's gasping.' He disappears down the first aisle, finding the milk in the fridges at the back of the shop. 'It's the pub's *grand opening* tomorrow. You should come.' Tomasz places the bottle of milk on the counter. 'Although I'm not sure it's going to be as grand as Mum's making out. It's just a few nibbles, really. But Grandad's making wuzetka. It's a—'

'Polish cake.' I remember, though I wish I didn't. Franciszek Nowak baked delicious cakes, and the chocolate sponge cake squares filled with whipped cream and plum jam were a firm favourite of mine. I haven't had a piece since Tomasz's grand-mother's funeral.

'Have you had it before? Because even if you have, you need try Grandad's. He used to have it back in Poland, before the war, and he craved it so much that he tried to make his own. It was a *disaster*, according to Gran. But he tried it again. And

50

again and again, until he got it right. I don't think it's exactly the same as the ones he used to buy, but they're amazing. You should definitely come and try it. Tomorrow, from two.'

'I'll try my best.' I can't say anything else; I don't want to commit but neither do I want to pop Tomasz's enthusiasm bubble. I know how much he cared about his grandparents, and it shines through whenever he talks about them.

Tomasz pays for the milk and heads for the door. Part of me is glad he's going, but another part wants to beg him to stay for a bit longer. To tell me the story of how Franciszek and Irene met, here in Little Heaton, and how they'd held on to each other for so long. I open my mouth to make the request, but the door bursts open, almost taking Tomasz out with it. He stumbles backwards to avoid the impact as my sister charges into the shop. She stops when she sees me behind the counter, her eyes narrowing to slits.

'You *are* here.'

I open my arms wide. 'Just like I said I was.' I'd finally replied to Heather's text, to let her know I'd started my shift at the minimarket and therefore – unfortunately – I'd have to bow out of the loft clear-out. 'Did you think I was lying?'

Heather shrugs. 'Wouldn't put it past you. You were messing about in the woods like an overgrown kid earlier instead of helping.'

I wish I had a witty or scathing comeback, but this is true. 'Did you want something, or are you just here to check up on me?'

'Mum wants wine for tonight.' Heather wanders to the right-hand side of the shop, where the booze is stored. I follow, safe to step out from behind the counter now that Tomasz has gone.

'What's tonight?'

'Duh.' Heather grabs a bottle of red and tucks it under her arm. '*Celebrity MasterChef*. Laura's coming round so they can perv over Sam Nixon again. It's so gross. He's young enough to be their grandson.'

'Grandson? He's older than us.'

51

'But he *looks* about twelve . . .' Heather plucks a packet of hand-crafted crisps from the aisle we're walking down. 'And it's so embarrassing the way they lust over him, like he's the only bloke left on the planet.'

'You'll find a bloke you'll lust over one day.'

Heather stops, turns, and stares me dead in the eye. 'I doubt it. I have much more important things to concentrate on than boys. Like my degree and getting out of this place.'

'I'm getting out of here too.' I've reached the counter again and I spot the Walkman tucked away on the shelf, the earphones' wires wound around it. A reminder of my life away from Little Heaton.

'You?' Heather snorts as she places the wine and crisps on the counter. 'Where are you going? You've got no qualifications.'

'I do have qualifications.' I scan the wine aggressively, zapping the label while imagining I'm zapping Heather's stupid face. Four years away clearly hasn't been enough.

'What, GCSEs and that tourism thing you did at college? You really put that to good use, didn't you?' She looks around the shop before smirking at me.

'I wouldn't be too smug if I were you.'

'Oh?' Heather grabs a Wispa Gold from the rows of chocolate bars strategically placed for impulse buys at the till. 'Why's that?'

'Because I will get out of here.' I snatch the chocolate bar and scan it before thrusting it back at my sister. 'And you – with your degree – are going to be stuck here, in Little Heaton.'

'We'll see.' Heather sings the words, the smirk back on her face. I don't tell her that I *have* seen it. That I'm not simply daydreaming about the future. I have a life outside this village – I just don't know how to get back to it.

Ed and Yvonne are waiting for me when I lock up the minimarket, perched on the war memorial's base while they giggle at something on the phone held between them. It's after eleven and the village is still in a way that LA never is. I can almost hear my own thoughts in the calm.

'At last. We nearly went without you.' Yvonne hops down onto the pavement and slips the phone in her jacket pocket. She's no longer wearing the Mickey Mouse T-shirt she was earlier. She's changed her entire outfit and is wearing a hot pink skirt and a cropped white top. The Sacha effect. He's been in the village for less than a day and he's already changing things.

'*Bonjour jolie fille.*' Ed pushes himself away from the plinth and heads for the minimarket.

'You what?' I pull the shutter down over the shop's window and door, giving it a wiggle once I've locked it to make sure it's secure.

'*Bonjour jolie fille.*' Ed rolls his eyes as I frown at him. 'Hello, pretty girl.'

Of course. I get it now. This was around the time Ed went to France, working at a campsite for the entire summer, which is why we were in the woods earlier. Ed, Yvonne and I hadn't spent more than a couple of weeks away from each other since we were four years old, so Ed going away for three months felt like a huge deal, like we were proper grown-ups now, with lives heading off in different directions. Obviously we already *were* grown-ups, with jobs – Ed was a youth worker and Yvonne was a hairdresser – but we all still lived at home and none of us had any real responsibilities. So living in a different country for three months was a massive wake-up call. Massive and scary, and we'd reverted back to the comfort of our old selves, just for one day, before he left.

'Do you have to do that?' Yvonne sucks in a breath and lets it out in a giant puff.

'What?' Ed slings his arm around me, pulling me in tight and kissing the top of my head. 'Tell this girl that she's the prettiest thing since sliced bread?'

'Sliced bread?' I elbow Ed lightly in the ribs. 'You know that comparing me to bread isn't a compliment, right?'

'I was talking about the French thing.' Yvonne mimes strangling Ed. 'It's so annoying and if you don't pack it in, I'm going to shove a baguette up your arse, you pretentious knobhead. Although you'd probably like that since you've just admitted you fancy bread. Weirdo.'

'Wow.' Ed loosens his grip on me as he turns to Yvonne. 'First of all, maybe chill the aggression? And second of all, I'm impressed. Not only did you use the word *pretentious*, you used it in the correct context. I didn't know you had it in you.'

'Are you saying I'm thick?'

'Absolutely, but in the nicest possible, I-love-you-to-death kind of way.'

'Pretentious *and* patronising. You're the full package, Edward Carter-Brown.' Yvonne sets off along the pavement, away from the minimarket and towards the footbridge over the canal, and already her gaze moves to the right, seeking out the Royal Oak. 'I pity the French having to put up with you for the next three months. I reckon they'll shove you on the first ferry out of there.'

'I know what you're doing.' Ed and I have caught up with Yvonne, and he links his arm through hers, forming a three-person chain. 'You can't deal with how much you're going to miss me, so you're masking your pain by going on the attack.'

Yvonne snorts. 'All right, Dr Frasier Crane.'

'I'll miss you too, you know. But we'll keep in touch. I'll even send you a postcard.'

Yvonne snorts again, but there isn't nearly as much derision this time. 'What, like it's the old ages? Just send a text or email like a normal person.'

I lean my head on Ed's shoulder. 'I'd love a postcard. Nobody keeps a text forever.'

I didn't keep the postcard either, though I wish with all my heart that I had. But I was careless. I had no idea how precious it was until it was too late. Still, I'm here with Ed now and I should treat it as the precious gift that it is.

'Are you okay?' Ed kisses the top of my head. 'We came to find you, once I'd managed to prise Yvonne from the pub, but you weren't there. You should have seen her flirting. Shameless!' Ed laughs at the look Yvonne shoots him. 'Heather said you were at work and we didn't want to get you in trouble with the dragon.'

'Again.' Yvonne stops suddenly and points ahead. 'Isn't that the new guy from the pub?'

'See? She's obsessed.' Ed's teasing Yvonne, but my stomach has dropped to the pavement at her words. It drops further when I spot Tomasz and not his brother up ahead, perched on the rail of the footbridge across the canal. It's grown dark outside, but he's caught between the streetlights either side of the bridge, which are casting him in a warm glow. He looks almost angelic sitting there, so still and peaceful, his hands clasped on his lap.

'Thomas!' Yvonne holds up a hand and jiggles it about. 'Thom-*as*.'

Yvonne rolls her eyes at Ed. 'Whatever, bread perv.' She turns back to Tomasz and breaks her arm free from Ed's. 'What are you doing out here on your own?'

Tomasz hops down from the rail and shoves his hands in his pockets. 'Just having a nosy round the village. It's quiet, isn't it?'

'That's one word for it, I guess.' Yvonne bounces up the steps onto the bridge and leans over the rail to look down into the canal, wrinkling her nose. In the sunshine, the canal glistens prettily, but in the dark the water looks like brown sludge. 'Want to come on an adventure with us?'

'An adventure?' Tomasz tilts his head to one side, his eyes narrowing. 'What kind of adventure?'

And there's another stark difference between Tomasz and his brother. Sacha wouldn't have hesitated for a second. He wouldn't have questioned, wouldn't have even *thought* to ask. In fact, he'd be the leader of the pack, the one forging ahead without care or consideration of the consequences.

'We're reliving our youth.' Yvonne pushes herself away from the rail and heads across the bridge. 'It'll be fun.'

Tomasz looks at me and Ed, his pale eyebrows rising up his forehead. Ed fills in the blanks before we hurry across the bridge to catch up with Yvonne before she disappears into the woods on her own.

Chapter 8

'This. Is. *Amazing*.'

Yvonne swipes a finger up her chin towards her bottom lip, scooping up the marshmallow goo before licking it from the tip of her finger. It's nearly midnight and we're sitting in the woods, cross-legged in front of the campfire Ed has set going, showing off his Scouting skills. He's brought a rucksack of supplies with him, including a couple of torches and a pack of giant marshmallows.

'Will you have these every night while you're away?' Yvonne waves her stick before pulling the remaining blob of marshmallow off with her teeth.

'Doubt it.' Ed reaches into the bag of marshmallows and passes one to Yvonne so she can reload her stick. 'I'll probably be stuck cleaning the bogs or something.'

'There are worse jobs.' Tomasz pulls his own marshmallow away from the fire and blows on it before taking a tentative bite. He catches my eye but I pretend I haven't noticed.

'Your grandad will kill you if he finds out you nicked these marshmallows from the Scouts' cupboard.' I check on my marshmallow but it isn't ready yet.

'He can't kill me. He's a man of the cloth and all that. He'll just have to go all red-faced and threaten me with the fires of Hell.

57

Again. Which is fine with me.' Ed lifts the bag of marshmallows. 'Toasted marshmallows every night.'

'It must be such a pain in the arse having a vicar as a grandad.' Yvonne slides her marshmallow onto the stick and pushes it towards the flames. 'My grandad is proud about the fact he hasn't stepped foot in a church since his wedding day.'

'My grandad was brought up Catholic, but he gave up on God during the war.' Tomasz takes a big bite of his marshmallow. The oozy middle is hot and his eyes widen as he flaps a hand in front of his mouth. 'Shit, that's like fucking lava.'

Ed grins. 'As hot as the fires of Hell. I'd better get used to it.'

'Tell us about your grandad, Tomasz.' Yvonne checks her marshmallow but it's barely changed colour and she returns it to the heat. I'd once loved the story of Franciszek and Irene, but I'm not sure I'm ready to hear it again. I have no choice in the matter, however, as Tomasz loved telling the story as much as we'd loved hearing it.

'Grandad's Polish, but he ended up here, at Durban Castle, during the war.' Tomasz turns slightly, towards the direction of the castle at the top of the hill at the edge of the village. I watch intently as he starts to speak again, watching the way his mouth moves, the slight twitch of his lips on the right-hand side before a full-on smile breaks out when he gets to a particularly wholesome part. He's mesmerising in a way I didn't notice at the time, not until much later.

'The castle was being used as a hospital then, for wounded soldiers. Grandad went there and that's when he met my grandma, Irene. She lived in the village, near the church. They fell in love but when Grandad was better, he had to go back out to fight. After the war, he stayed in Britain and ended up building houses down in Coventry. He set up in business with one of his war friends and ended up in Nottingham. He never forgot about Irene, though, and once he had enough money to support them both, he came back to Little Heaton and asked her to marry him.

58

They moved to Nottingham, where they had Dad and my aunt and uncle, but Grandad always promised they'd come back to Little Heaton one day.'

'And now they have.' Yvonne sighs and checks on her marshmallow while I use the sleeve of my stripy T-shirt to wipe my damp cheeks. I thought I'd have forever to hear that story, but like everything in life, it had to come to an end.

'You're not telling that barf-inducing story again, are you?'

There's the snap of a branch behind us. I twist around and see Sacha Nowak making his way towards us, his scuffed-up biker boots creating cracks and crunches as he passes through the woodland. Yvonne's face lights up brighter than the flames in front of us.

'Want a toasted marshmallow?' She proffers her stick, where the marshmallow has started to char at the edges. 'They're delicious.'

Sacha shakes his head, barely looking at her or the marshmallow. 'Nah, you're all right.' He crunches his way to where his brother is sitting and nudges him in the back with the toe of his boot. 'Mum's worried about you. Thinks you've got lost, though how you'd get lost in this tiny shithole is beyond me. You could fall in the canal and drown, I suppose.' Sacha seems cheered by this suggestion, a smile spreading across his face. 'I'd be an only child. The one getting all the attention. And I wouldn't have to go out looking for my brother like he's still a baby.'

Tomasz scrunches up his nose. 'How did you even find us out here?'

Sacha aims the toes of a boot towards the flames. 'I could see the smoke. Thought I'd check it out.'

'You're dead clever.' Yvonne gazes up at Sacha, her eyes shining in the campfire light. 'You should be a detective. Like Sherlock Holmes but without the dorky hat.'

Tomasz stands up, brushing the soil and tiny twigs from his jeans. 'Why didn't Mum phone me?'

'Because you left your phone at home.' Sacha pushes the side of his brother's head, sending Tomasz's hair flopping. 'Dickhead.'

I stand up too. I want to shove Sacha, to tell him that *he's* the dickhead. That everyone around this campfire will have their life ruined because of him. I want to shove him harder, and tell him how much I despise him. I want to hit him. Again and again. I want to hurt Sacha Nowak as much as he's hurt me and the people I love, but I don't think that's even possible. I don't think I could ever come close.

'You okay?' Ed is standing beside me, his voice a murmur beside my ear. I want to shake my head, because I'm not okay, but I nod instead, flicking my lips upwards as I unfurl my fists.

'I'm a bit tired. I think I'm going to go home.'

'Me too. I've got a set of highlights booked in first thing.' Yvonne shoves her marshmallow in her mouth, swearing as the molten goo burns her mouth. She spits it out, flashing Sacha a sheepish look as it plops onto the ground. But Sacha has his back to us, already heading back towards the trees. Ed calls to him, offering him one of the torches, but Sacha simply holds up his phone and continues on. We put out the fire and pack everything away before we make our way through the woods.

Ed nudges me as we near the lane. 'You're quiet. You've been acting a bit odd today.'

There's no point denying it. I'd be surprised if I hadn't been acting weirded out given the circumstances. I've tried to mask the fact I'm an interloper by saying as little as possible, but that's only made me stick out even more.

'I'm just going to miss you. Every single day.'

'Aww, Elodie.' Ed puts his arm around my shoulders and pulls me in close, kissing me on top of the head. 'I'll miss you too. Hey, are you actually crying?' Ed stops, holding me by the shoulders and turning me to face him. He studies me intently as I look down at the ground, another tear loosening and gliding down my cheek. It's all too much. Being here, on this day where everything changed.

I didn't realise it at the time, but this day was seismic in our lives: Tomasz and Sacha's arrival, Ed's camping adventure, the cassette tape. Three unconnected events that will shape our futures and we didn't even know it.

'I won't go.' Ed runs a thumb along my cheekbone, gathering up the tears that have settled there. 'I'll stay. Here, with you.'

I shake my head, swallowing down the huge lump in my throat. 'You have to go. You have to go and have the most amazing time. Promise me. Promise you'll live your best life out there.'

There's a smile playing at Ed's lips as he watches me swipe at my face with the sleeve of my jacket. He doesn't get it. He doesn't understand. Not yet.

'Promise me, Ed. Be happy.'

He huffs out a confused laugh, but he nods. 'I promise. Anything for you, *ma belle fille*.'

We emerge out onto the lane, where Sacha's sitting astride his motorbike. He revs the engine as we approach. 'Want a lift?'

He aims the question at Tomasz, but it's me who answers.

'He doesn't have a helmet.'

'So what?' Sacha looks at me. Properly looks at me, for far too long. I can't stand it and have to drop my gaze.

'It's dangerous.'

Sacha snorts. 'You getting on, bruv, or are you pansy like your little friend?'

Tomasz passes me and Ed, slowing his pace slightly. 'It isn't far. I'll be all right.' And then he climbs onto the back of his brother's motorbike. Without warning, they zip away with a roar, Sacha swerving left and right across the lane to taunt me further.

'Are you okay?' Yvonne shuffles over, so she's standing next to me. She reaches out to place a hand on my arm as I stumble. The ground seems to shift beneath my feet and there's concern etched on Ed's face as I reach out for him, but I'm still unstable even with my two best friends holding me up. I lurch backwards, and I'm falling. Towards the ground. Towards . . . nothing.

My ears are filled with a deep roar, and I clasp my hands over my ears and squeeze my eyes shut as I continue to plummet.

'This is ridiculous.'

And just like that, the roar stops and I'm on solid ground. Or rather, I'm up in the air, back on the plane, safe and well as though nothing has happened. The man next to me is still snoring and Dolly is complaining as she turns away from the cabin crew. It *was* a dream after all and I'd laugh at myself for even thinking – however briefly – that I'd time-travelled, if I wasn't freaked out by how real it had all felt.

'All we wanted was one little drink.' Dolly frowns at me. 'Are you okay, honey? You've gone very pale.' She pats me on the arm. 'Do you need the barf bag?'

I shake my head. I'm totally weirded out, but I don't think I'm going to hurl. 'Did you feel that?'

Dolly's rummaging in the seat pocket. She whips out the sick bag. 'Feel what?'

'The turbulence.'

Dolly hands over the sick bag. She smiles kindly at me. 'What turbulence? I didn't feel a thing.' She pats me on the arm again. 'Shall I get you some water, honey? Surely they can't say no to *that*.'

Dolly reaches up to press the assistance button. *Bong!*

The rumble starts. There's a roar. I know it's happening again, whatever 'it' is. I squeeze my eyes shut as the roar and the rumble increases in force until I think I can't take it for another second. And then it tails off. When I open my eyes, I have to shut them again straight away to block the super-bright light. Is this it? Death has caught up with me ('So sorry I'm late, Ms Parker. You wouldn't believe the queues. So much red tape when travelling these days!') and now it's finally time to step into the light?

I peel my eyes open slowly, adjusting to the light. It isn't Death sitting across the room from me, and the light is simply sunlight shining through the window. I was expecting it to be dark. I was expecting the woods, and Ed and Yvonne. But while I'm no longer on the plane, I haven't been delivered back to where I was only a moment ago, ready to pick up where I left off. Ready to say goodbye to Ed.

Chapter 9

'Turn that rubbish off, Elodie.'

I'm sitting in my parents' living room, my feet tucked up underneath me as I sit on the sofa. Gran's sitting in the armchair under the window, her slipper-clad feet crossed at the ankles, and she's wearing a thick cardigan over a jumper even though it's blazing hot. She waves a dismissive hand towards the telly, her lips and nose scrunched up in distaste.

'I can't listen to another second of this Brexit nonsense. In, out, who cares? It's over with now, so let's just get on with normal life.'

I tune in to the news report on the telly. From what I can gather, the referendum took place only a few days ago, so Gran's in for a shock if she thinks she can escape hearing about it any time soon.

'What time is the tennis on?'

I grab the remote from the coffee table and bring up the guide. 'Not for another half an hour.'

Gran tuts and throws her eyes up to the ceiling, as though I'm personally responsible for making her wait, as though I've given up my job at the minimarket and become a TV scheduler. But wait. This isn't the same time period I hopped back to last time, when Sacha arrived in the village and Ed left for his French adventure. I do some quick calculations in my head, taking into account the fact Gran appears to now live here and the whole Brexit thing, and conclude that it's the following year. Which means I *don't* work at the minimarket anymore.

I look down at my outfit. I'm wearing unflattering navy trousers and a white tunic, which confirms my suspicions that I'm now free of Mrs Gacey and the minimarket, though I haven't gone far. I haven't made it to America, or even managed to stray out of the village; I'm now working as a chambermaid at the castle on top of the hill, which was turned into a hotel sometime after its requisition as a hospital during the war. The money isn't great, but it's more hours than Mrs Gacey was offering, plus I now know this is my ticket out of here. I didn't know it at the time, but I am firmly on the path out of Little Heaton and I want to high-five past me and let her know that her Kim Wilde plan isn't a silly wish, that her dreams will come true. At least, some of them.

'When's your mother due home?'

I'm flicking through the TV channels. There's an ancient episode of *The Bill* on, which I know Gran likes, so I switch it over. 'I'm not sure. Isn't she at work?'

'You tell me. I never know where she is. She's always off gallivanting. She was in the pub until almost ten last night.'

'It's called having a life, Gran.' I dump the remote back on the coffee table. 'She's allowed to let her hair down and enjoy herself.' Even if the extent of the entertainment is bingo and quiz night at the Farmer's Arms.

'Without your father?' Gran's tone goes up, scandalised at the very notion. 'My Roy wouldn't have stood for it. Your father needs to put his foot down.'

'Mum and Dad are fine. They don't need to spend every minute of every day together.'

Gran tuts and shakes her head. 'You youngsters. You haven't got a clue. It's no wonder there's no ring on your finger.'

I hold out my left hand, splaying the fingers. All of them are bare. But so what? I'm still young. Ish. There's plenty of time to find The One. Or The Two, since I've already found and lost the person I thought I'd spend the rest of my life with.

'I was married with three children by the time I was your age.' Gran says this as though it's something to envy, but I can't think of anything worse. I wasn't ready for babies when I was twenty-five, and I'm about to say so when there's a rap at the front door to the tune of *Inspector Gadget* that snatches my attention.

'Does he *have* to do that every single time he knocks on the door?'

Gran recognises the signature knock and so do I, even after all these years. My lips spread into a huge cheesy grin in response, because as annoying as I found it at the time, I missed it once it was gone. I fly into the hallway to wrench the door open. Ed's standing on the doorstep. He's grown his hair long on top and even though it's warm out, he's wearing a leather jacket over his *South Park* T-shirt and jeans. He leans in to kiss me on the cheek and I get a whiff of warm leather that makes every cell of my body ping with the nostalgia hit. I'm really back here, back with Ed, and I know it's crazy, that time travel isn't possible, but how can something feel, sound and *smell* so real if it's a figment of my imagination? And I hopped back to the present, didn't I? Even if it was only for a few seconds. I was back on the plane with Dolly as though not a second had passed before hopping back in time again.

Oh my God. I've actually travelled back in time. To be with Ed. To be with Tomasz. How or why doesn't seem to matter and I couldn't explain it even if I tried so hard my brain exploded all over Ed's lovely leather jacket.

'Pub?' Ed's voice pulls me away from my internal babbling. I'm still standing on the threshold and Ed has made no attempt to step into the house. 'Yvonne's finishing up at the salon and then she'll meet us there.'

I pull at my tunic top. 'I'll have to get changed first. I've only just got home from work. Which is where you should be, isn't it?' I'm stalling, because although I'm beyond excited to be back with Ed and Tomasz, there are serious consequences with time travel. What if I'm able to actually change events but I mess it all up? I've seen *The Butterfly Effect*. One little tweak in the past could change *everything*. What if I inadvertently send us on a completely different path in which my sister ends up marrying Sacha Nowak instead of the head teacher of Little Heaton's primary school? Or worse. What if I come to on the plane and realise I'm heading back to England to witness Heather marrying *Tomasz*?

'I had a dentist appointment so I took a half-day, remember?' Ed looks up at the sky, squinting as the sun makes a sudden break from the clouds. 'And it's a gorgeous day. Perfect for sitting out with a pint.'

Sitting in the beer garden of the Royal Oak sounds blissful. It's been ages since I've had a pint on a sunny day. The bars just aren't the same in California and the atmosphere is lacking. But can I sit with Ed and the others, pretending everything is fine? And if not, what is the alternative? I can't tell anyone what's happening to me, because who would believe that I'm not really from here, that I'm really Elodie from the future? I can't quite believe it and it's actually happening to me, so I can't expect anyone else to think I'm anything but losing the plot big time.

'Give me two minutes.' I pull Ed into the hallway and shut the front door. He immediately pulls at the collar of his leather jacket, wafting it back and forth while puffing up his cheeks. 'Sorry. The heating's whacked up to the max again. Gran can feel draughts even in summer. Try not to melt while I get changed. I'll be as quick as I can.'

Ed steps into the living room and I can already hear him chatting to Gran as I head up the stairs. The airing cupboard has been removed and the bathroom squished up to make room for the new set of narrow stairs up to the loft, and I'm glad I've skipped the whole loft conversion because it was bad enough living through the chaos and the dust the first time around. The area has been cleared and transformed into two small rooms, giving me and Heather our own space for the first time. I'd longed for my own room for so many years and I get that same thrill I did back then as I step into the bedroom on the left.

The space is small, but it doesn't feel cluttered. There's my bed, neatly made out of habit after working at the hotel, with a slim wardrobe on the left and a chest of drawers under the window. On top of the drawers is a jar, half-filled with pound coins and fifty-pence pieces, with a handwritten label and a red, white and blue stripy ribbon. My America fund, set up last summer after I'd discovered the Kim Wilde cassette and a seed had been sown. Propped up against the jar is the postcard Ed sent me from France last summer, and next to it is the Walkman, loaded with the Kim Wilde cassette as always, and the poster is tacked to the front of my wardrobe.

Pulling my phone from my trouser pocket, I check the date, confirming my suspicions as I sink onto the bed. I am replaying a summer day from seven years ago, and the latest photos on my camera roll further corroborate it: the last photo I took was of Ed and Yvonne, champagne glasses in the air as they toasted Ed's mum and stepdad on their fifteenth wedding anniversary. I swipe to see Laura and Jim dancing, her arms draped loosely around his shoulders as she gazes at her husband, radiating pure adoration, and swipe again to see Ed and his mum cheek to cheek, grinning at the camera. There are so many photos from that party, mostly of Ed and Yvonne, but a few of Mum, Dad and Heather have slipped in, and there's even one of Gran dancing with Reverend Carter. I delete the photo of Gran and Ed's grandfather and throw my phone down on the bed. I don't want to look at that man, knowing what he is. Knowing how tangled up he is in Ed's death.

I change out of my work uniform, pulling on a floral slip dress and a pair of sandals before hurrying back downstairs to rescue Ed from Gran. She's currently berating him about his lack of commitment, between bites of the sandwich he's presumably made for her, so he looks like he could weep with relief when I drag him outside.

'Sorry about that.' I close the front door behind us and thread my arm through his, holding on extra tight as we wander along the path towards the gate. Although I was only back on the plane for a matter of seconds and didn't have time to process my feelings – relief that I was back to normal, confusion over the weird timeslip thing, sadness that I'd never get to see Ed again – I felt such a rush of joy when I saw Ed standing on the doorstep. I still have no idea what's going on, but *Ed is here* and I can't wish that away, even if it means being back in Little Heaton.

'It's fine. I quite like being told I'm feckless. I don't hear it enough, to be honest.'

I scrunch my whole face up, squeezing my eyes shut as I groan. 'You are not feckless. You are feck*full*. Overly full of feck if you ask me.'

'A massive fecker, you might say.'

'Easily the biggest fecker in Little Heaton.'

Ed places a hand on his chest. 'That's the nicest thing anyone has ever said to me.' He swings the gate open and I'm forced to unlink my arm from his so we can step out onto the pavement, but I grab hold of his hand as we fall into step side by side. This feels glorious. The sun is shining. I'm joking around with one of my best friends. And we're on our way to the pub. My heart feels full and I can't remember the last time I felt this content, the last time I felt this relaxed and free, as though the world is full of goodness again.

'Little Heaton looks so pretty in the sunshine, don't you think?'

Ed gives me a puzzled look. 'Are you feeling okay? You never say nice things about the village. Ever. Not even when they light up the high street at Christmas and give out free mince pies and mulled wine.'

'I just think it looks lovely today.' I look around me, at the window boxes bursting with blooms, at the hills dotted with sheep in the distance, at the bunting left over from the last street party.

'Exactly how much do Yvonne and I have to drink to catch up with you, because you're obviously pissed.'

I nudge Ed with my elbow, though there's no intent there, and we chat as we wander towards the pub. Yvonne's already there when we arrive, and she's bagged one of the picnic tables out in the beer garden at the back with Tomasz. Her heart doesn't look full. Her mouth is downturned and she barely moves her head to look at us as she rests her cheek on her upturned hand.

'Hey, you.' I plonk myself next to her and swing my legs over the bench. I can feel Tomasz's eyes on me but I'm trying not to look at him because I'll want to leap across the table and snog his gorgeous little face off and I'm pretty sure that if I *can* alter things here in the past, kissing Tomasz now would get the butterfly's wings flapping and turn the world as I know it to utter shite. So I focus my full attention on Yvonne. 'Ed doesn't think we tell him how much of a fecker he is, so feel free to let rip.'

'Apparently, I'm the biggest fecker in the village.' Ed sits next to Tomasz on the opposite side of the table. I look at Yvonne. Really, really hard. But there's nothing from her. Not even a hint of a smile.

'She's sulking because my brother isn't here.' Tomasz stands up and I sneak a peek at his hands as he gathers the empty glasses and crisp packets from the table. Tomasz has a smattering of pale freckles across his nose and there's a cluster of them near his thumb that almost form a heart shape. Yvonne shifts, the movement causing me to drag my eyes away from the heart-shaped freckles, and when I look at her, her features have morphed into a glare that's aimed straight at Tomasz. But he doesn't see as he's already turned around and is heading across the lawn towards the door. He's tossed the grenade and now he's running away, and he knows it by the flash of a grin I clock as he looks back at us over his shoulder. His eyes lock on to mine and I almost snap my neck as I twist back round to face Yvonne.

'It is not that *at all*.' Yvonne swipes a clump of hair off her forehead. The clouds have started to thin out and her forehead is shining from the heat. 'I don't even *care* where Sacha is. I'm totally over him.'

Ed catches my eye and I can tell he's holding in a belly laugh, because Yvonne was totally *not* over Sacha Nowak. She'd spent the past year following him around the village, but she wasn't alone in her adoration. It seemed like the female population of Little Heaton had fallen for the village bad boy, and there'd even been a rumour that he'd had a fling with the married owner of the local hairdresser's, which made for an awkward situation for Yvonne, who was green with envy, no matter how much her boss rebutted the claim. The salon was the perfect breeding ground for gossip, and the affair became more salacious with every snip of the scissors.

'Where is Sacha?' Ed spots a fragment of crisp and flicks it off the table.

'Where do you think?' Yvonne's shoulders sink. 'Nottingham. Again. I swear he's there more than here. Why did he move in the first place if he'd rather still be down there?' She folds her arms across her chest and scowls at a pigeon who's working on the flicked-away crisp.

'Because if he hadn't moved here, you wouldn't have fallen madly in love with him.' Ed yelps. I suspect he's received a swift kick to the shin under the table. 'You *are* in a mood today.'

'I am not.' Yvonne's scowl deepens, to prove she isn't in a mood. But if she isn't in a mood right now, she's about to be. Craig Radcliffe, the ex-boyfriend of her youth, is sauntering towards us across the lawn. His ego had never quite recovered from Yvonne dumping him so he used every opportunity to beat his chest in front of her, like a gorilla, albeit with a weaker grasp of the English language, fewer manners and far worse dental hygiene than an ape.

'Whoa, what happened to your hair?' He points at Yvonne's hair, which is dyed pastel pink. 'You weren't ugly enough with its normal colour?' His mean face is creased up, his yellow teeth on display as he chortles.

'What happened to your knob? Stopped growing at birth?'

The laughter ceases and Craig's lip curls as he looks at Ed. 'Why are you so interested in my knob?' He grabs his crotch and jiggles his fist up and down. 'Wanna suck on it, eh?' Craig was the typical school bully who hadn't grown out of picking on anyone he saw as inferior. Last I heard, he was doing a stretch for battering his girlfriend in a drunken rage. Nice chap.

'Oh, look. It's Tom-ass.' Craig sticks his butt out to the side and jabs his index finger into its cheek as Tomasz makes his way over to the table with a tray of drinks and more crisps. 'Do you like his ass, Ed? Is he your boyfriend?' Craig lifts his hand and makes a flopping motion with it.

'Is that your latest baby mama?' Tomasz nods across the beer garden, to the woman and small child sitting at a picnic table in the corner. 'How many kids you got now? Too many to count? Defo too many to actually look after. Wasn't your Riley nicked for shoplifting last week?'

Craig's face scrunches up, making him look meaner than ever. I think about Craig Radcliffe of the near-future. Of the drunken rage. The photos of his girlfriend's swollen and bruised face in the papers. Perhaps best not to poke the beast.

'Why don't you just go back to your family?'

Craig sneers at me. 'Why don't *you* just shut your gob?' But he starts to back away, kicking out at the pigeon who's searching for more crisps on the ground. The pigeon takes off in a flap and, satisfied he's riled the bird at least, Craig turns and saunters back to his girlfriend and child. I reach across the table and take Ed's hand. It's okay. He's safe. For now.

'What did you ever see in that loser?' Ed is still watching Craig as he swaggers across the grass, so I pull his chin gently to bring his focus back to us.

72

'It was the alcopops, and don't pretend you didn't enjoy them as well.' Yvonne yanks a packet of crisps open and shoves a handful in her mouth. 'Thanks for sticking up for us, Tomasz.'

Tomasz shrugs and plonks himself down on the bench next to Ed. 'We get idiots like that in here all the time. You get used to it.'

'But this isn't even your job.' Yvonne shoves another handful of crisps in her mouth, wiping her greasy fingers down the front of her dress before she pats Tomasz on the arm. 'So we appreciate it.'

Tomasz rolls his eyes. 'When your mum and dad run a pub, it's always your job. You have to get good at creeping around unseen, otherwise they rope you in.'

'You're lucky though.' Yvonne grabs another handful of crisps. 'Rumour has it Shaz is selling up Lady Dye, so who knows if I'll have a job if she does. With your mum and dad here, you've got a job for life.'

But she's wrong, because the Nowaks will move on. How could they stay around in a place like Little Heaton after what happened to Ed?

Chapter 10

Unlike Yvonne, I'm glad Sacha isn't around as it allows me to unwind and enjoy the afternoon with my two best friends. The clouds have almost vanished by mid-afternoon and I close my eyes, losing myself in my friends' chatter. I've barely said a word to Tomasz as I'm afraid of blurting out how much I've missed him and I'm gutted when he leaves to carry out a quote for a plastering job.

'Shall I get another round in?' Ed stands, not really in need of an answer, but Yvonne shakes her head.

'Not for me. I've got a shampoo and set booked in at three.' She turns to me and pulls a face. 'Your old boss, Christine Gacey. Her grandson's visiting so they're going out tonight for tea. She wouldn't shut up about it when she booked the appointment – Dominic this, Dominic that – and she's going to be even worse when she's in the chair.'

Dominic Gacey. I heard a lot about him when I worked in the minimarket. Mrs Gacey was incredibly proud of her grandson, and you wouldn't know that she'd only seen him a handful of times by the details of his life she went into. She knew *everything* about the boy and wasn't averse to sharing it. I felt like I knew Dominic before I even met him.

'I'd better get going too, actually.' Ed gathers up the glasses and crisp packets from the table. 'I said I'd pop round to the church to speak to Grandad about some volunteer work.'

Yvonne swings her legs over the bench and stands up. 'Aren't you busy enough with your job and being Deputy Scout Leader?'

'It's *Assistant* Scout Leader, and the volunteering isn't for me. It's for some of the young people I work with. I'm hoping Grandad will let them do some gardening and odd jobs around the church grounds and the hall, to boost their confidence and give them something to put on their CVs. But you know what Grandad's like – he's all for preaching Christianity and helping others but he doesn't always put it into practice himself.'

Yvonne grabs her mini rucksack from underneath the table and hoists it over her shoulders. 'Why wouldn't he want a free bit of labour?'

Ed rolls his eyes. 'He thinks I only work with ex-convicts.'

'And are they ex-crims?'

Ed starts to walk across the grass, with me and Yvonne following. 'We all make mistakes. And we all deserve a second chance. Jesus would have let an ex-convict trim his hedges. Probably would have paid them for it too, but there's no way Grandad will be reaching into his pocket.'

We head through the pub and emerge back into the sunshine on the street. Across the road, a couple of young children run along the pavement, giggling as balloons attached to ribbons trail after them while their mums follow behind as though they have all the time in the world. I don't remember Little Heaton feeling so glorious, so carefree. When I think about the village, it feels grey and oppressive. If it wasn't for Heather's wedding, I don't think I'd have made the journey back at all.

'I'll come with you to see your grandad, if you'd like?' I work hard not to gag at the thought of seeing Reverend Carter again, but I don't want to let Ed go. I could be pulled back onto the plane any minute now so I want to soak up every bit of my best friend that I can before I'm forced to leave him behind again.

'Thanks, but I think it's better if I go on my own. Grandad might think we're ganging up on him, making it harder for him to say no to the volunteer thing.'

'Isn't that a good thing? Making it harder for him to say no?'

'Not with Grandad. If he feels backed into a corner, he'll dig his heels in. He's a stubborn old git.' Ed leans down and kisses my cheek. 'I'll call you later. Maybe we could all get together? Go see a film or something?' He's already backing away, and he raises a hand before he turns and heads off for the church.

Yvonne nudges me with her shoulder as we cross the road. 'When are you two going to stop arsing around and get together?'

I start, my eyes flicking left and right. I had no idea Tomasz was back. But then I realise Yvonne is still watching Ed as he disappears around the corner.

'Me and Ed?' I almost laugh until I remember how it was back then. Everyone thought Ed and I would end up together because we were so close and nobody really believed that a man and woman could be just friends. And it isn't as though I hadn't had the same feeling myself every now and then. I loved Ed and he was attractive (as my teenage diary would tell you with mortifying frequency) but somewhere along the way I'd pushed beyond the crush.

'Yes, you and Ed.' Yvonne rolls her eyes as we step up onto the pavement. The salon is only a few yards away from the war memorial and we wander towards it. 'It's so obvious that you're into each other with all that touchy-feely, lovey-dovey stuff.'

'He's my best friend. He's *your* best friend too.'

'But he doesn't kiss me. Or hold my hand. He calls me a dickhead and gives me nuggies.' Yvonne touches her hair, as though Ed has just rasped his knuckles over her head. 'He's different with you, so stop being a scaredy-cat and go for it. You need to seduce him.' She nudges me with her shoulder again. 'Get some sexy underwear. Some proper slutty stuff to blow his mind.'

76

I place my hands over my ears, knowing she is about to utter the words *crotchless panties*, which still makes me feel icky all these years later. Yvonne drags my hands away from the sides of my face.

'Don't be such a prude. This is why you get a peck on the cheek, mate.'

'I don't think me wearing . . . those things . . .' I can't even bear to say it out loud and instead wave my hands in front of my foof '. . . is going to do anything for Ed.'

'Are you kidding? You're a hot fox.' Yvonne throws her arm around my shoulders and pulls me in close, and I laugh even though she's squeezing me a bit too tight. I've missed this. Yvonne and I talk all the time, and I see her face when we chat on FaceTime, but it isn't the same as having an actual, physical squish from your bestie.

'Come on, say it.' Yvonne releases me from her grip, but she holds me at arm's length by the shoulders. 'Say I'm a hot fox.'

'You're a hot fox.'

Yvonne stamps her foot on the ground, pretending that her lips aren't twitching in amusement. 'I'm serious. Say it. Say "I, Elodie Parker, am a hot fox".' Yvonne's lips are no longer twitching. Her face is still, intense. When I don't speak, her eyebrow quirks, ever so slightly.

'Fine.' I flick my eyes up towards the cloudless sky. 'I, Elodie Parker, am a hot fox.'

'And I'm going to blow Ed's mind by wearing crotchless panties.' Yvonne's hands are suddenly snatched away from my shoulders, and she plasters a huge smile on her face as she leans to the side to see past me. 'Hello, Mrs Gacey. Do you want to pop inside and I'll be with you in one minute?' Her grin remains fixed until there's the click of the salon door closing, and then her face crumples as she stoops to press her forehead against my chest. 'Oh. My. *Fuck*.'

'It's fine.' I give my friend a reassuring pat on the back. 'She probably didn't hear.' She probably did. One of the things I learned while working at the minimarket – other than the entire biography of her grandson – was that Mrs Gacey had superhuman hearing capabilities. That woman could have heard a spider fart from the other side of the village.

'You're so lucky.' Yvonne peels her face from chest. 'I don't even have anyone to show my snatch off to.' Her gaze automatically strays to the pub across the road. 'Though not for want of trying. I'd have a drawer full of crotchless panties if I thought it'd entice Sacha.'

'Can you please stop saying . . . that.'

'What? Crotchless panties?'

I grab Yvonne by the shoulders and turn her body so she's facing the salon. 'Have fun with Mrs Gacey.' I give her a little nudge so she shuffles towards the door. 'She definitely heard you.'

Gran's fallen asleep in the armchair under the window with *Wimbledon* still playing out on the telly. I creep through to the kitchen, where I'm relieved to find my sister. As annoying as Heather can be, her company is better than being on my own with questions and fears buzzing around my head.

'I'll have a tea.'

Heather turns to give me a dark look, even though she's just boiled the kettle and it will take very little effort to make one more brew.

'You're as bad as Gran. I came home for the summer for a break and I've ended up playing care assistant instead.' She drags open the cupboard and snatches a mug from the shelf. '*Unpaid* care assistant. I should start charging. I bet I'd earn more than I do waitressing, being on call twenty-four hours a day.'

Twenty-four hours a day? As if. Heather didn't roll home until the early hours during her summers at home. Not that I could blame her. She'd been working hard at uni, plus working part-time at a restaurant, so she deserved to blow off a bit of steam. It wouldn't be long before she was back to studying.

'Sit down.' I pull out a chair at the little table tucked away in the corner. 'I'll finish that.'

Heather pauses, a teabag still pinched between thumb and finger above the mug. 'What have you done? Did you borrow my velvet trousers? Because I specifically told you that you weren't to even *look* at them. Do you know how many tables I had to clean to buy those trousers? How many times I had my arse touched by minging old men or how many times I was called "oi" or beckoned over like a dog?'

'I haven't touched your trousers.' At least I don't think I did. If it's the trousers I'm thinking of, the ones that looked like the pair of Gran's old curtains that she hung in the winter to keep the draughts out, then I definitely did not borrow them. 'I'm just trying to be nice. To be a caring big sister. You're right – you do deserve a break.'

Heather releases the teabag so it plops into the mug. 'But we don't do that.'

'What? Be nice to each other?' She has a point. I can count on my fingers how many times we've spoken on the phone since I flew out to California. 'Then maybe we should. Starting now. You sit down and I'll make the brew.'

Heather narrows her eyes. She isn't moving towards the table. 'And what do I have to do in return? Because I'm serious about those trousers. You are *not* to touch them. You still owe me for the dress you dunked in the manky river last year.'

No wonder Heather is so good at her studies; she remembers everything.

'You don't have to do anything in return. Just sit. Enjoy your tea.' And forget about the dress and the money owed, because I don't want to dip into the America fund. Past me worked hard for that money. Waitressing may not have been the most pleasant job, but neither was trying to avoid stains while stripping beds and scrubbing toilets.

Heather doesn't look convinced, but she sits anyway and I finish off the tea. Gran's still asleep but I leave a cup on the little table next to her, just in case she wakes, before returning to the kitchen. Heather frowns as I sit opposite her, squeezing into the small gap between the table and wall. It takes some manoeuvring, but I've still got the knack and eventually slide onto the seat.

'So we're going to just sit here – together – and drink our tea?' The crevices on Heather's forehead deepen as she attempts to comprehend the idea.

'Yes, because we're family. Sisters. And one day we won't be able to just sit like this and you never know, you might miss it.'

Heather snorts. 'I doubt it.' She stands up and grabs her tea, taking it up to her bedroom to drink alone.

I glance around the kitchen, which always felt too small and cluttered but now feels warm and familiar. Comforting. Maybe it won't be so bad coming back here for Heather's wedding, just to see Mum, Dad and Gran, and Yvonne – even Heather, I suppose. Because I have missed them, even if I don't always admit it to myself. The bright lights of LA don't shine quite so bright when you're on your own.

Chapter 11

I was transported back to the plane around midnight the previous time – a bit like Cinderella with the magic wearing off – and it's already late afternoon so I figure I don't have much time left. I want to make the most of my time in the past but I'm also anxious in case my actions do alter my timeline (imagine the fallout if I prevented Heather from marrying her hunky head teacher and she ever found out! She'd make a noose out of the horrible granny curtain trousers and do away with me) and since Ed is with his grandfather and Yvonne's working, my options are limited. So I watch the tennis with Gran, which is actually quite nice if you ignore her constant jibes at the players, and then I help Mum make tea when she gets home from work, offering to chop the onions, which she hates doing. It gives me the excuse to have a little weep, if I'm honest, because it's all a bit much: being back home, coming face to face with Sacha again, trying so hard not to kiss the heck out of Tomasz and seeing Ed when I know his fate. It's lovely and horrid and confusing, all wrapped up in layers of wacky and inexplicable and I'm exhausted from it all.

'Here you go.' Mum hands me a sheet of damp kitchen roll and I dab the cool tissue against my stinging eyes. 'Better?'

I nod, though I'm not sure I *do* feel better, because I'm still here, aren't I? Somehow re-enacting events from my past. It's impossible, yet I am twenty-five years old and desperate to escape Little Heaton all over again. There's a jar half-full of loose change up in my bedroom to prove it.

'Everything okay?' Mum takes the chopping board to the stove and slides the diced onion into the pan with a knife. I would have brushed off her concern the first time round, assured her that everything was fine. There's no way I would have confided in her. We didn't have one of those chummy mother–daughter relationships. I didn't see her as a friend. She was Mum. Authoritative. Annoying at times. She wasn't someone I'd offload on – that's what Ed and Yvonne were for – but maybe I should now. Because how much damage could a teeny convo with my mother make, even if I could change the past?

'What is it?' Mum's sensed the hesitation. Knows that there has to be something, otherwise I would have dismissed her concern before she'd even got the initial question out of her mouth. 'Is it work? Or something else? Some*one* else?' She turns back to the onions, prodding at them with a wooden spoon, and not having her looking at me helps me to open up more than I normally would.

'I like someone. Really like them.'

'Oh? Really?' She glances over at me, her lips turning up at the corners slyly.

'It isn't Ed.'

'Of course it's Ed. It's so obvious. You've been following that boy around the village since you could toddle.' She adds chopped carrots and celery to the pan with a little self-satisfied hum.

'Mum.' I fight a sigh. *This* is why I never used to confide in her. 'It really isn't Ed.'

'Who else could it be?' She has an annoying air about her now. A smug look that says she knows what's going on here. Even though she's so very wrong.

'There are lots of men in the world.'

Mum snorts. 'But we live in Little Heaton, where there is a shortage of everything, according to you. I assume that means potential boyfriends. Unless . . . No.' Mum shakes her head, turning back to the stove to add the garlic. 'Not the lad from the pub. Please don't tell me you have a thing for the lad from the pub.'

I'm silent. I don't tell Mum I have 'a thing' for Tomasz because it's so much more than that. I'm utterly in love with him, even now, four years on, but it's hopeless because Tomasz is no longer in love with me. I imagine he hates me for what I did and I don't blame him.

'He's a wrong 'un, Elodie.' Mum places the knife down on the chopping board as the room fills with a delicious garlicky smell. 'He nearly ran over Reverend Carter outside the minimarket the other day.'

'Did he?' I didn't know that. Tomasz never mentioned it and he was always a careful driver, unlike his brother. Oh. *That* boy from the pub. 'Sacha nearly ran over Reverend Carter? On his bike?' If only. It would have stopped the argument with Ed a few years later. Stopped Ed climbing on that same bike just to get away from his grandfather.

'He mounted the pavement and nearly took the reverend out. Silly boy. You need to stay away from him. He's bad news.'

'Yeah. You're right.' I run the tap to wash my hands of the onion. 'I'll keep my distance from Sacha.' I'd happily never set eyes on Sacha Nowak again.

We eat our spaghetti off lap trays in front of the telly. *The Chase* is on and although I probably watched it the first time round, I still perform poorly. Even Gran gets more questions right than me and she's having to concentrate really, really hard to get the spaghetti to twirl round her fork so is only half-listening. Afterwards, Mum takes Gran to the knit 'n' natter group at the church hall and Heather locks herself in the bathroom, where she'll soak until she resembles a prune. So it's just me and Dad, which is quite nice as I haven't spent any quality time with him yet and I'll be leaving in a few hours.

'You're coming out to the *gourden* with me?' Dad sounds surprised as I follow him out of the back door, but then I'd never have normally come out here with him. The garden – or the gourden as he'd rebranded it – was Dad's domain. He'd really got into growing his own veg since watching *Gardeners' World* with Gran, and he'd taken a particular shine to gourds, which he'd planted at the bottom of the garden. Mum said he'd only gone to the actual effort of growing anything to prove he had an interest in gardening rather than only watching the program to lust over Frances Tophill, but whatever the inspiration for his green fingers, he was certainly passionate about it now and it would be the one hobby he stuck at for more than a couple of weeks.

'Hey there, Betsy.' Dad crouches down in front of the trellis he's set up along the wall, reaching out to tenderly touch the leaves of the first plant. 'You're looking good today. And you, Antonia. You're growing fast!' There are five plants set out in front of the trellis, and each has its own name, which is quite sweet. The gourds, unfortunately, won't last as Mum will deem them 'too ugly' and 'creepy-looking', so next year Dad will be encouraging crops of sweetcorn and broad beans to grow.

'We have to be on the lookout for powdery mildew.' Dad wriggles his phone free from his trouser pocket, tapping at the screen before angling it towards me. There's a zoomed-in photo of a leaf with fuzzy white patches. 'I haven't seen any yet, but apparently it's bad. Or *not gourd*. Not good. Get it?' Dad chuckles to himself as he slips the phone back into his pocket. 'Would you like to water them?'

I would, oddly enough. I'm enjoying seeing this passionate yet playful side of Dad. I didn't notice it before, and not because Dad didn't show it to me. I simply wasn't interested enough to look for it. I'd been so fixated on getting out of Little Heaton, especially after what happened with Ed, that I'd stopped seeing what was in front of me. Only the future mattered, which would be funny, being back in the past, if it wasn't so baffling.

I water the plants under Dad's watchful eye and he tells me what he plans to do with the gourds once he's harvested them. His face is all lit up in a way I haven't seen before and I vow to take more of an interest in the future. I'll ask about his garden when we're on the phone and I'll definitely help him to care for his plants when I'm back for the wedding.

Mum and Gran are back in time for *Holby City*, which Dad takes as his cue to head to the Farmer's Arms for 'a swift pint'. Heather's out of the bath by now but she doesn't look impressed by Gran's TV choice. I ask her if she wants to go for a drink and the shock when she agrees should be enough to zap me back to the plane in the present day. But I remain in Mum and Dad's living room in the past while Heather dashes upstairs to change out of her loungewear and throw on some lippie. She must really dislike *Holby* because I don't think we have ever been to the pub together. I don't think we've ever socialised at all together. Heather was always just my annoying little sister, and we didn't have time for each other, but I realise now that I've missed her while I've been away. Absence really *does* make the heart grow fonder.

Ed hasn't called me like he said he would, so I send him a message, asking how it went with his grandad and letting him know we'll be in the pub if he fancies joining us. I invite Yvonne along and think about asking Tomasz too, but even though I'd survived being in his company this afternoon, I don't want to push my luck. Obviously, as we're going to the Royal Oak, there's a chance we'll bump into him anyway, and I'd suggest we head to the Farmer's instead but it'd be completely out of character. Plus, there's no way Heather would even think about drinking in Dad's local. Once again, living in a small village is biting me on the arse. In LA, I could disappear, blend into the background, choose any bar to spend an evening in and nobody would know me or my life story. Yes, it can be lonely, but it feels safer. I can't have my heart broken again if nobody has easy access to it.

Heather's wearing the velvet trousers, and they look even more hideous than they did on the hanger with their ridiculous turn-ups. Not that I say this to Heather as I value my life and tonight is about connecting with my sister. Spending a couple of hours together before our lives splinter off all over again. Ed and Yvonne are already at the bar when we get to the pub, and Ed raises his eyebrows and nods towards Heather when she heads straight to the loos to check her lipstick.

I shrug. 'She's my sister.'

'I know. And that's my point. You've never voluntarily been in the same room before.' Ed lifts his hand to catch the attention of the bar staff, and he orders a round of drinks.

'I'm sorry about your grandad and the volunteer thing.' Yvonne's managed to bag the only free table near the door and we join her with the drinks. 'That sucks.'

Ed sighs. 'It does. Grandad was definitely at the back of the queue when they were giving out Christian values.'

'Luckily, you were at the front.' I reach across the table and give Ed's hand a squeeze. 'And I'm sure you'll find something else for them. I could have a word with Gillian at work if you want?' Too late, I realise I can't do this. For one thing, I barely know Gillian Quinn yet and also, I'll be leaving very soon to return to my normal, present-day life.

'That would be amazing.' Ed's face has lit up at the idea, and I push away any qualms because Ed's smile fills me to the brim with warmth and joy.

'Do you think you could get me some work?' Heather plonks herself down on the stool next to me and takes a sip of her vodka Coke through a straw. 'Not volunteer, though. I'll need paying. I'm proper skint and I want to go to Kendal Calling next month. Tickets are a hundred and thirty-five quid, but that includes camping, and Keeley went last year and said it was the best festival she's ever been to. I think it's the *only* festival she's ever been to, but . . .' She shrugs and takes another sip of her drink.

'Camping?' My eyes flick to Ed and then Yvonne, who look as bemused as I feel. 'You?' I can't imagine my sister sleeping in a tent, with bugs and spiders and questionable toilet facilities.

Ed shares a look with me before he turns to my sister. 'You know you have to sleep in a tent, right?'

Heather heaves a sigh and shakes her head. 'Of course I know you have to sleep in a tent.'

'And that tent's on the ground? And you'll probably end up with someone's big toe up your nostril during the night?'

Heather looks suitably horrified at the big toe bit. Ed looks like he's enjoying himself.

'You spent three months at that campsite last year.' Heather arches an eyebrow at Ed. 'If you can survive that, I can make it through a weekend. Although you were in France, which is a lot nicer than the UK, actually. Less rain?' She aims the question at Ed but he doesn't answer. He no longer looks amused. His chin has dropped towards his chest, his shoulders hunched forwards, and his cheeks have taken on a pink tinge.

'You'll be fine.' My tone is overbright. Too chummy. False. 'It'll be fun. A good chance to let your hair down after all your hard work at uni.'

'Exactly.' Heather nods and slurps the dregs of her drink through the straw. 'Shall I get another round in?'

'Yes please.' I'm overbright again, but at least Ed is perking up. He gives the tiniest nod, an even tinier smile, and thanks her.

'I'll come and give you a hand.' Yvonne shuffles out from behind the table and heads to the bar with Heather.

'Can we talk about last summer? When you were in France?'

Ed looks stricken, his Adam's apple bobbing as he swallows hard. He covers his mouth with his hand, as though he might throw up over the table. But I have to do this. I can't believe

87

I never noticed the agony Ed had been carrying around with him because it's as clear as day right now.

'Have you seen my brother?'

Sacha Nowak is standing over us, his full lips set in a pout, as though he's a model on a shoot, and a pair of sunglasses perch on top of his blond curls. The sun has lightened the dirty blond and his skin is tanned. I can see why Yvonne was so smitten with him back then, at the same time as wanting to lamp him.

'Not since this afternoon.' Ed stands up, taking a step away from the table. From me and the conversation I've tried to initiate. 'Do you want me to help you look for him?'

'Nah.' Sacha's backing away, reaching for the sunglasses, which he slips down over his eyes even though he's still indoors. 'You're all right. He'll turn up. Not like you can get lost in this shithole.'

'Little Heaton isn't a shithole.' I'm not sure whether I'm bigging up the village because I mean it or simply to argue with Sacha.

'It is a bit small.' Ed hasn't sat back down, and he's fidgeting, as though he's deciding whether to stay or leg it while he has the chance.

'A bit small?' Sacha's laugh is mean. Mocking. 'You can't take a piss without someone else knowing about it. Does my head in. Wish I hadn't come back from Nottingham.'

'Wish you'd stayed with Ronnie?' I tilt my chin so I'm looking directly at Sacha. I feel commanding, for the tiniest fraction of a second. As though I'm in control for once.

'You what?' The sunglasses are shielding Sacha's eyes, but his mouth is pressed into an angry-looking line, and I feel vulnerable with him towering over me. All the power is zapped away in an instant. 'Why? What has our Tomasz said about Ron?'

'Nothing.' My heart is hammering, but I somehow remain outwardly calm. 'He hasn't said a thing.' *I know your secret*, I think to myself but I'm not brave enough to form the words out loud. Instead I watch silently as Sacha backs away.

'Good, because whatever he says, he's lying. Got it?' He turns and saunters away, and it isn't until he's pushing the pub's door open that Yvonne notices him. She turns to me, her mouth wide open. She mouths something at me but I don't catch it because I'm too busy willing myself to disappear back onto the plane, because as much as I've been enjoying spending time with my friends and family, Sacha's appearance has reminded me about Ed and what is to come and I really, really don't want to be here a moment longer.

Chapter 12

Seeing Sacha and being reminded of the night Ronnie arrived has put me on edge. It isn't as though I've ever forgotten that night – how could I? – but I don't allow myself to dwell on it. If my mind ever wanders there, I snap it back to something else: cleaning, taking on mundane tasks at work that I'd usually delegate, compiling shopping lists – anything so I don't have to picture the night Ed died. But there's no real escape here in the past. There are reminders everywhere and I can't cope with it. I need to go back. To the plane. To real life. To the time when my only real worry was having to attend my sister's wedding. At least then the terrible thing had already happened and I didn't have to dread the day it would play out all over again. I wish I knew for certain that I could change the past, but what use would I be here, years before the accident? I don't think begging Ed to never ever get on a motorbike without a sane explanation will work.

'What did he say?' Yvonne plonks a couple of pints down on the table and flops down onto her seat. 'Did he say anything about me?'

'What *didn't* he say about you?' Ed slides one of the pints across the table so it's sitting in front of him. 'We couldn't shut him up. It was Yvonne this, Yvonne that. The man's smitten.'

Yvonne heaves a sigh as she slumps back in her seat, crossing her arms aggressively. 'Shut up, you clown.' She narrows her eyes at Ed for a moment before she turns to me. 'What did he really say?'

I take the pint Heather is proffering and set it down on the table. 'He was looking for Tomasz.'

'Oh.' Yvonne unfolds her arms, resting her elbow on the table and resting her cheek on her upturned palm. 'Boring.'

'Sorry.' I try to sound convincing, but I'm not sorry. I wish Yvonne had never met Sacha. I wish none of us had. He's poison. At least he won't be here when I'm back to my normal life. Little Heaton will be safe in that respect. 'How did it go with Mrs Gacey this afternoon?' We need a change in topic, even if we do run the risk of straying into crotchless panty territory again.

Yvonne scrunches up her nose. 'Did you know her grandson is visiting? Because I do – she told me fifteen million times. And she wasn't in the chair for long – she only had a shampoo and set. I sometimes wish Shaz *would* sell up so I wouldn't have to put up with Christine and her tales of her super-duper grandson.'

'But then you'd be out of a job.'

Yvonne shrugs off Ed's point. 'I'd find a new job. There are other salons out there. More modern ones, where the average age of the clientele isn't seventy-two.'

'Sounds like you love your job.' Heather hides a smirk behind her glass. It's the look of someone who has yet to start their career and discover it isn't quite what you thought it'd be.

'I do. Or I would if the salon was run to its full potential. Shaz is never going to make any real money from pensioner specials.'

'And how is she going to make any real money in Little Heaton? We're a tiny village with rubbish access. Nobody is going to make a special journey here, no matter how modern the salon is.'

Yvonne opens her mouth to argue, but the door to the pub opens and she's distracted as she strains her neck to get a better view. I can see the moment she realises it isn't Sacha returning: her face falls and she slouches back down in her seat, snatching up her pint for an angry swig. I slouch down in my own seat, my eyes focused on the table so I don't catch their attention, because it's Tomasz and his grandparents. I cover my face with my hands and will myself back on the plane.

'Are you falling asleep?'

Ed has poked me in the side, and he's looking at me with his head tilted to one side, the corners of his lips lifted slightly in a bemused half-smile.

'Sorry.' I fake a yawn, too loud and too dramatic. 'Early start at the hotel.'

'I used to work at the hotel.' I could kick myself as Irene Nowak stops besides us, smiling fondly. 'Back during the war. It wasn't a hotel back then. I'm not sure what it was before it was requisitioned, actually.' The lines on her forehead crease as she tries to remember. She beckons her husband over and my heart drops when Tomasz follows as well. He is way too cute to be standing there unkissed. 'What did they use the castle for, before the war?'

Irene's husband shakes his head. 'No idea. A residence, maybe, for someone very wealthy?'

Irene smiles and pats him on the hand. 'I bet that was it.' She turns to me. 'How's it going working there now? I bet it's posh, isn't it? Franciszek has promised to take me for afternoon tea, but we've been here for a year and it hasn't happened yet.' She nudges her husband, but you can tell from her tone and the smile playing at her lips that she's only teasing him. 'You used to work at the shop, didn't you? With Christine?' Irene stoops and lowers her voice. 'She seems like a bit of a battle-axe to me. Reminds me of my old neighbour, Mrs Newton. She was always telling us off when we were little. Said we were making too much noise. We were only playing, the miserable old goat. Then there was the lady at the butcher's who never had a kind word to say about anybody, not even her long-suffering husband. She disappeared one day, you know. Rumour had it that the husband had snapped and strangled her before feeding her through the mincer.'

'That's a bit grim, Gran.'

Irene dismisses Tomasz's qualm with a wave of her hand. 'It wasn't true. The postmaster had also done a flit at the same time. Turns out they'd run off together. Been carrying on together for months, apparently. You've never seen a man as happy as that butcher when he was set free.' Irene chuckles, her cheeks plumping up and her eyes almost disappearing behind the crinkled-up skin. 'Happy as Larry, he was. He ended up having a great love affair with a lady from up the road. They were never married but they had three strapping lads – quite scandalous, back then – and they were together until the butcher died in his nineties. Went peacefully in his sleep with his lady by his side.'

Tomasz's grandfather smiles fondly at his wife. 'You always were one to spin a good yarn. The stories you used to tell to keep us entertained while we stuck in that hospital. Like a little ray of sunshine, you were.'

I sit up straighter, fully alert now as I realise I've never heard the story of Franciszek and Irene from her point of view. It's always been through her husband or its retelling via Tomasz or his mum. It'd be nice to hear the story from Irene's perspective.

'Can you tell us the story of how you and Mr Nowak met?'

Irene smiles, her eyes crinkling at the corners again. 'My favourite love story of all time. You can keep your Romeo and your Prince Charming. This man is the only hero I'll ever want.' She turns to her husband and even though I can only see part of her face, it's lit up with adoration. 'Obviously, it didn't start off so well. There was the war on and everything.' Ed has given up his seat for Irene, and she sits down, tucking her wellington-boot-clad feet under the table. Ed spies a couple of free chairs, which he squeezes around the table. He and Franciszek sit down to hear the story while Tomasz leans against the wall behind me. I can't see him but I can feel him there. I focus intently on Irene's words to try to dispel the discomfort of having him so close without being able to touch him.

'I had two choices back then: work in one of the munitions factories or help out at the castle. They'd turned the place into a temporary hospital and while I'd never had any aspirations for nursing, it seemed like the better option.'

'All those young soldiers.' Franciszek wiggles his bushy eyebrows up and down. Behind me, Tomasz makes gagging sounds while Irene taps her husband lightly on the arm.

'Don't be saucy. It was the travelling. We didn't have a car between us back then, so my sister and I would have had to cycle miles to one of the factories. The castle was right there, up on the hill, so that's where we decided to do our bit. Those young soldiers were an added bonus.' Irene winks, and there are more gagging noises from Tomasz while his grandfather whoops with laughter.

'Now who's being saucy?'

'But I only had eyes for one soldier.' Irene smiles at her husband, her head leaning in towards him, and her adoration for him is written all over her face. I'd loved like that once and it takes every ounce of energy I possess to not turn around to look at Tomasz. It had been inconceivable that our love story would ever end, but life can be cruel.

'It was that Martin Fellowes, wasn't it? All the ladies fell for his classic handsome looks.'

Irene tuts at her husband. 'I'm talking about you, you old fool, and you know it. It was love at first sight.' She turns back to her audience around the table. 'At least for me. I used to practically run up that hill every morning to see him and I'd practise saying his name, over and over again. I'd never heard anything so exotic.'

'You were still getting it wrong up to our wedding day.'

Irene taps her husband on the arm again. 'I was not. I'd mastered it long before you left to go back fighting.' The light from her eyes dims. 'When we had to say goodbye. I never thought I'd see him again. We'd fallen in love and then he was gone. Back to fighting. Back to Poland if he survived.'

'What did you do?' I know what Franciszek did – he secured

a future for the pair, working to afford a home for them to start their new life together. But what about his wife?

Irene shrugs. 'What could I do? I got on with life. There was no other choice. The war ended. The hospital closed. I started working in the post office. Got engaged.'

My eyes widen. 'You got engaged? To someone else?'

Irene chuckles, her cheeks at full plump. 'Why not? I never thought I'd see Franciszek again. I didn't even know if he was still alive at this point.'

'Why didn't you write to Gran?' Tomasz's voice is full of accusation, despite the years and the happily ever after that passed.

'Because I'm a fool.'

Irene nods at her husband's assessment of himself. 'A big fool, but he got there in the end.'

'So what happened?' I lean forward in my seat in my eagerness to hear more. 'You were engaged to another man and then . . .'

'Then this great lump showed up, out of the blue.' She smiles indulgently at her husband. 'And it was love at second sight. I knew I couldn't marry Sid, lovely as he was. It was Franciszek who my heart belonged to and this was our second chance at love. I took it with both hands and I've never regretted it for a second.'

I think about what would happen if I was given a second chance at love. Would I take it with both hands, or would I run away all over again? Tomasz is right behind me and I can't bear to not look at him for a second longer. I could start our love story early. Or snog his face off one last time before I'm dragged away to the present. I brace myself to do it. To turn around and ask Tomasz if I can have a word with him outside. Once alone, I'll tell him how I feel, or at least a watered-down version because I don't want to scare him away with a full-on declaration of undying love before we've even had our first kiss.

I turn around, my heart beating painfully hard and fast. I'm going to do it. No more scaredy-cat Elodie Parker.

'I need to get going.' Tomasz is looking at his watch. He pushes himself away from the wall and shuffles over to kiss his grandmother's cheek.

'Meeting Holly?'

Irene's question glues my mouth shut. I won't be asking Tomasz for a private word. I won't be confessing anything tonight. Because Tomasz has a girlfriend.

Chapter 13

My head is still full of the Nowaks and second chances at love as Ed walks me home. It really is too late to put things right between me and Tomasz. I can't erase those terrible things I said, can't take away the pain of losing Ed, and I'll be leaving this place, this time, any minute now. But I still think about Tomasz, even before I came back to Little Heaton in these weird time-travel stints, no matter how hard I try not to. Little things bring Tomasz back to me. A stranger in the street who looks a bit like him from behind, or has the same walk or mannerisms. A bubble of laughter that grows and grows until there are tears to be wiped away. And I dream of him, often. Happy dreams, not tainted with the anguish of reality, and I both cherish and despise those dreams in equal measure, because as lovely as they are in the moment, there is always the waking up to do, when real life douses the fantasy. I don't allow my thoughts to linger on him when I'm awake, because then I'd have to face up to the truth.

I made a massive mistake. I paint Sacha as the villain, because it's easier than admitting that it was me. I was the one who cracked mine and Tomasz's relationship. Who picked at it and picked at it until there was nothing but scraps of love left. Scraps that seemed impossible to thread back together. And then I left him. I abandoned everything – our life together, our future – and jetted off for a new start. And the worst bit is, I'm not even living happily ever after. I'm miserable and lonely and I'm beginning to realise how much I've been missing everyone. How much I've been missing out on. I *want* to hear about Dad's veggies, I want to cook with Mum and I want to get to know my sister, to get beyond the annoying spats we had as kids. My sister is getting married and I've done nothing but complain instead of sharing her joy.

But it isn't too late. I can be there for Heather. I can tell her how happy I am that she's found the person she wants to spend the rest of her life with. How proud I am of her for working hard to achieve her dreams. They may not be the dreams she envisioned for herself in the beginning, but things change. *People* change. I didn't get that. I thought Heather had failed by not escaping our childhood village, but who is happier right now? Me, in my one-bed apartment with a view of a brick wall and neighbours whose names I only know because their mail was once posted into the wrong mailbox? Where I have one friend, who I barely see these days because she's moved to another state? Or Heather, with the husband-to-be who adores her, a job she loves, and her friends and family all within easy reach?

I can cook with Mum when I come home, and tell her how sorry I am that I've put such a distance between us, both physically and emotionally. And I can take an interest in Dad's gardening. I may even pay proper attention to his political rants from time to time. It isn't too late to mend the broken threads of my family, and Heather's wedding has presented the perfect opportunity. All I have to do is get myself back on the plane.

'I can't come in.'

I start at the sound of Ed's voice. I've been so lost in my thoughts, I hadn't realised we'd made it to my front door.

'I've got an early start.' Ed shoves his hands in the pockets of his leather jacket and shifts his weight from one foot to the other. He won't meet my eye because the conversation I tried to start earlier is still hanging in the air. He steps forward, taking one hand out of his pocket so he can rest it on my shoulder as he stoops down to kiss me on the cheek, still avoiding eye contact. He's about to pull away, but I snatch him to me, my arms around his shoulders, pulling him in close. My nostrils fill with the scent of warm leather as I burrow my face in his chest. I should have talked to him about the France thing but I can't rush it and time's running out.

'I love you, Ed.' I release him from my grip, but I don't let him go completely. Not yet. My hands hold his face as I reach up on tiptoe to rest my forehead against his. 'I always will. No matter what.'

I kiss him on the cheek and hope my words are enough.

The house is quiet when I step inside. Heather got a taxi to meet up with some old school friends in town and the others are already in bed. I creep up the stairs, pausing on the landing outside Mum and Dad's room. I'll be back soon, to put things right. I climb the narrow staircase up to my bedroom and kick off my sandals before easing myself down on the bed, reaching for the postcard Ed sent me almost a year ago. On the front is a picture of the Eiffel Tower, overlaid with facts about the country. I turn the postcard over and run my thumb over Ed's words, over the mishmash of print and joined-up letters that is unique to him. I read these words over and over again while he was away, my heart aching with how much I missed him, counting down the months, the weeks, the days, the *hours* until he was home again.

I press the postcard to my chest now, wishing I'd taken more care of it. Been more like Mum and kept hold of everything that was important to me. If I could, I'd take this postcard with me. Rescue it. Because I will regret losing it forever.

I prop the postcard against the America fund jar and lie down on the bed, shattered suddenly. I close my eyes and will the roar to start, to let me know that I'm on my way back.

* * *

I don't hear the roar. It's another sound. Sharper. More piercing. And much more annoying.

'Shurrup.'

My voice is slurred, my dry mouth struggling to form the words. I must have fallen asleep while I waited for the transfer to the plane and my eyes feel heavy as I peel them open. I shut them again. I'm not on the plane. I'm still in my loft bedroom. Still wearing the slip dress I wore to the pub. And the noise is coming from the set of drawers next to the bed.

I sit up, squinting against the light pouring through the window. The blind hasn't been closed and the light is dazzling.

'Shut up.' I find the source of the noise: my alarm clock. 'Ssh!' I jab at the button to silence it and drop my face into my hands. I'm not on the plane. I'm still in Little Heaton, still seven years in the past judging by the crumpled dress I'm wearing. My handbag has dropped to the floor and I rifle through it in search of my phone, which confirms my suspicion that I haven't travelled anywhere. It's only a day later. I'm still reliving the past.

This can't be right. I can't *still* be here. Last time, I visited for just a day before I hopped back to the plane. Why am I hop-free?

My mouth is desert-dry. I need water. Or wine. Wine would be very good right now. Maybe things would start to make more sense if I was blind drunk. I stumble across the bedroom, my body still sluggish, still half-asleep, and move carefully down the two sets of stairs. Mum's in the kitchen, filling the kettle, and she frowns at me as I stagger into the room.

'Did you sleep in your clothes?' Her voice is laced with judgement as she looks me up and down.

'Yep.' I yawn loudly as I head for the cupboard and it takes enormous effort to drag the door open and reach for a glass. I feel as though I've been hit by a truck.

'What time did you get in last night?'

I shrug, leaning against the sink for support as I turn on the tap. 'Just before midnight, I think.'

100

Mum's tut is in sync with the switching on of the kettle. 'No wonder you look like you've been dragged out of a cave. You need to get a decent night's sleep.'

I turn the tap off and take a sip of the water. 'I would have had a much better night's sleep if my alarm hadn't woken me up.'

'But then you would have been late for work.' Mum reaches up to open the cupboard and grab a mug. 'Cup of tea?'

I shake my head as I groan. Work. I have to go to work. Here, in Little Heaton, back down on the bottom rung. And it isn't as though the money will be worth the effort. Plus, I won't even get to spend it, as presumably I'll be spirited away back to the present day. This sucks.

It takes every ounce of energy I possess to drag myself back up the stairs. I get myself ready for work, pulling on the trousers and white tunic that makes up my chambermaid outfit, and head across the village. The commute isn't bad, I suppose, and Little Heaton feels peaceful at this time of the morning while most people are still slumbering and the shops and the pubs aren't open yet. There's a stillness I've never experienced in LA, which had been a plus point – you can't dwell on the past if you're rushing forward – but I find I quite like hearing the birds chirruping as I head up the path towards the gates of the castle.

Durban Castle is fairy-tale-like beyond the gates, its turrets stretching up to towards the sky, the vast pale-bricked building surrounded by lush grass and wild flowers. There's nowhere as pretty as this in the LA I inhabit. Nothing so dreamy or uncon-strained. Everything was uniform in the places I ventured out into, with its grid-like roads and carefully spaced trees, and I wish I'd appreciated the rebellious nature of Little Heaton while I'd had the chance.

'Name badge!'

The bark of the head housekeeper makes me jump as I step through the staff entrance at the side of the building, and my stomach lurches once I process her words. I'm not wearing my name

101

badge and I have no idea where past me would have put it. On the drawers, next to the America fund jar? I can't recall seeing it there when I picked up the postcard last night, but then I hadn't been on the lookout for it. In my handbag? I unzip it and rifle through, but there's no name badge to be found.

'Well?' Linda arches an eyebrow as my shoulders slump in defeat.

'I don't have it.'

Linda's lips purse, scrunching up tight so there's just a little pink, wrinkled 'O' where her mouth should be. She watches me with her mouth all puckered up for ages, as though the name badge will appear if she glares at me for long enough.

'Your name badge is part of your uniform. Would you arrive at work without your trousers?' Linda sweeps her hand in the general area of my legs.

'It depends how drunk I'd got the night before.'

I think this is amusing. Linda does not, and the flaring nostrils of my manager wipe the smile straight off my face.

'No.' I look down at the carpet, which isn't nearly as plush as it is out in the public areas of the castle. It isn't shabby exactly, but your feet don't sink into it. 'I wouldn't show up without my trousers.' Which really isn't the same as forgetting your name badge, especially when you haven't worn that name badge for seven years. She's lucky I've turned up at all if you think about it, because I'm going through the motions here, living the life of seven-years-ago-Elodie, but I don't have to. I could tell Linda to stick the name badge up her arse and go and sit in the pub until I'm shaken out of this time-hop thing. I could strip off and run around the hotel in my undies and it wouldn't matter because this isn't really my life now. But then I remember the butterfly effect and reason that if I am overriding the past here, then getting sacked would impact my present-day self quite a lot.

'Everything okay here?'

Linda stiffens, her shoulders jerking back and straightening her spine. I half expect her to salute as Gillian Quinn stops beside her.

'Ms Parker has forgotten her name badge.' Linda pierces me with her eyes even though she's speaking to the hotel manager.

'Oh dear.' Gillian turns sharply and starts to stalk away. 'Thank you, Linda. I'll deal with this now. Come with me, Ms Parker.'

Linda's lips twitch as she watches me leave. I bet she's dying to rub her hands together with glee. *I'm* dying to tell her to get bent, but I resist and instead remain silent as I trail after Gillian. I need to not get sacked more than I need to vent, just in case my actions now do affect my future. We head along the corridor, turning off to the left, and then to the right. The castle is a warren of corridors and I'm not sure I'll remember my way around. Linda will be thrilled if I get lost within the maze of passageways.

Gillian stops at one of the doors along the latest corridor, pushing down on the handle and swinging it open. She indicates that I should step inside her office before following me inside.

'Take a seat, *Ms Parker.*' She catches my eye and I realise she's smirking. Mocking Linda. 'Here.' She sits down at her desk pulls open a drawer. She grabs something, which she pushes across the desk towards me. It's a name badge, but it isn't mine. It's an old badge of Gillian's, from when she was the events manager of the hotel. 'It'll have to do for today. It'll keep *Ms Peterson* happy, at least.'

'You think?' I don't mean to say it out loud, and I clamp a hand over my mouth, my eyes widening in shock. But Gillian snorts, her lips pressing together to prevent full-on laughter, and I'm reminded why we're friends. Not now, seven years in the past, not yet. But we will be.

'You have a point, but stick it on anyway, just in case. Linda can't pull you up on not having a badge if I've told you to wear that one temporarily.'

'Thank you.' I pick up the badge and pin it to my top.

'No worries.' Gillian shrugs. 'We all make mistakes, and this one is tiny in the grand scheme of things. There's no need to make someone feel small over it.'

Gillian always was a good boss. She was firm when she needed to be but always fair. And she was kind and encouraging. I wouldn't have fulfilled my America dream if it wasn't for her. I bet if I'd offered to ask Gillian about the volunteer work for Ed's young people, she'd have agreed to it. I could ask now. Float the idea and test my theory, even if it hadn't actually happened in reality. It's a good thing so it can't have a negative impact on the future, surely.

'I have this friend.'

Gillian had turned to her computer screen, probably expecting me to pin the badge on and scuttle off to start my morning duties, but she doesn't look annoyed that I'm disturbing her work. Her eyebrows rise, ever so slightly, and she nods, encouraging me to go on.

'He's a youth worker.' Why is my mouth so dry? This is *Gillian*. My friend. She's seen me fall out of a cab onto the pavement, so drunk on champagne that my legs wouldn't function properly. She's seen me cry so much I was in danger of vomiting. And she's still my friend, even when she's seen me at my worst. She's the only real friend I have out in America. 'And he's trying to organise some volunteer work for some of the people he works with. Some gardening, maybe? To give them a confidence boost. Something to put on their CV. That kind of thing.'

Gillian's head tilts to one side. 'And you want them to volunteer here? In the gardens?'

It's hard to swallow, but I give it a go. 'Maybe. If it was something the hotel was up for.'

Gillian holds my gaze for a moment, her eyes narrowing slightly. I'm regretting asking when she finally speaks.

'Leave it with me. No promises, but I'll look into it.'

I sag against my seat. 'That's brilliant. Thank you so much.'

104

'No worries. It's a great idea in theory.'

I push back my chair and stand up while Gillian turns back to the computer screen, but I hesitate as I reach the door. Dare I push this a bit further?

'Gillian?' I dare. I'm shocked but pleased. 'You don't happen to have any jobs going, do you? For my sister? She's home for the summer and is looking for some temp work.'

Gillian grabs the mouse, her eyes still on her computer screen. 'If she's as hardworking as you are, then definitely. Get her to shoot her CV over.'

'Brilliant. Thanks again.' I propel myself out of the office and into the corridor before I start asking for a promotion. Two favours in one morning is enough.

I look up and down the corridor, the passage stretching on and on both ways. I need to find my way to the breakfast room, and fast, before hungry guests start to arrive and Linda gets in another tizz.

Chapter 14

There is something very, very wrong. A week has gone by and I'm still stuck in the past. June has crept into July and I have yet to come to on the plane. Instead, I've remained in Little Heaton, remained twenty-five (which, admittedly, I'm not going to kick up a fuss about) and I've played along with whatever trick is occurring. I get up and go to work – with my own name badge pinned to my tunic, which I'd found in the top drawer beside my bed – and help out with breakfast before cleaning the bedrooms, bathrooms and suites of the guests. I go home and make Gran's lunch and watch the tennis with her before meeting up with Ed and Yvonne in the pub. I shower and eat and chat with my family as though this is all perfectly normal, that I belong back here, and I'm starting to question whether this *is* my real life and I dreamed up the whole moving to America thing and the last seven years have been a figment of my imagination. Is it possible that I wanted it so badly, fantasised about escaping Little Heaton so much, I believed I'd achieved it?

'Raf's proper dishy, isn't he?' Laura's come round for the evening and is squeezed on the sofa with me, Mum and Ed. There's a bowl of hand-cooked crisps and a second bottle of wine open on the coffee table. Laura aims a crisp at *Holby City* on the telly. 'And he's a doctor, which is proper sexy.'

'Mum.' Ed screws up his face. 'Don't say sexy.'

'But he is. I definitely would. Wouldn't you, Elodie?'

I hold my hands up. 'Don't drag me into this.' I take a sip of my wine. 'Though he was good on *Strictly*.'

Laura frowns at me. 'But he hasn't been on *Strictly*. I'd remember that. All those tight tops and sequins and his sexy swivel hips.' She winks at Ed, just to wind him up. It works, and he pretends to stick his fingers down his throat and vomit over his lap. Luckily, it takes the attention away from my gaffe. When was Joe McFadden on *Strictly*? It was before I left the UK, I'm sure of it. But what if Joe McFadden *hasn't* taken part in *Strictly* and it's all part of my made-up fantasy world? The world I've created in my head and plotted out seven whole years of, including the tragic death of one of my best friends and the destruction of my relationship with Tomasz. Oh, God. What if there was no relationship at all? What if my life with Tomasz was yet another fabrication and he doesn't even fancy me?

I drain my glass of wine and top it up. I don't have a clue what's going on. What's right, what's wrong. Past, present, future. It's all jumbled up.

'I think we should go to the pub.' Ed wriggles free from the sofa, where he was wedged between me and his mum.

'I'd rather stay here.' Laura points another crisp at the telly. 'That supernatural drama's on after *Holby*. It was quite good last week.'

'I was talking to Elodie.'

Laura rolls her eyes at her son. 'I know. I'm pulling your leg.' She pops the crisp in her mouth, her lips lifting into a smirk as she crunches it.

'I wouldn't go in the Farmer's if I were you.' Mum gives Laura a nudge with her arm, encouraging her to shift over into the space Ed has created by moving. 'I sent Gordon in there after tea. I was up to here with listening to him going on about leadership contests and people quitting parties.' Mum rests her hand against her hairline, to demonstrate the upper limit of her tolerance for Dad's political rants. I bet he was gutted to be shunted off to the pub. 'He'll still be going off about it now, I bet. *The country's in bloody turmoil.*' She adopts a gruff voice for the last bit, which sounds more like Al Pacino in *The Godfather* than Dad. 'Honestly, Laura, he never stops going off about it all.'

He'll still be going off about it all in seven years' time.

Maybe.

Who knows? I certainly don't anymore.

'Pub.' I heave myself up off the sofa. 'Let's go and get falling-over drunk.'

The pub is pretty quiet, so I spot them almost as soon as I step inside. Sacha's sitting in the far corner, his biker-boot-clad feet propped up on a stool, with Tomasz sitting to the left of him and Yvonne sandwiched between the two. Ed starts to head towards the back of the pub once we have our drinks, but I grasp his arm to stop him. I've avoided Tomasz over the past week because although I've been pining for the boy, he's with Holly at this moment in time and I have never gone for another woman's bloke, even if I know they aren't destined to last until Christmas (perhaps I should warn Tomasz not to buy that limited-edition Gucci perfume?).

'Let's sit over here.' I nod towards the opposite corner, to a table beneath the bay window at the front of the pub.

'But Yvonne . . .' Ed aims his pint in our friend's direction.

'Yvonne's fine. She's with Sacha. She won't even notice we're here.'

Ed smirks. 'That crush isn't going away, is it? She thinks he's the best thing since toasted bread.'

'It's *sliced* bread.'

Ed shakes his head. 'I vehemently disagree. I've thought about it and toasted bread is by far the superior invention.' He sets off for Yvonne's table and I don't try to stop him this time. It'd look far too suss if I pushed it any further.

'All right, Elodie, love.' Nigel Gacey is slumped in his seat, his mouth downturned at the corners while his wife is sat ramrod-straight, her hands clasped neatly in her lap, her eyes flitting across the pub as though someone is going to jump out of a hiding spot and attack at any moment. Neither looks particularly thrilled to be sitting in the Royal Oak this evening, yet here they are. Nigel lifts his glass and gives a nod as we pass, and I stop, my legs rendered useless with the shock. Nigel's communication when I'd worked for him and his wife at the minimarket had been restricted to the odd grunt. I wasn't even sure he knew my name, to be honest.

'Hello, Mr Gacey.' I flicker a smile on my face, not fully committing to the gesture as I'm uncertain what is happening here.

'Your dad in the Farmer's?'

'He is.' Probably mid-rant about the state of the UK right now. A warm-up, really, for what's to come over the next few years.

Nigel takes a sip of his pint, his eyes narrowing as his gaze lands on his wife. He slams the pint down on the table and folds his arms across his chest, slumping even further down in his seat. I don't think I've ever seen Nigel in the Royal Oak, and it looks like he'd rather it had stayed that way. Christine pretends she hasn't noticed her husband's mood and twists in her seat so she can beam up at Ed.

'Edward. How lovely to see you. Come and meet my grandson.' She reaches across the table and squeezes the arm of the young man sitting there. 'This is Dominic. Dominic, this is Reverend Carter's grandson.'

'Hey.' Dominic smiles, lips stretched wide and showing off a row of neat, white teeth. 'Nice to meet you, Edward.'

'It's Ed.' He throws his arm around my shoulders and pulls me in close. 'And this is Elodie.'

'Hey, Elodie.' Dominic hasn't stopped smiling – he has one

of those faces that always seems to be full of joy – but it widens even further as he looks at me. 'Beautiful name.'

'Is that an American accent?' Ed looks from Dominic to me. 'Elodie's *dying* to visit America. New York or California, preferably.'

'I'm Canadian.' Dominic shrugs, still smiling away. 'Mum and Dad are from England but they moved to Canada not long after they got married.'

Mrs Gacey purses her lips. I know from the time I spent working at the minimarket that she'd never forgiven her daughter-in-law for the move, even though it was her son's work that had taken them to Canada.

'How long are you here for?'

Dominic doesn't have time to answer Ed's question because Yvonne suddenly descends, popping her head between me and Ed as she clamps a hand down on each of our shoulders.

'What's going on here then?' She spots Dominic sitting at the table with the Gaceys. 'You must be Dominic. Christine's told us all about you.'

'Has she?' Dominic, still smiling, looks at his grandmother.

'We couldn't shut her up.' Yvonne laughs, though she isn't joking. I could write an essay on the life of Dominic Gacey.

'I'm just proud of you, that's all.' Mrs Gacey reaches across the table to squeeze Dominic's arm again. 'And I'm so pleased you came all this way to see us. It's a shame your father couldn't make it. Or your mother.'

'Work.' Dominic rolls his eyes good-naturedly. 'As always.'

'Dominic's from Canada.'

Yvonne pats Ed on the back. 'I know. Quebec. He's fluent in French and is learning Japanese.' She opens her mouth to reel off more facts that have been drummed into her, but Ed gets in there first, his face alight with this new knowledge.

'*Tu parles français? Étonnante! Moi aussi.*'

Yvonne groans. 'Oh no. Not again. What's he saying?' She looks

110

at me, but I shrug. I don't speak French. She gives Ed a pointed look. 'Remember what I said about the baguette?'

Ed holds his hands up. 'I was just saying that I speak French as well. It won't happen again.' His lips twitch as he tries to contain a cheeky grin. '*Je promets.*'

Yvonne looks at Dominic, who translates: *I promise.* Yvonne holds a finger up at Ed, her eyebrows pulled down low.

'Final warning, mister.'

'Sorry.' Ed hangs his head, but probably only so Yvonne won't clock his smirk. 'Won't happen again.'

'Good. Now buy me a drink as a proper apology. I'm sitting over there.' She points at the table, where Sacha and Tomasz are still sitting.

'Why don't you join them, Dominic?' Mr Gacey is out of his seat before his grandson has had the chance to answer, and he shushes his wife as she protests. 'Let him sit with the younger ones. He doesn't want to be stuck with a couple of old farts.' He grabs his pint and downs the dregs. 'And that way, I can go to the Farmer's for a quick half.' Swiping at his mouth with the back of one hand, he raises the other in farewell before he bolts from one pub to the other.

'Well.' Mrs Gacey's mouth is pinched up tight as she stands up. 'I guess I'll go and check in on Olivia at the shop.'

'You don't mind if I stay for a bit, do you, Grandma?'

Mrs Gacey looks very much like she does mind, but she gives a brief, tight-lipped smile. 'No, of course not.' She presents her cheek as Dominic stands up and leans in to kiss her goodbye. 'You've got your key to the flat, haven't you?'

Dominic pats the pocket of his jeans. 'I have.'

Mrs Gacey looks at me and then Yvonne with a stony face, her features only softening when her gaze lands on Ed. 'You'll look after him, won't you?'

Dominic laughs lightly. 'I'm twenty-eight. The flat is a matter of yards away. I'll be fine.'

111

Mrs Gacey nods. She doesn't look convinced, but she leaves anyway. Yvonne waits until the door to the pub swings shut before she claps her hands together.

'Right then. Shots!'

Chapter 15

Dominic Gacey, with his warm, brown eyes beneath neat eyebrows and curly hair, and his perma-smile and chilled-out nature, seems to breathe life into Little Heaton. The dull village becomes vibrant overnight, as though the dimmer switch had been cranked up to the max as soon as that first shot in the Royal Oak went down. (It was Yvonne who tipped the first one into her mouth, obviously.) It didn't matter that we had work in the morning – 'we' being everyone but Dominic, whose only responsibility for the rest of his visit was to inject energy and sparkle back into our lives. We were like kids again, more so than when we were building campfires in the woods the previous summer, because it was the carefree attitude Dominic instilled in us rather than the activities that gave us back that sense of freedom.

We explore Little Heaton for the next few days, discovering its hidden charms as though it is *our* first foray into the village. We rent a barge and somehow bring it back again in one piece, picnicking along the way and chatting to walkers. Yvonne tries to befriend a goose, which doesn't go as planned and she ends up locking herself in the barge, peering through the little curtained window until the goose gives up waddling furiously after us. We watch a cricket match even though none of us really know the rules apart from Tomasz, who tries not to become exasperated by the constant questions, and we take part in karaoke and bingo at the pub. But best of all, for me at least, is our walks, where we amble for miles, enjoying the countryside that until now we've taken for granted.

'Still want to escape us?'

Ed and I are lying in a meadow of wild flowers while Yvonne, Tomasz and Dominic attempt to fish down by the river. I have no idea where we are, but it feels idyllic with the sun shining down on us while a cooling breeze ruffles the grass and leaves around us.

'It's not you I want to escape from.' I prop myself up on my elbow, so I can look down at Ed. 'It's never been about escaping from you.'

'So I can come with you on your American adventure?'

I smile sadly at Ed. No, no he can't come with me. I wish he could. I wish I could hold on tight to him and never let him go, but Ed won't get the chance.

'Oh my God.' Ed laughs, leaving his mouth gaping open in outrage. 'You actually don't want me to come with you. You want to leave me here, on my tod.'

'That isn't true.' I keep my face neutral, even though I can feel the corners of my mouth tugging. 'You won't be on your own – Yvonne will be here.'

Ed's eyes widen. 'And that's supposed to make me feel *better*?'

'Stop it.' I nudge Ed and settle back down so I'm looking up at the sky again. 'You love Yvonne to bits.'

Ed sighs. 'It's true. I do. She's like the sister I never had. The really annoying little sister. Like Heather.'

'Heather isn't so bad.'

Ed sits up, twisting around so he can look down at me. 'Who are you and what have you done with the real Elodie?'

If only Ed knew I really wasn't the Elodie who is supposed to be here.

114

'What? She isn't. I know I used to think she was a pain in the arse – and she can still be a pain, actually – but she's mostly okay. Gillian at work loves her, which makes her like me even more since I recommended her for the job. I'm getting brownie points all round – for Heather and for your volunteers.'

'You deserve all the brownie points.' Ed's hand finds mine and our fingers entwine. 'You're amazing. I hope you realise that.'

I squeeze my fingers tighter around Ed's. There's something happening. A churning, deep in the pit of my stomach, and my heart rate is picking up, thumping a gallop in my chest. My mouth is dry, making it difficult to swallow and when I speak, my voice cracks.

'I hope you realise how much I love you, Edward Carter-Brown.'

Ed squeezes my hand back. 'I love you too, Elodie Parker. Always.'

'You don't have to tell me about France.'

Ed's grip of my hand slackens so it's only me holding on now. 'France? What do you mean?' His voice is hoarse, barely even there at all.

'You don't have to tell me about it, but know that I will listen if you ever want to talk. I will hear you. I will love you. No matter what.'

Ed doesn't say anything. We don't even look at each other. We stare up at the blue sky, my heart rate slowing with every breath, and I feel at peace for the first time in forever. I wish it could always be like this, but at some point I will have to return to reality.

Ed lifts our hands, properly entwined once again, and he presses his lips to my fingers.

'Elodie! Ed!'

We prop ourselves up on our elbows. Down by the river, Yvonne is jumping up and down, her arms waving about. Next to her, Tomasz is holding a hand up to his forehead, shielding his eyes from the sun. I can't see who he's looking at from over here but it feels like his focus is entirely on me. Wishful thinking, maybe.

'Come and look what we've caught!'

I look at Ed. He smiles, sadly. He doesn't understand that it really is okay. I lean across and kiss his cheek.

'Last one to the river has to buy the first round in the pub tonight!'

I'm up on my feet before Ed even has the chance to register my challenge, but he still beats me to the river, where Yvonne proudly presents the smallest fish I have ever seen outside of a goldfish bowl.

'Are you sure that isn't a slightly overweight tadpole?' Ed leans in close to the fish, squinting as though he can hardly make it out. Yvonne whacks him on the arm.

'It's a fish, and I caught it all by myself.'

'Impressive.' Ed frowns. 'Though it isn't every day that the chips are bigger than the fish.'

'Shut up, you fanny.' Yvonne whacks him again, harder this time, and Ed rubs at his arm. 'You've never caught anything other than a cold and if you don't stop winding me up, I'll be chucking you in the river and not Gilly.'

We head back to the village and Ed walks me home. I have to force myself to prise my hand from his and once upstairs in my bedroom, I pick up the postcard, rereading it for the millionth time before propping it back up against the America fund jar. One day Ed won't be a fixture in my life and I won't even have this postcard, with his mishmash handwriting and humour, as a memento of our time together.

Chapter 16

I think I'm stuck in the past. It's been a week since the fishing trip at the wild flower meadow and I'm still here in the village instead of thousands of feet up in the sky in the present day. Heather's staying with her mates for the weekend, Gran has refused to leave her armchair while Wimbledon's on and Dad's spent every free minute patrolling the garden for pests eager to chomp through his crop. Life has continued with no hint that I'll be going back to my real life any time soon and, with every day that passes, I've become more convinced that I've hallucinated a life spanning several years into the future.

'Are you sure you won't come with us?' Mum's hovering by the living room door, one foot in the room, the other in the hallway. She's going into town to watch the *Absolutely Fabulous* film with Laura. Part of me does want to go with her because I've already seen the film and if I can predict the plot beforehand, it'll prove that I haven't made up the next few years at all.

'I can't. I'm meeting the others once I've changed.' I've not long got back from work and am still wearing my uniform. 'We're going for a bike ride.'

'Are you sure you won't join us?' Mum's addressing Gran this time, but she simply waves the question away, her eyes never leaving the television screen. It's the men's final, between Andy Murray and Milos Raonic. She definitely won't want to miss this. I'd quite like to watch it too as it's another way to settle the time travel versus delusion debate that's going on in my head. But I leave Gran to her tennis and go upstairs to change, shoving on a pair of leggings and a T-shirt. My old bike is in the shed and I'm pleased to see it isn't too rusted. We used to ride our bikes all the time – Ed, Yvonne and I – and we'd ride to our secondary school and back each day because it was more convenient than waiting around for the crappy bus service. I haven't sat on a bike for years though – at least not one that isn't static at the gym – so I'm hoping the saying about never forgetting is true.

I wheel the bike through to the front of the house, guiding it out of the garden and out onto the road where I climb onto the seat, one foot on the pedal, the other safely on the ground. I take a deep breath. I can do this. The handlebars wobble, but then I'm off, sailing past the cricket grounds and across the iron bridge. Yvonne and Tomasz are already waiting at the war memorial, Yvonne straddling the familiar red bike with the black seat and handlebars. Tomasz's bike is silver and black and without a hint of rust.

'Look at you with your fancy new bike.' I pick at a piece of loose paint on the handlebars of my bike. It flakes off and flutters to the ground.

'It's my dad's. He bought it last year but I don't think it's been further than the Farmer's Arms.'

'If you were going to borrow a bike, you should have gone with Sacha's.' Yvonne twists her hands back and forth over the handlebars of her own bike and makes revving noises. 'I'd have hitched a lift.'

'I don't think you'd have wanted a lift with me. I don't have a licence. I've never even had a lesson, so we'd probably end up wrapped around a tree.'

I wince at Tomasz's words, but Yvonne isn't put off. 'But at least I wouldn't have to pedal. I'm knackered already and we haven't even left the village yet. Whose stupid idea was this bike ride anyway?'

'It was mine.' Dominic skids to a stop beside us. Like me and Yvonne, his bike is old, probably pre-dating even ours. The tyres are super-thin and the handlebars curl round like rams' horns and the blue paint of the frame has faded to a pale grey, apart from a few sparse patches.

'Cool bike.' Yvonne is smirking as she says this. 'Where'd you get it? The *Antiques Roadshow*?'

'Close. It was in storage at my grandparents' with a load of dusty old junk. I think it was my dad's.' Dominic pats the curly handlebar. 'Still works though.'

Yvonne bursts out laughing, but it isn't Dominic's vintage bike that's causing the amusement. She's looking past Dominic and when I turn, I see Ed pedalling towards us in what at first glance appears to be a retro bike with a cream and brown frame but is much more modern on closer inspection.

'Nice basket.' Yvonne is trying to keep a straight face but is failing. Hard. 'Whose bike is that? Your mum's?'

'First of all, the basket is indeed very nice. I brought snacks.' Ed reaches into the wicker-style basket and pulls out a bulging carrier bag. 'And second of all, no, it isn't my mum's bike. I've borrowed it from the church hall. I think it's getting flogged in the jumble sale at the summer fair next week so it won't be missed.'

'What happened to your own bike?' Yvonne turns her bike round and we set off towards the iron bridge.

'My grandad happened to my own bike.' Ed dings the bell attached to his handlebar three times as we pass a woman with three yapping dogs. 'You know what he's like – he'll haul anything you take your eyes off for a minute to the church hall. He's very charitable, though he never seems to donate his own stuff. My poor bike helped pay for the cracked window at the back of the church.'

'He must have got at least fifty pence for that old thing.' I shoot Ed a grin and he responds by sticking his tongue out at me before speeding up to join Dominic at the front of the pack. Ed hasn't said anything to me about the France thing, but me bringing it up in the meadow last week hasn't made things awkward between us, which is a relief.

'Where are we actually going?' Yvonne is already red in the face and we haven't even made it to the bridge yet, never mind out of the village.

'Wherever we like.' Dominic glances behind from where he's leading the bike ride to call out his answer.

'I'd like to go home.' Yvonne grimaces as she pedals harder to keep up.

Yvonne complains until we stop for a break at a reservoir, laying our bikes down on the grass beside a picnic bench. The reservoir and surrounding area are picturesque, with lush trees reflected in the water, and the top of a church's stone tower can be seen in the distance. There's wildlife all around, with ducks and swans on the water, birds and squirrels in the trees, and butterflies fluttering around. It feels open, vast, but also sheltered and protected at the same time. A tranquil space only half an hour's ride from Little Heaton and yet somewhere I hadn't explored until now.

Ed empties his plastic bag of goodies out on the table and we gorge on sour cream Pringles, Haribo Supermix and sharing bags of Maltesers and Revels. A couple pass, nodding in acknowledgement as they call for their dog when he sniffs at our snacks, but other than that we're out here on our own.

'Didn't you think to bring any drinks?' Yvonne lifts the empty Maltesers bag, as though a bottle of water might be hiding under there.

'Did you?' Ed folds his arms across his chest, a proper miffed look on his face.

'I haven't got a pretty little basket on my bike.' Yvonne lifts the Revels packet. There's no water under there, but an undetected chocolate rolls out onto the table. Yvonne snatches it up and pops it into her mouth, scrunching up her nose after a couple of chomps. 'Ugh. Coffee. Now I really need a drink to take the minging taste away.'

Ed twists in his seat, so he's facing the reservoir. 'There's a load of water right there. Go nuts.'

'We passed a kiosk.' I swing my legs over the bench and stand up. 'I'll go and get us some drinks.'

'I'll give you a hand.' Tomasz gathers up the empty wrappers and tubes from the table, shoving them in the bin we pass. Ed and Yvonne are still bickering, their voices growing quieter as we follow the path's curve. The trees are overhanging, giving a welcome relief from the hot sun. It's no wonder Ed and Yvonne are cranky.

'It's hot today.' I reach up to touch my head, where my parting exposes the now-tight skin. I should have worn a hat. It's the first time Tomasz and I have been alone during this summer and I feel shy and awkward, which is ridiculous. I know this man inside out. I know all his secrets. His dreams. Or at least I used to. Maybe he has new dreams now with someone else.

Tomasz pulls at the collar of his T-shirt. 'Yeah. It is.' He picks up a rock and studies its smoothness before rejecting it back onto the path.

'Didn't Holly fancy a bike ride?' It's the first time I've brought her up and it feels weird talking about his girlfriend. My shoulders stiffen and I have to force her name out of my mouth.

'It's her sister's birthday. They're going shopping and getting manicures or something.'

I didn't know Holly had a sister. I didn't know much about her, to be honest, because I'd never bothered to find out. She was around for a few months and then she was gone, leaving nothing behind but a gift-wrapped bottle of perfume that Tomasz gave to his mum instead. Holly hadn't really registered all that much the first time round because I wasn't all that interested in Tomasz's love life. But I am now. I'm jealous of the time she gets to spend with him. How open she can be with him, because I've been holding everything in and I think I may implode.

'Do you . . .?' I tail off, not sure I can ask. Not sure I can take the answer. 'Do you love her?'

'Holly?' Tomasz stoops down to pick up a rock. 'I like her. A lot. But I don't think I love her.' He skims the rock across the reservoir and we watch it bounce across the water – once, twice, three times, plop. 'Is that bad?'

I shake my head. 'It isn't bad at all.' It's flipping fantastic. I want to do a happy little jig but I fight it, scooping up a smooth-looking rock for Tomasz instead.

'I don't look at her the way Ed looks at you.' Tomasz skims the rock but it fails to skip across the water and instead dunks straight under the surface.

I pull back my chin. 'You think Ed looks as me as though he's in love with me?'

'Isn't he?'

I think about Ed. About France. I shake my head. 'No, Ed isn't in love with me.'

'Are you . . .?' Tomasz pulls at the collar of his T-shirt. It's still hot despite the shade of the trees. 'Are you in love with him?'

My stomach starts to churn and I feel my pulse pick up its pace. I'm going to do it, whatever the consequences, because what's the worst that can happen? I've already lost Tomasz and Ed in the future and this could be my one chance to grasp a bit of happiness, even if it's only short-lived. I'm going to do it. Now. Goodbye, scaredy-cat Elodie Parker. Make way for the braver version who's going to tell Tomasz that I'm not in love with Ed. That it's him I'm in love with.

Chapter 17

'Tomasz.' I wipe my sweaty palms down my leggings and take a deep breath. 'I'm not in love with Ed and he isn't in love with me. We're friends, that's all. We will never be more than that.'

'But I've seen the two of you together. You're all . . .'

'Touchy-feely, lovey-dovey?' I remember Yvonne's words from the time she thought I should go for it with Ed with the aid of a pair of . . . nope, still can't think about it without wanting to vomit all over the place. But if Yvonne thought we were into each other, it's no wonder Tomasz was under the same impression. Is that why it took so long for us to get together? Why he never admitted that he liked me all that time? My palms are sweaty again already so I try to subtly wipe them down my leggings once more. I'm doing this, right now. I'm telling Tomasz how I feel and I'm going to grab his gorgeous face in my hands and kiss him over and over again to make up for the lost four years.

'Elodie! Tomasz!' Yvonne is making her way towards us, her face all red and her hair sticking to her forehead. 'Wait up! I need to get away from those two. They're talking French again. I swear I'm going to swing for Ed. He's such a tosser sometimes, showing off with his stupid I-can-speak-two-languages knobheadedness.' She places herself between me and Tomasz, pushing her arm through mine and then his, so we set off for the kiosk as a linked trio, with Yvonne in the middle like Dorothy on the way to Oz with her pals. 'Sacha doesn't speak another language, does he?'

Tomasz snorts. 'He barely speaks English.'

'Good, because that's how I like my men: dumb as a box of frogs but with an arse I can sink my teeth into. Does Sacha have a hairy arse, by the way?'

Tomasz looks appalled. 'He's my brother.'

'Exactly. You can't tell me you haven't seen his arse, so spill.'

'I haven't seen Sacha's bare arse since we were little kids sharing a bath. I don't want to think about his butt, never mind look at it.'

'Spoilsport.' Yvonne jabs Tomasz in the side with her elbow. 'I'd take a sneaky peek for you.'

'You'd spy on my brother's naked butt for me?' Tomasz pulls his chin back. 'Thanks. I appreciate the sacrifice.'

Yvonne jabs him in the side again, but lighter this time. 'Not at Sacha, you plank. At a girl you liked. Elodie, for example. If you fancied her, I'd tell you what a cracking pair of tits she has. Her nipples don't point down or anything.'

'Yvonne!' I shove my friend, forgetting Tomasz is connected on the other side of her so that when she stumbles, she knocks into him like a domino. Luckily, neither falls over.

'What? They don't. They're annoyingly perky, you lucky cow.'

'They're not *that* perky.' I place my free hand over my chest. 'And you don't have to broadcast it.'

Yvonne shrugs. 'It's only Tomasz, and it isn't as if he fancies you. If he did, I'd have to warn him that you don't wax in the winter.' Squealing with laughter, Yvonne unthreads her arms from me and Tomasz, and leaps out of the way before I can wallop her. She turns, facing us as she scuttles backwards. 'What's your problem? He's just your mate. It isn't as though I'm telling Ed your yeti secret.'

This is my chance. I can tell Yvonne – tell them both – that I wouldn't want Ed to see me without my kit on in a million years, but I would like Tomasz to see me naked, thank you very much. But I don't say a word as Yvonne resumes her place in between us, her arms threaded through ours. If Yvonne is Dorothy on her way to Oz, I am very much the Cowardly Lion.

We ride on after we've finished our drinks from the kiosk, finding ourselves on the high street of a small town. Yvonne spots a pub and begs for another pit stop and none of us argue. We sit outside, our bikes propped up against the wall, and savour every last drop after cycling in the sun. My scalp feels even tighter now and my thighs and arse cheeks are burning, but I feel content, despite everything. I remember enjoying this day out the first time round, but I didn't appreciate it as much as I do now.

'I need an ice cream.' Yvonne points down the street, to a newsagent's with a vintage Wall's ice cream sign in the window. 'Who wants what? Or shall I just get a selection?'

'Just get a selection.' Ed is slumped against the table, too knackered to even sit up straight never mind schlep down to the shop to choose an ice cream from the freezer.

'I'll give you a hand.' Again, it's Tomasz who offers to help, and the two wander down to the shop. Ed twists in his seat, propping his feet up on the bench in the space Yvonne has left. I close my eyes, tilting my face up to the sun, listening to the bustling of the shoppers around us. It's much busier here than at the reservoir but I still feel at peace.

'You guys.' There's a rustle and thud as Yvonne drops the ice creams on the table a few minutes later. 'There's a tattoo place around the corner.' She indicates that Ed should move his feet, which he does, slowly, and with a groan. 'I've wanted a tattoo for ages. We should all get one.' She plonks herself down on the bench and grabs a Twister from the pile of ice creams.

'I've already got a tattoo.' Dominic rolls the sleeve of his T-shirt up to show off a wolf's face made up of geometric shapes. It's all sharp edges but somehow beautiful at the same time.

'Then get another.' Yvonne peels the wrapper off her Twister and turns to Tomasz. 'Have you got any tattoos? I know Sacha's got loads – that one on his neck is *awesome*.'

Tomasz shakes his head. 'Nope. None.'

'Me either.' Ed opts for a Fab lolly. 'But they are pretty cool. We should do it.'

Yvonne's eyes light up. 'Yeah? You're up for it?'

Ed shrugs. 'Yeah. Why not?'

Dominic takes the lime Calippo and peels the lid off. 'I'm in.'

'And me.'

Yvonne squeezes Tomasz's arm, giving a happy little squeal before she turns to me, eyebrows rising. Tomasz has taken the Solero, leaving me with the Magnum, which I take, slowly removing the wrapper and pretending I don't feel everybody's eyes on me. I didn't get a tattoo the first time round. I'd claimed somebody needed to keep an eye on the bikes, but the truth is I hadn't been brave enough. Am I brave enough now? I wasn't brave enough to open up to Tomasz earlier and I know I'll regret it forever. Do I want to add to my list of disappointments so soon?

'Let's do it.'

'Really?' Yvonne's eyes are flitting between the others, as though she's waiting for one of them to crack and reveal it's a wind-up. 'You're getting one? *You*? The scaredy-cat?' Yvonne whoops with joy, forgetting the exhaustion of our cycling as she jumps up to do a little dance on the pavement. My stomach is churning so much I don't really enjoy the Magnum, but I go through with the tattoo and it isn't as bad as I'd always imagined it would be. Yvonne has a little dancing hedgehog inked onto her ankle while Tomasz opts for a series of little stars, trailing from his thumb to his inner wrist and Dominic has another wolf, this one smaller, more lifelike, sitting under his collarbone. I go for a dainty sprig of wild flowers because I was drawn to the design for some reason and couldn't drag my eyes away from it once I'd spotted it.

'Finally.' Yvonne sighs, long and hard, when Ed emerges from the tattoo parlour. The rest of us are outside with the bikes, our tattoos finished ages ago. 'What did you get?'

Ed holds out his wrist and pulls back the dressing to reveal *South Park*'s Butters, dressed in a blue bunny onesie.

'Oh no.' Dominic covers his eyes with his hands. 'You don't like *South Park*, do you?'

'Love it, mate.' Ed claps Dominic on the back. 'It's hilarious.'

Dominic removes his hands from his face, but he shakes his head as he looks down at the tattoo. 'You do know that's forever, don't you?'

'I love it.' I reach up on tiptoe to kiss Ed's cheek. I wish it was forever, more than anything.

'I think it's cute.' Yvonne kisses his other cheek. 'Not sure your grandad will approve though.'

'Oh, shit.' Ed secures the dressing back over the tattoo. 'I didn't think about that.'

'Who cares what your grandad thinks?' I grab my bike, dragging it away from the wall with more force than is necessary and stumble backwards. Tomasz holds out a hand to stop me from falling on my arse, and I smile my thanks before I turn back to Ed, the corners of my mouth already downturned. 'You shouldn't live your life in his shadow, tiptoeing around him. Be yourself. Be *happy*.'

Ed snorts. 'Easy to say. Not so easy to put into practice.' He grabs his bike and guides it out towards the road.

'Do we *have* to ride all the way back home?' Yvonne trudges towards her bike, as though she's being led to a guillotine with a blunt blade. 'Can't we get a taxi?'

'What about the bikes?' Dominic hops onto his bike, using his foot to push it onto the road.

Yvonne shrugs. 'I'm willing to sacrifice mine. It's a rusty piece of crap anyway.'

'Come on.' Dominic's pedalling now, leading the way as he calls over his shoulder. Yvonne groans but she follows. I set off too and my handlebars wobble beneath my hands. Perhaps it wasn't such a good idea to have that beer earlier. It was only one bottle but I feel rather unsteady and the tarmac looks as though its undulating in front of me.

And that's when I hear it. The roar, loud and close, as though there's something howling right down my ear. It's unbearable and I squeeze my eyes shut, afraid of the sound, of the way my bike is rocking from side to side, the road almost liquid beneath my tyres now. The bike is whipped out from under me and I'm falling. I want to scream but my mouth won't open.

'Here you go, honey. Small sips.'

I'm back on the plane with the unused sick bag on my lap and the snoring guy next to me, as though no time has passed at all. Dolly pushes a plastic cup of water into my hands.

'Better?' Dolly watches me intently as I take a sip. My mouth is parched and I remember the heat of the bike ride, of the sun beating down on us. I lower the cup of water and Dolly's eyes flick down to the empty sick bag on my lap. I pick it up, contemplating opening it up and vomiting into it but although I do feel pretty queasy, it's starting to pass. I slip the bag into the pocket on the back of the seat on front of me, to show her that I'm not about to throw up. 'You still look awfully pale, honey. Maybe a little nap would help. I have a sleep mask?' She lifts her eyebrows and offers an encouraging smile but I shake my head. The last thing I need is sleep. I need to stay awake. Alert. In the present. 'Are you sure? I can shut that guy up for you, no trouble.' Leaning across me, she pokes a finger into the arm of the snoring guy next to me. He snuffles and bats at his arm before pulling the fleecy aeroplane blanket over his head. His snoring resumes immediately. Dolly gives a heavy eyeroll as she sinks back into her seat.

'Dolly?' I flip the little table down in front of me and place the cup of water into the indented circle. 'Do you ever get déjà vu?'

'I should have got déjà vu when I met my ex-husband.' She

rolls her eyes again, even heavier this time. 'He was just like all the others: a liar and a cheat. Though he did mix it up a little by stealing my mom's car as well. They're all the same.' She shoots daggers at the lumpy blanket next to me. 'It's just some are more handsome than others.' Her lips turn up on one side and she shrugs. 'And I'm a sucker for a handsome man. Can't resist them. Are you married?'

I shake my head.

Dolly lifts her left hand, displaying a ring-free finger. 'No, me neither. Though I gave it three goes, more fool me. All of them handsome. All of them liars and cheats. Well, no more.' She shakes her head and slips her hand beneath her thigh, as though she can protect herself from any wayward engagement rings. 'Have you ever been married?' I shake my head again and Dolly pats me on the arm. 'Good for you, honey. *Good for you.*'

I push a smile onto my face but I'm not feeling it. I'm not sure never marrying was good for me. It isn't as though I'm happily single, and I'd wanted the whole husband, house, kids thing. I came close to it, once upon a time, but life threw us a massive curveball and we never recovered from it.

'Do you have kids?' There's an ache I haven't allowed myself to acknowledge since the day I flew out to California, heavy like a rock in the pit of my stomach. Being reminded of the hopes and dreams of the past has let it nudge its way back in.

'Three.' Dolly holds up the fingers on her right hand, the left still tucked safely under her thigh. 'Two boys and a girl. All grown up now. Two married, one still keeping his options wide open. He reminds me of his father in a lot of ways, unfortunately.'

'I don't have any.' There's that ache again, pushing itself outwards. 'I wanted them, but it didn't happen.' Ed died and the grief had taken over, overwhelming and all-consuming. I'd acted irrationally, made huge mistakes and ended up alone. At the time I believed that was what I wanted. What I needed. Now I know it wasn't but it's too late. I'm still on the fence about this whole time travel thing, because now I'm back to reality, the idea is ludicrous. But if it wasn't all made up in my head, I had my chance to start again with Tomasz but I blew it because I was afraid.

'Are you a sucker for a bad boy too?' Dolly sucks in a breath and gives a slow shake of her head. 'They're lethal.'

My mind goes straight to Sacha. He was a bad boy, and definitely lethal, and he did break my heart into a million pieces with his reckless behaviour. I've never been able to put it back together in the same way since. They say that time heals but that's a load of bollocks if you ask me. Some wounds remain, no matter how well you mask them from the world.

'Still, life would be boring without them, wouldn't it?' Dolly chuckles throatily while I try to imagine a life without Sacha. A life where Franciszek didn't keep his promise to Irene, where the Nowak family remained in Nottingham instead of moving to Little Heaton. A life without meeting Tomasz.

The ache's back, but it isn't for the babies-that-never-were this time. It's for him. My perfect one. The one I was supposed to live happily ever after with, to have the babies with, to tell our story to over and again like Irene and Franciszek. Now, I'm not saying the story would be as epic as theirs, but the love would have been just as strong, just as real. But our story isn't a love story at all. It's a tragedy and no amount of daydreaming can change it.

I'm on edge for a little while, waiting for the rumble and the roar that will set me off into the past but nothing happens. I sip my water. The guy next to me snores under his blanket. And Dolly talks. A lot. When she nips to the loo I take the opportunity to plug my headphones into the in-seat entertainment system, smiling when she flops back into her seat but not removing my headphones. Dolly plugs in her own headphones and taps at the screen as she searches for something to pass the time. I'm starting to relax as I lose myself in the film – it's one I've seen before, lots of times, so it's familiar and comforting – when I feel agitated movement beside me. I lower my headphones so they're off my ears and resting around the back of my neck.

'Everything okay?'

Dolly growls as she jiggles the headphone jack in the socket. 'Stupid things aren't working. The sound keeps cutting out.' She jiggles the wire again, more aggressively. 'Ah, there we go.' She grins and gives a nod of triumph before settling down in her seat to watch her film. I slide my headphones back into place but I can't seem to unwind again. I keep thinking about home. About Ed and Tomasz. I'm too hot. Too enclosed. I remember the expanse of the reservoir, the space, the air, the chirrup of the birds and the fluttering of the butterflies. I can almost taste the tang of the sour cream Pringles. It had to have been real. As crazy as it is, I had to have been there only a few moments ago.

I take a sip of water but it doesn't help. I feel as though I'm boiling inside and the heat is pulsing out of me. I'm still wearing my cardigan, half unbuttoned, so I slip it off, folding it and wedging it into the pocket on the back of the seat in front to keep it out of the way. Dolly taps me on the shoulder and I expect to hear another complaint about the faulty headphones, but she's smiling at me.

'Love it. Very pretty. Bohemian, almost.'

'I'm sorry?' I look at the cardigan. There's nothing bohemian about it and I wouldn't describe it as pretty. It's mid-grey with small, plain buttons. Functional rather than fashionable for the flight.

Dolly's smile fades. 'I've got my first husband's name tattooed on me. I won't tell you where.' She grimaces and shakes her head. 'I wish I'd got something pretty instead of branding myself with that jackass forever.' She pulls at her collar, revealing three small Chinese symbols. 'I've got these as well. They're supposed to mean love, faith and serenity, but who knows? I wish I'd gone for something beautiful like yours.'

Like mine? I don't have a tattoo. I was too chicken. I stayed outside with the bikes while the others got theirs. Except when I went back in time and threw caution to the wind and did things differently.

'Excuse me.' I whip the headphones off and squeeze past Dolly, stumbling out in the aisle because I haven't given her enough time to move aside. There's already somebody in the loo, so I fidget outside, as though I'm desperate for a wee when really I'm just on the brink of freaking out. Finally, the bar on the lock slides over to vacant and I rudely push myself inside before the current occupier is fully over the threshold. I can't care about manners right now though. Shoving the door closed, I lock it before standing in front of the sink, twisting so I can see my shoulder blade in the mirror.

And there it is. A sprig of wild flowers that shouldn't be there because I wasn't brave enough to get the tattoo in real life. But it's there. *It's really there.* I reach for the tattoo, half expecting it to come away as I run my fingers over it, the ink smudging because it isn't a real tattoo. It's a fake. An illusion. But it doesn't disappear. It's doesn't smudge. It stays fast. Permanent. I touch it again, pressing hard, until it hurts.

It is real. The tattoo is actually there, inked onto my skin the day of the bike ride. But that means it definitely wasn't a daydream or an hallucination. It means I really did go back in time, revisiting past events and I *changed them.* And that means if I go back again, I can save Ed. I can stop the accident. I can save his life.

Chapter 18

There's no way I can concentrate on the film now. I need to go back, back to Little Heaton before the accident, but how? I'm not in control of this thing – whatever it is – and I could weep with frustration. I wasted so much time. Squandered the opportunity to save my best friend. Instead of whining about being back home, instead of pissing around on rope swings and bike rides, I should have been doing *something* to protect Ed, because there's nothing I can do now, back on the plane in the present day. I need to get back but I don't know how, or if I *can*. It's been over an hour since I was plonked back on the plane and I haven't heard even a murmur, let alone a full-on roar, and there hasn't even been a hint of turbulence to suggest something is about to happen.

'I give up.' Dolly snatches her headphones off her ears and unplugs them from the socket, winding the wire around the headset and shoving them in the seat pocket. 'I think they're coming round with food anyway.'

My stomach rumbles as I'm hit by the smells wafting from the trollies making their way along the aisles. I didn't eat breakfast this morning as I was too nervous about the journey home so the only things in my stomach right now are the cocktails I had in the airport bar and the tiny glass of wine from the drinks trolley a little while ago. Still, despite the grumbling stomach, my appetite has packed up and left. I can't eat right now, not while I've got so many thoughts whizzing through my brain at a gazillion miles an hour.

'Pasta or beef?' The cabin crew member is grinning at me, her red lips stretched over super-white teeth. I'm about to turn down the meal when my stomach growls. Loudly. It would sound ridiculous if I claimed not to be hungry now.

'Pasta.' I force my lips to flick upwards. 'Please.' I take the tray and place it on my table, my stomach rumbling again as the smells reach my nostrils. I don't know if it smells delicious or disgusting. Or somewhere in the middle.

'Pasta or beef, sir?'

The guy beside me has finally stopped snoring and is looking up at the cabin crew member through bleary eyes. He yawns, his mouth cavernous, before he mumbles his response. He's handed a tray and the trolley is dragged backwards to the next row of passengers.

I peel back the plastic cover on the pot of salad and nibble at a slice of tomato. It's bland and is doing nothing to inspire the return of my appetite. I give a piece of lettuce a go, which, unsurprisingly, does nothing for me either, not even with the addition of the dressing. I give up and move on to the pasta, which smells pretty decent but tastes like cardboard with a sprinkling of cheese.

'Not hungry?' Dolly unscrews her mini bottle of water and takes a sip.

'Not really.' I admit defeat and place my knife and fork down on the tray.

'It's the nerves, I bet.' Dolly gives me a sympathetic arm squeeze as she places her bottle of water on her tray. 'But you're doing really well. I flew out to Ohio with one of my girlfriends last fall and she was so scared of flying, she squeezed my hand the whole way. I thought she'd fractured a finger or two by the time we landed.' I'm about to tell her that I'm not actually afraid of flying when she holds out a hand to flex her fingers and knocks the bottle of water over. 'Oh, shoot!' She springs into action, picking up the bottle and attempting to mop up the spilled water with the serviette provided. I hand my serviette over, which still isn't enough. When I ask the snorer beside me if we can have his, he grunts in response, and I have no idea whether that's a yes or a no.

Bong!

Dolly has reached up to press the assistance button as her tray is still swimming. She's managed to rescue her pot of crumble and her cheese and biscuits, popping them onto my tray before they end up soaked. I turn to the snorer, to ask again for the serviette, but my voice is lost in the roar. My seat begins to shake and I'm filled with a mixture of fear and relief that it's happening again.

My shoulder is aching against the hard ground beneath it and I'm cold, chilled right to the bone, as though I will never feel warmth again. There's a weird, earthy smell – not unpleasant but not enjoyable either – and though it's bright, there's a greenish hue when I open my eyes. My brain is foggy and my mouth feels as though it's lined with cotton wool as I try to swallow. I shift to ease the pain in my shoulder, stretching out my stiff limbs, and there's a crinkle as whatever has been thrown over me moves. I wince as I sit up, squeezing my eyes shut against the brightness of the room for a moment, trying to compose myself. Everything hurts: cold bones, stiff muscles, thumping headache. I feel as though I've been hit by a lorry. A really, really big one that's been filled with concrete.

'Time's it?'

My eyes are wide now as I twist around in search of the owner of the mumbled voice. There's someone here. A man, lying on the floor, chest exposed and an arm flung over his face to shield his eyes. We're in a sleeping bag, in a small tent, with sunlight streaming in through the fabric.

'Babe?' His arm moves, sliding away from his face until it's just his hand covering his eyes, his fingers and thumb rubbing them vigorously. 'What time is it?'

'Er, I don't know.' My voice is raspy. Barely even there. I look around the small space for my phone. Or a glass of water.

'Too early.' He rolls over, his arm back over his face, his back to me. He has a mole on the back of his neck. It's tiny, almost heart-shaped, and I want to reach out and touch it.

There's movement from outside the tent and I can make out a figure crouching by the canvas.

'Knock, knock.' There's a whoosh and brighter sunlight bursts into the tent as it's unzipped. 'You're not shagging, are you?'

Yvonne is crouched on the other side of the opening, one hand covering her eyes while the other still holds on to the zip. She's wearing a denim skirt and a white T-shirt with writing printed on the front in pink, and a pair of black utility boots. Her hair has been cut into a choppy bob and dyed a silvery platinum blonde, and there's a pair of hexagonal-lensed sunglasses perched on top of her head.

'Nah.' The bloke beside me pulls the sleeping bag over his shoulder. 'Too early.'

'It's never too early for a good shag. Or even a bad shag.' Yvonne pulls the zip open a bit more. 'You getting up? We want to grab some breakfast.'

'Time is it?' I search for my phone as my tent-mate asks the question again. There's a rucksack next to the sleeping bag with a pair of jeans spilling out of it.

'Nearly ten.' Yvonne stands up, so I can only see her legs now.

'Too early.' The sleeping bag is dragged over my tent-mate's head. Otis's head. My ex-boyfriend. Current boyfriend if I've time-travelled again. 'We only went to bed four hours ago.'

'I know. My head's banging.' Outside the tent, Yvonne's boot rubs up and down her calf. 'It was a great night though, wasn't it? Probably shouldn't have had all those shots though.' She crouches down again and sticks her head into the tent. 'Are you coming with us or not? I need food. *Now.*'

It's the summer after the tattoo, six years in the past, and I'd been seeing Otis for nearly seven months. We met at a New Year's Eve

136

night at a club in town, just before the countdown, and we were snogging before Big Ben's bongs. Otis is twenty-nine. He works in HR for a manufacturing company and he likes football, live gigs and his pug, Arnold. He doesn't live in Little Heaton – which was a major attraction – and house-shares with a police officer and a shop assistant. Arnold was originally his ex-girlfriend's dog, but when she moved out, her new place didn't allow pets and so Otis adopted him as his own.

'All right, all right.' Otis groans as he whips the sleeping bag away. He's only wearing a pair of boxer shorts, which isn't a bad look, actually. Living outside Little Heaton wasn't the only attraction.

'Jeez, give a girl a bit of warning.' Yvonne stands up, so only her legs are visible again.

'Don't worry, the goods are tucked away.' Otis grabs a pair of jeans and shoves his legs into the them. The tent really is quite small, so he has to stoop to pull them up over his hips. I've slept in a pair of shorts and a vest top and I change the shorts for the jeans spilling out of my rucksack, using the sleeping bag as cover, before hunting out my wash bag and a clean outfit. I find my phone too, and I scroll through the photos as I wait in the queue for the loo. Surprisingly, Heather is in most of my latest pics, sticking her tongue out at the camera as she perches on Ed's lap or grins as she holds up bottles of beer or colourful shots. With some careful questioning of Yvonne as we wait outside the shower block, I learn that we're on day two of a music festival, which I definitely didn't attend first time round, and I've missed out on seeing the Happy Mondays and Franz Ferdinand, which is ultra-annoying.

I feel slightly better once I've had a good wash, brushed my teeth and changed into clean clothes. I've slipped on a pair of sandals, but I realise my mistake when I see the state of the path. No wonder Yvonne's wearing boots – the path seems to have been swallowed by a bog after heavy rainfall. I'd quite like to nip back to the tent to shove my wellies on but Yvonne's having none of it – 'I'm *staaaaaarving*' – and so I'm forced to tread as carefully as I can through the mud. My feet are filthy by the time we make it to the food stands but I'm not at all bothered as I'm hit by a wall of deliciousness and my gurgling stomach lets me know that I'm *ravenous*.

Otis had gone ahead while I changed, and he's sitting with Ed, Heather and Tomasz. My heart flutters when I see Tomasz sitting there, laughing at something my sister has said, and my stomach fills with butterflies when I think about the possibility of not only saving Ed with this time travel thing but saving myself too. I can allow myself to love, to be loved, and I don't have to let go. Ever. This is my second chance, and this time I won't mess it all up.

Chapter 19

It rains quite a lot during the festival but we don't let it dampen our spirits. We listen to fantastic bands, we sing and we dance and we eat good food, and I'm having such a great time with my friends that I almost forget that I'm here to save Ed. In a year, he'll be gone and I can't let the opportunity to prevent the accident slip through my fingers. I can't sit back and let it happen. There has to be something I can do, even now, to make sure it never happens.

'You look lost in thought.' Heather flops down next to me on the patch of dryish grass that I've managed to bag and hands me a bacon butty.

I feel lost in general, to be honest, but I don't say this to my sister. 'Just soaking up the atmosphere before we have to leave.'

Heather pulls a face. 'Wish we didn't have to go.'

'Be a bit boring once all the beer tents and food stands have gone and it's just us and a massive field.'

Heather shrugs and unwraps her own bacon butty. 'Better than going to work though.'

'Good point. It's been a laugh though, hasn't it? Thanks for inviting us.'

Heather shrugs. 'Had to. Keeley and the others backed out and I couldn't come on my own.' Heather smirks at me before she sinks her teeth into her sandwich. I know she's only messing and I play along, digging her gently with my elbow. This is the first festival I've ever been to, because Heather didn't invite me originally. I think she'd rather have boiled her own head than spend a long weekend with me and the feeling was very much mutual, but there's been a shift in our relationship. A thawing that has allowed us to connect in a way we never had before and I'm learning so much about my sister that I never knew.

Last night, as we sat outside Yvonne and Heather's tent with a bottle of vodka and a pack of playing cards, Heather had entertained us with impressions of people from work, and although the others hadn't known who any of our co-workers were, they'd howled with laughter. Heather's talent for capturing and exaggerating the essence of those around her had been a revelation to me and the impression of the head housekeeper had been my favourite.

'Do your impression of Linda again.'

Heather swipes at her mouth with the back of her hand and clears her throat. With a straight back and her chin tilted in the air, she adopts an over-the-top posh voice.

'I am Linda Peterson, queen of this castle and you, peasant, are a scruffy urchin. Tie your hair back! Remove those *disgusting* false nails *at once*. How *dare* you smile in my presence?' Heather rolls her eyes, back to being herself again. 'She's like Mrs Gacey with a fucking feather duster.'

I almost choke on my sandwich as I bark with laughter at Heather's assessment of the head housekeeper, because it's spot on.

'You're funny.' I'd never realised it before because I was too caught up in the pain-in-the-arse parts of my sister.

Heather nods. 'I know.'

I roll my eyes, but good-naturedly. 'And modest.'

'You forgot stunningly beautiful.'

140

I shove her with my shoulder. 'Get lost.' But I'm smiling because I feel like I've not only found my sister, I've also discovered a new friend.

'I could sleep for a week when we get back.' Otis yawns, covering his mouth with the back of his hand. 'Pity we've got work in the morning. I'll be falling asleep at my desk.' He groans and thumps his fist down lightly on the steering wheel. 'I forgot about that meeting first thing, with Geoff and Marjorie. I'll definitely be falling asleep having to sit through that. What time are you in work tomorrow?'

I'm only half-listening to Otis so I don't respond. Instead, I turn to look out of the window, back towards the car park we've just left. After an amazing weekend, we're heading home.

'Poor bugger.' Otis has glanced back too, and he thinks I'm watching the car that's stuck in the mud, with three festival stewards helping to push it forward. But I'm really on the lookout for Tomasz's car. He's driving back with Ed, Yvonne and Heather, and I haven't seen them since we said goodbye in the swampy car park. I'd been in Otis's arms at the time as he'd carried me across the mud, bride-over-the-threshold style, even though I was wearing my wellies.

'Did you text your mum? To let her know we're on our way back?'

It's sweet of Otis to remind me to do this, because Mum will have spent the past few days worrying, even though Heather and I are old enough to look after ourselves. I'm twenty-six and Heather has just finished her second year at uni, where she's proved she's more than capable of taking care of herself, but I remember the previous summer, when Heather had gone to the festival with her mates and Mum had almost worn a hole in the living room carpet with her anxiety-induced pacing.

'I'll do it now.' I wriggle my phone free from my jeans pocket. The lock-screen image is a selfie of me and Otis, grinning drunkenly at the camera, heads squeezed close together so we both fit in the frame. Being with him was fun and carefree, but he isn't The One. The One is in another car, driving my best friends and sister back home to Little Heaton. As lovely as Otis is, I'm a bit put out that I'm not travelling with any of them. The others all gravitated towards Tomasz's car while Otis carried me to his, and I didn't want to come across as dumb by asking why the cars weren't more evenly split.

'What time are you in work in the morning?' I'm vaguely aware that Otis has already asked me this question, but I don't know the answer. 'Hopefully I'll have time to drop you off so you don't have to mess about with the bus.'

So we're staying at Otis's place tonight, which makes the travel arrangements make sense. The others are all going to Little Heaton and we're not, and this, strangely, makes me feel a bit sad. It seems odd to not be going home to Mum and Dad's after living there again for the past few weeks.

'Elodie?'

'Sorry.' I tap at my phone so I can check the calendar, where I add my shifts. 'I'm on a ten-six.'

It's been over a year since I started working at the hotel and I'm no longer a chambermaid. I'm a receptionist now, with some extra administration duties on top. Gillian has really taken me under her wing and is encouraging me up the career ladder.

'Great. I'll drop you off at home in the morning before I head into work.' Otis yawns, covering his mouth with the back of his hand again. 'Getting up is going to be a killer though.'

'Make sure you don't fall asleep at the wheel.' My tone is jovial, but I am a little concerned, to be honest. We didn't sleep much during the festival; once the acts were finished for the night, we stayed up, playing cards and drinking until we couldn't keep our eyes open a moment longer.

'We should have brought the L-plates with us.' Otis stops at a junction and checks for traffic before turning off. 'You could have had some practice.'

Yes! I can't help my lips spreading into a wide smile as I realise what this means. With the extra hours and money from work, I'd been paying for driving lessons – another step towards freedom from Little Heaton.

'I don't think having the supervisor napping counts when you're a learner.' Not that I need supervising – I've had my licence for nearly six years. Passed first time – though I'm not sure I could use time travel as an excuse if we were pulled over.

'Good point.'

I slide my phone back into my pocket and turn the radio on. It's 'Despacito', which I haven't heard for *so long*. It was everywhere this summer and then it was gone. I turn it up and Otis and I sing along to the 'despacitos' and the occasional 'oh, yeahs', neither of us able to manage the rest of the lyrics. Otis taps out the beat on the steering wheel and I nod along. The windows are open and there's a breeze whipping up my hair, and this moment sums up my relationship with Otis. Fun. Carefree. Liberating. Showing me that there *was* a life beyond Little Heaton. And I didn't even need to fly all the way to America to find it.

I'd forgotten how pretty Otis's house is with its arched windows and roses climbing up the white rendered walls. Inside, the walls are pale grey and the floors are a glossy oak, the furniture and décor kept to a minimum, giving the place a clean, clutter-free look (though Otis claimed this was because he and his housemates couldn't be arsed shopping for bits and pieces for the house rather than by design). The rooms are large, apart from the kitchen, which is tiny, like an afterthought squeezed in at the last minute, and there's a separate walk-in shower in the bathroom, which I make use of as soon as we're inside, rinsing the grime of the festival from me. As fun as camping was, it was pretty grubby, especially with the bogginess caused by the heavy rain.

I'd loved this house. It didn't have the ancient, swirly-patterned carpet that should have come with a health warning due to its headache-inducing capabilities that we had at home, and we could usually watch what we wanted on the telly because Otis's housemates were barely at home in the evenings. I didn't have to sit through *Fake Britain*, or *Gardener's World* or that Gary Barlow search-for-a-band thing that Mum loved and wouldn't let us speak – or cough, or sneeze, or even breathe, practically – through.

Otis's house is calm. It's fresh and light and neat, and as far away as you could get from my family home. But I sort of miss the chaos of home right now. I miss Gran complaining about the cold, aggressively buttoning her cardigan up to her chin while death-glaring at whichever poor sod happened to be in the room. And I miss Mum lusting after Gary Barlow or Sam Nixon or any other vaguely attractive male on the telly, and I miss Dad talking over everything (apart from the Gary Barlow search-for-a-band thing, because he valued his life). I even miss despising Heather's reality TV.

'Are you okay, babe?' Otis is lounging on the sofa, his legs draped over my lap, Arnold the pug curled up against his chest, but I'm sitting upright. Stiff. Uncomfortable in a place I used to feel at ease.

'Yeah.' I smile, overbright, overcompensating for my discomfort. 'Just tired. The weekend, you know?'

Otis grins. 'It was good though, wasn't it?'

'Yeah.' I relax against the sofa a bit more. 'Really good.'

'Are you watching this?' Otis juts his chin out, indicating the telly. *EastEnders* is on but I haven't been paying attention. I stopped watching it when I moved to California and I only half-watched it before that. I shake my head and Otis turns it over, flicking through the channels before he finds an old sitcom. I watch for a little while but my eyes are heavy and I'm struggling to keep them open. I must drift off because the next thing I know, Otis is gently shaking me awake. We go to bed – there's a pair of clean pyjamas in the bottom drawer, along with a few other bits and pieces – and I fall back to sleep again pretty much straight away.

I dream about Ed, about Yvonne and Sacha and Tomasz, and I wake early, before Otis, before either of our alarms, with a tight knot in my stomach. I have to do something to stop the accident, but what? The accident involved Sacha but he wasn't the catalyst. It was Ed and his grandfather, and I don't know how to prevent the conflict between them. I feel helpless, but there must be a reason that I'm here, in the past. It should be impossible, but I'm jumping back in time and I'm able to change things. *Prevent* things.

The question, though, is how do I prevent the drama of that day – Ed and Reverend Carter, Yvonne and Sacha and Ronnie – and stop the tragedy. That day changed absolutely everything, changed every*one*, and I must find a way to alter the events that led up to it.

Chapter 20

Being back behind the reception desk at the hotel isn't too bad; I can still remember how to manage the switchboard and use the booking systems, and the admin is light, with just a bit of photocopying and filing to do. It's a lovely day, with no sign of the rain from the weekend, and Gillian joins me out in the courtyard to the side of the castle, where we sit on the iron bench under the shade of a tree. Heather's working in the restaurant over the summer again and she stops by the reception desk before the start of her shift.

'Hey, you.' She grins at me, really, really wide and toothy, as though seeing me is the highlight of her year. Which is sweet but a bit weird and I'm not quite used to the new dynamic that has developed between us. As lovely as spending the long weekend with her at the festival was, I'd never in a million years imagined I'd willingly choose to go camping with my sister. It's an adjustment and living the past few summers in brief snatches hasn't given me the same amount of time to wrap my head around it as Heather.

'Hey.' I try to return the smile as enthusiastically as my sister but I'm not sure my mouth can physically stretch that much. 'Recovered from the weekend yet?' Mentioning the weekend makes me want to yawn. I woke up feeling pretty refreshed but I seemed to hit a brick wall of fatigue around lunchtime and I'm becoming increasingly knackered as the afternoon wears on. I'd quite like to curl up on the floor behind the reception desk and have a nap but unfortunately I'm not a cat with an idle day ahead of me.

'What? Oh. Yeah. The weekend was great.' Heather grins at me again. It's quickly dropped its sweetness and is now simply weird.

'Aren't you going to be late for your shift?'

'Nope.' Heather leans her elbows on the reception desk and rests her chin on upturned palms, tilting her head so she's looking up at me. 'Got ten minutes. It's fine.' Her lips spring into life again, stretching to reveal her gnashers. I take a step back, unnerved by the display. This is getting creepy now. What the hell is going on with my sister? Heather has always been annoying but this is different. This is disturbing. Have I done something to upset the world as we know it with my time-travelling? It's an odd leap from getting a tattoo to turning my sister into a psychopathic grinner but doesn't the butterfly effect theorise that the small action of the flap of a butterfly's wing can cause a typhoon or something? Or maybe she took something over the weekend. Something slow-reacting that's only now taking effect. I'd prefer that option, if I'm honest, because it'd mean it isn't my fault that my sister is broken.

Heather continues to beam at me, her eyebrows rising as I look down at her and her unnerving grin. Eventually, when I've done nothing but plan my escape route should things get even creepier, Heather heaves out a giant sigh. She straightens and folds her arms across her chest.

'I can't believe you haven't noticed.'

'Noticed what?' That my sister has taken a strange turn? I've definitely clocked that. I couldn't miss it.

'My teeth.'

147

I nearly laugh, because I couldn't miss them with her shoving them in my face like the Cheshire cat.

'My braces.' She bares her teeth again, this time jabbing her index fingers in their direction.

'Your *braces*.' My shoulders slump and I do laugh this time as I'm flooded with relief. 'They're gone!'

'Finally.' She juts her chin in the air and side-eyes me.

'How does it feel?'

Heather runs her tongue over her naked teeth. 'Weird. I'm so used to them being there.' She runs her tongue over her teeth again. 'I'm sure I'll get used to it though.'

'I'm sure you will, and you look great.'

Heather rolls her eyes. 'You didn't even notice they were gone.'

This is totally unfair. Yes, I didn't click straight away, but I'm more used to seeing Heather *without* the braces than with these days. For me, Heather's braces have been gone for six years, so it isn't that I'm unobservant. Not at all.

'Anyway, I'm off to start my shift.' Heather takes a couple of steps away from the desk. 'Gio's on tonight and I love it when he yells at me for getting orders wrong.' She fans her face with her hand. 'I think I might *accidentally* drop a plate tonight. That really gets him going.'

The mention of the 'accidental' plate-drop gets me thinking about Ed. I'm still not sure what I can do to prevent an accident that isn't going to happen for another year but now I know for sure that I *can* prevent it, I need to keep him close so I can seize any possible chances to save him. I want to wrap my arms around him, hold him tight, tell him that he isn't going to leave me after all. Ed is going to live. He is going to live the happy, fulfilled life he deserves.

Ed's dad died when Ed was a baby so Laura moved back in with her father until she married Jim and they moved into their own cottage. The vicarage was sold a couple of years ago – after

Reverend Carter had left the village and his replacement was housed in a more modest cottage – and is now a B&B that sleeps nine, with a sauna, gym and hot tub. Laura and Ed's cottage is tiny in comparison, with two bedrooms tucked into the eaves and an open-plan kitchen and living area, but it's always felt warmer than the reverend's place. Less showy and much more cluttered but bursting at the seams with love. The garden to the front is minuscule, barely big enough to fit the set of wheelie bins beneath the window, but there are hanging baskets bookending the glossy red front door, spilling tiny blue and pink flowers, with a pair of potted conifers underneath. The knocker is a brass hare, and I smile as I think about all the times I've rapped at the door with him over the years. Too many to count.

'Elodie!' Laura beams at me when she sees me on the doorstep but her smile quickly dims. 'Is everything all right? With your mum? Your gran?'

'Everything's fine.'

'That's good.' The beam returns, but only for a moment before a slight frown appears on her face. 'Would you like to come in? We're out in the garden.' It seems a bit odd – Laura wouldn't usually ask if I'd like to come in – the door would be opened and I'd bound inside in search of Ed – but she opens the door wider and steps aside after the initial hesitancy. The door leads straight into the living area, with a narrow staircase opposite leading up to the bedrooms and shower room, and two large, squishy sofas take up most of the living room to the side. Beyond, separated by a small breakfast bar, is the kitchen and the door leading out to the garden. While the cottage is petite, the outdoor space at the back is vast, with a long, narrow lawn stretching out towards the hills beyond. A stone path leads to a patio area, where Jim and Reverend Carter are sitting on rattan chairs beneath a wide parasol.

'Can I get you a cup of tea?' Laura pauses on the threshold while I step out into the garden. There's a tea tray set on the table, with a tea-cosied pot and matching cups and saucers, and a plate of bourbon creams and pink wafers. The tea set is for the reverend's benefit; Laura usually has her tea in one of the mismatched mugs from the cupboard.

'No thank you.' I move my gaze away from the reverend, who's relaxed back in his chair with feet crossed at the ankles, nodding along to whatever it is Jim is saying. Loathing boils in the pit of my stomach, threatening to spill over. 'I just popped over to see Ed.'

Laura has started to walk along the stone path towards the patio, but she stops to turn back to me. 'He isn't here, sweetheart.'

As a youth worker, Ed often worked in the evenings. I should have sent him a text but I was too focused on seeing him, away from the festival, away from the others.

'Do you know what time he finishes work today?'

Laura shakes her head. 'No idea. Sorry. Why don't you give him a ring?' She jerks her head towards the table. 'Are you sure you won't have a cup of tea with us, while you're here?'

I look again at Reverend Carter. I'd rather wear shoes filled with dog shit than sit with that man. Why Ed ever listened to a word he said is a mystery to me and I can't stomach having to look at him, having to listen to him, and there aren't enough pink wafers in the world that could entice me over to that table.

'Thanks but I should get going.' I'm already backing away, back into the kitchen. 'I'll see myself out.' I hear Laura and Jim calling out their goodbyes but I'm already striding across the kitchen, away from that man. I've always blamed Sacha for what happened to Ed, but surely the reverend has to take some responsibility too. If it wasn't for him, for his evil words . . .

'Hello?'

I've dialled Ed's number while I scurry through the cottage, and he picks up as I'm closing the gate behind me. It's a relief to hear his voice, as though seeing his grandfather will have made him vanish all over again. But he's here. He's still here.

'Hi.' I try hard to keep my voice casual, pushing down the dread and anxiety Reverend Carter has brought on. 'I was wondering if you wanted to get a drink or something? After work?'

'I'm not in work. Booked an extra day off. I didn't fancy facing all those kids with a hangover I'd been curating for four days. Though I don't feel too bad, actually. Definitely up for a drink.'

'Great.' I place a hand on my stomach, hoping the churning will stop now. 'Where are you?'

'At home.'

I stop. Turn to face the cottage I've just left. Frown. 'No, you're not.'

Ed snorts out a little laugh. 'I am. Been here all day, apart from when I had to go out for bread and milk. A bar of chocolate fell into my basket as well. For medicinal purposes, obviously.'

'You're not at home.' I'm still watching the cottage. Still frowning.

'I definitely am. Ask Yvonne. She's been moaning at me since she got home.' I hear Yvonne in the background, yelling about Ed being a lazy arse. 'She's just jealous because she had to go into work this morning while I had a *massive* lie-in. Didn't get up until after one. *Ow.*' Ed laughs. 'And now she's chucking stuff at me. *Do not* throw that. I swear if you do . . .'

Ed *is* at home, but his home is no longer at the cottage with Laura and Jim. I'd forgotten that he moved into the flat above the hairdresser's with Yvonne after Christmas, once the sale of the salon and flat had gone through and Shaz had moved out. Yvonne had asked me if I'd wanted to move into the second bedroom but I'd decided to stay at home, where I paid minimal board and could funnel as much money into the America fund as I could, so Ed had taken it instead. A fresh wave of exhaustion crashes into me. This time travel stuff is hard to keep up with sometimes.

* * *

Ed and Yvonne meet me at the pub. We sit outside under the newly erected pergola, with music playing through the attached speakers. Later, as it grows dark, the strings of amber lights draped along the roof will give off a magical feel and outdoor heaters will make sure we keep warm, but for now we enjoy the evening sunshine. I haven't eaten since my lunchbreak, so I fill up on smoky bacon crisps and roasted peanuts. Otis phones while I'm on my way to the loo, but it's just a quick call, just checking in, really, and I remember that's one of the things I liked most about our relationship. It wasn't full-on. We weren't in each other's pockets. After living in a close-knit community, not knowing every little thing about the other person had been refreshing.

'I'm quitting.' Yvonne plonks a tray of drinks down on the table before throwing herself down in her seat.

'As a barmaid?' Ed lifts up one of the drinks, watching as lager drips from the bottom into the puddle on the tray. 'I don't think anyone would hire you in the first place.'

Yvonne gives him a dark look. She is not in the mood for playing. 'As a hairdresser. Or rather, as a hairdresser at Lady Dye. It's so shite since Carolina took over: the hours, the fact we have to share our tips, the lack of innovation.'

Ed lifts his eyebrows at Yvonne's use of the word 'innovation' but cleverly keeps his gob shut and instead takes a sip of his pint. He doesn't even complain about the drips on his T-shirt.

'I suggested I go on a course for eyebrow-threading, so we could expand our services – I was even going to pay for it myself – and she said no. She said our clients don't want their eyebrows threading. They want a cut and blow or a shampoo and set. I said maybe they'd want their eyebrows threading if we offered it, but she just walked away and told me to sweep the floor.'

'To be fair, I don't think the likes of Christine Gacey wants their eyebrows shaping.'

Yvonne slaps Ed on the arm. 'But *that's my point*. Our clientele is mainly pensioners, but that's because we only cater for pensioners.

152

That place hasn't been updated since 1985. If we update it, bring it up to modern standards, maybe we'd get younger clients. Clients who want their eyebrows threading or a bit of nail art. We don't just have to stick to curling grannies' hair. Do you know what the old butcher's is opening as?' Yvonne looks from Ed to me. She folds her arms and sits back in her chair. 'A tanning shop. Now, you tell me the likes of Christine Gacey is getting a spray tan. So there must be other customers in mind. Customers *we* should be encouraging through *our* doors.'

'Oi.' I playfully tap Ed's hand as he reaches for my bag of nuts. 'Get your own.' I wait for Ed's best wounded look before I offer him the packet. 'You never know, Carolina might not last that long.'

Yvonne's eyes widen. 'You mean she might snuff it? Why? What've you heard? Is it cancer? Because she's always chaining it out the back. And then she makes me sweep up the cigarette butts from the yard, obviously.' Yvonne snatches up her drink, flicking out droplets of lager, and mutters something about Carolina being a lazy cow.

'I mean she might sell up.'

Yvonne scrunches up her nose. 'So what? I'll only end up with someone else with no vision. And the flat.' She nudges Ed with her foot. 'If Carolina goes, we might lose the flat.'

'But you probably won't.' In fact, I know they won't. The new owner will keep them on as tenants, and he'll modernise the salon. Maybe not to the extent that Yvonne is envisioning, but they'll get a new set of backwashes and a rebrand. He'll even throw in a bit of paint to spruce the place up.

'But we *might*.'

'That's the way it goes with renting, I suppose.' Ed shrugs as he shoves the last couple of peanuts in his mouth. 'There's no guarantee.'

'I guess not, but there's no way we could afford a place round here. Have you seen the price of the new houses they're building?

I wouldn't be able to afford one of those in a million years. I'm screwed if Carolina sells the salon.'

Well, there goes my attempt to comfort my best friend with my insider knowledge. I haven't made her feel better. If anything, I've made her more anxious for the future.

Chapter 21

'Now remember, love, just try to be calm. You'll get there. It takes practice, that's all.'

Dad's words are encouraging. His face is not. It's all scrunched up, apart from his eyes, which are wide and darting from my hand on the handbrake and the road ahead. We're sitting in his car, still parked up outside the house, and he's already in panic mode. As well as paying for lessons, I'd been practising my driving with Dad.

'Take it easy now. No rush.' His eyes bulge even further as I move off, and my smile of satisfaction as it goes smoothly does nothing to ease his anxiety. 'Eyes on the road, Elodie! Eyes on the bloody road!' He's clinging on to the dashboard as though he's on a speeding, loop-the-loop rollercoaster and not going at five miles an hour along a residential street.

'What happened to keeping calm?' I speed up, moving up into second gear as we near the cricket grounds.

'You're right. Sorry.' Dad takes in a deep breath, letting it out slowly. He repeats this, finishing off with a nod of his head. 'You're actually doing really well.'

'You sound surprised.'

'Last time we came out, you nearly took out the war memorial.'

'It came out of nowhere.' I turn to smirk at Dad, but he jabs his finger towards the windscreen, his eyes nearly popping out of his skull again. 'I remember that day. I was swerving to avoid the pigeon.'

I also remember Dad's fury, his hand clutching his chest after he'd screamed at me to pull over. His 'sod the bloody pigeon. That can fly out of the bloody way. *That can't*.' His hand had trembled as he pointed at the war memorial. Which was still standing. I hadn't even clipped it with my wing mirror. Dad was being dramatic.

'I'll never forget it.' Dad clutches his chest, as though his heart is still going at a million beats per minute, as though it hadn't happened six years ago. Though, thinking about it, it hadn't been six years for Dad. Maybe it hadn't even been six days.

'Sorry. It won't happen again.'

'I hope not.' Dad points up ahead. 'We're going to turn right. What do we on the approach?'

I carry out the manoeuvre, and Dad's impressed with the ease and accuracy of my driving until we reach the high street and a motorbike zooms right at us. There's an animalistic yelp from Dad, a cross between a screech and a whimper, before he waves his arms around.

'On the left! On the bastard left!'

I move over just in time, narrowly avoiding the motorbike, which I'm pretty sure is going too fast.

'Pull over.' Dad's voice cracks. I think he's going to cry and he's clutching his chest again. 'Please, for the love of Mary and every other bugger in the Bible, pull over.'

I pull up outside the salon. I can see Yvonne inside, her bum wiggling to whatever's playing on the radio as she snips at her client's hair. The new owner stands at the window, mug of tea in hand, probably wondering where all the customers are. I watch her take a sip of the tea instead of looking at Dad because I don't want to see the fury or the fear – whichever has claimed dominance – on his face.

'That was . . .' Dad takes a deep, shaky breath. 'My God, Elodie. My life just flashed before my eyes. I think I saw Jesus. What were you thinking?'

I was thinking I was still in LA. I'm so used to driving in the US that I was on the wrong side of the road. It's an easy mistake to make. Frightening, obviously, and I doubt Dad will ever sit in a car with me as the driver ever again, but understandable under the circumstances.

'Sorry, Dad.' I turn away from the salon but I still can't look at him, my gaze fixed on my lap instead. I hear the rumble, growing louder and louder, and I expect to be flung back onto my flight with Dolly. I'm half looking forward to it because although I haven't saved Ed yet, I'm not exactly thrilled that I've just made my dad swear. He never swears – not the bad ones, anyway, not even when he's ranting about the Tory government. There's the odd bugger (so to speak) but never anything stronger. But it isn't the time travel thing claiming me back. It's the motorbike, heading back our way. Sacha stops right in front of us, his tyre almost touching the car's bumper, and when he removes his helmet, he's glaring right at me. He stomps his way to my window, which I wind down just a little bit, keeping my finger on the button, ready to roll it back up should the need arise.

'What the fuck was that?'

I swallow and try to arrange my features into a look of contrition. 'Sorry about that. It was totally my fault.'

'Of course it was *your fault*. You were on the wrong fucking side of the road.'

'Now, now.' Dad leans across to speak to Sacha. 'There's no need for language like that.'

'You what? She could have fucking killed me. She shouldn't be behind the wheel.'

She could have fucking killed me. Is that the answer to the Ed dilemma? Off Sacha before he kills my best friend? I'll admit it's a tad dark, but it's something to mull over.

Dad holds a finger up at Sacha. 'She's a learner, as you can see from the L-plates clearly visible, and you didn't help with the speed you were going at. What were you doing then, son? Do you even know how fast you were going? Because it wasn't within the limit, was it now?'

Sacha kicks at a stone, his jaw clenching. 'Just be more fucking careful, yeah?' He continues to glare at me as he climbs back on his bike, and I know he's still glowering even when the helmet goes on and the visor's down.

'Thanks for that, Dad.' I pat him on the knee as Sacha roars away from view.

'Don't thank me.' Dad unclips his seatbelt. 'I agreed with every word he said. Even the bad ones.' I nod. I can't argue with that. 'Do you know what that pillock did the other week? He tore through the kiddies' playground on that bike. One of the little girls was so scared she wet herself on the slide. But do you know what? I'm sorry to say it, Elodie, love, but I'd feel much safer on the back of his bike than in this car with you behind the wheel.' He opens the door and twists his feet out onto the pavement. '*I'll* drive us home.'

Later, in the pub, Ed thinks my account of the driving lesson is hilarious. Yvonne is only interested in how sexy Sacha looked while angry.

'Where is he, anyway?' She looks around the pub. Micha Nowak is behind the bar while her husband is collecting glasses from the pool table area, ribbing Tomasz about the shot he's just taken. Even Franciszek and Irene are sitting in the alcove, enjoying a drink after their walk. The whole Nowak family is here apart from Sacha.

Ed catches my eye and flicks his gaze up to the ceiling, giving his head a small shake. 'Nottingham, probably. He's there most weekends. But what does it matter?'

'It matters to *me*.'

'But why?' Ed places his hand on top of Yvonne's. 'Look, you know I love you to death, even though you're a nightmare to live with and be around in general, but this crush is getting ridiculous. It's been, what? Two years? If nothing's happened by now, I don't think it ever will.'

If only that were true.

Yvonne snatches her hand away from under Ed's. 'You don't know that.'

'No, you're right, I don't know for sure, but I don't want to see you get hurt.' Ed picks up his empty glass and stands up. 'Another?'

I shake my head – I'm due in work in ten minutes – but Yvonne says it's the least he can do for bringing her down with the Sacha thing.

'He's right though, don't you think?' Ed's at the bar, being served by Micha, so I inch closer to Yvonne into the space he's left. 'Nothing's happened with Sacha over the past couple of years. Nothing even close. You should move on. Find someone who deserves you.'

I've decided – selfishly – that I couldn't handle a life stretch behind bars, so I'm not going to go down the murder route to save Ed. Instead, I'm going to go about it in a more roundabout way. If I can prevent the drama of that night from happening, Sacha and Ed will never be on the bike in the first place, and the best way to do that is to steer Yvonne away from Sacha.

'But I don't want to move on.' A smile flickers on Yvonne's face. 'He's the one for me. I know he is.'

'But why?' I can't think of any redeeming features. Yes, he's good-looking, but he's also moody and selfish and about as much fun as tap-dancing barefoot over Lego. I don't recall ever seeing him smile, at least not through genuine happiness. And then there's the Ronnie thing. Sacha is trouble.

'I can just feel it.' Yvonne closes her eyes, a smile playing at her lips, and I know she's imagining a blissful future Sacha simply won't deliver. I don't want to take a giant pin and burst her daydream, but I can't let my best friend sleepwalk into something that will devastate her – and everyone around her.

'Sacha isn't the one for you. He isn't good enough for you.'

Yvonne's eyes flick open. The smile is gone. 'Why would you say that?'

'Because it's true.' And because I know what will happen. I've been there and seen it play out already. Sacha Nowak is a liar and a cheat and I wish none of us had ever met him.

'It isn't true at all. How would you feel if I told you that Otis wasn't right for you?'

I'd feel that Yvonne's words were true. But again, this is only with the power of having lived through these events before. Otis is no more my true love than Sacha is Yvonne's, and it's something I'm going to have to face up to. But not now. Now I have to get to work.

'Just think about what we've said today.' I stand up and reach out to place my hand on Yvonne's shoulder, but she flinches away. I need to tread very carefully with this, because as much as I need to save Ed, I don't want to sacrifice my friendship with Yvonne in the process.

There's a weird atmosphere when I arrive at the hotel. Whispers. Shifty looks between staff. Is someone getting sacked? Is it me? Because I've been on top form these past few days, even if I do say so myself. They're paying for a receptionist/admin assistant but they're getting someone with much more experience and expertise right now.

I scurry to the restaurant before my shift starts. If Heather's here, she'll know what's going on. She's that sort of person. The kind who knows the right people to befriend so you're always up to date on gossip, so you're always one of the first to know what's going on. We've curled up on her bed gossiping and venting about work for the past few nights and it's been nice having someone to chat with who gets it. Who I don't have to explain everything to when I want to moan about Linda, or Marv and his drunken overfriendliness, or one of the others. It's like having a shorthand between us, so we can get straight to stuff that's irking us rather than having to wade through backstory first.

But Heather isn't on shift tonight so I have to leg it back to reception still in the dark. I'm checking a couple in when I spot Gillian crossing the foyer. She has her jacket draped over her arm and her handbag slung over her shoulder, so she must be on her way home. I rush through the rest of my welcoming spiel – directing the couple to the lift, which floor to head up to, do they need a hand with their luggage? – before I run after the manager. Gillian's at her car by the time I make it through the doors, her fob aimed, and I clatter down the stone steps, almost breaking my ankle on the loose gravel as I throw myself across the car park.

'Gillian!' I wave my hand about as I near, hoping to catch her attention. She's sitting in her car now but she hasn't closed the door behind her.

'Everything all right?' Gillian twists her legs out of the car, readying herself to step out again.

'Everything's fine.' I hope. 'I just wanted a quick word. About my performance.' My palms are sweating. I can't have travelled back in time and wrecked my career. That would be totally unfair. Plus, it'd leave me stuck here in Little Heaton. I really must be careful with how much I'm changing. One flutter of a wing can balls up my life. 'I hope you don't think I was wasting time setting up that database for the staff benefits yesterday? It's just Lawrence asked me how many friends and family passes he had left for the gym, and then Aggie wanted to know how many discounted drinks Marv had on his shift last night as she thinks he's taking advantage, and I thought it would save time in the long run to have all that information in one place, where it's easy to pull up the data.'

Gillian holds up a hand. 'The database is fine. Brilliant, in fact.'

'So I'm not getting sacked?'

Gillian laughs. 'Why would you think you're getting sacked?'

I shrug. It seems silly now. The odd atmosphere and furtive looks could have been my imagination.

'I just thought maybe I'd overstepped the mark. Nobody asked me to set up the database.'

Gillian shakes her head before resting it on one side. 'Not at all. I'm impressed by your initiative. In fact, I'm so impressed by your work lately that I was going to run something by you tomorrow, but we might as well do it now.' Gillian claps her hands together. 'How would you like to help organise the Christmas Food and Drink Festival? It'll mean more responsibility, and a lot more admin, so you'll be working in the office a lot of the time rather than on reception.' She twists so her feet are back in the car. 'You don't have to answer now. We can talk about it more tomorrow.' She reaches for the door. 'Keep up the good work, Elodie. It isn't going unnoticed.'

She pulls the door shut and I head back inside. I'm not getting sacked. I'm doing a good job and being given more opportunities. I'm definitely on the right track out of Little Heaton. Which is absolutely what I want. Isn't it?

Chapter 22

I'm kept incredibly busy over the next few days as I begin work on the Christmas Food and Drink Festival. Mel, the event manager at the hotel, is impressed not only by my enthusiasm but also by my 'natural ability' to organise and to prioritise, and he nearly loses his mind when I secure a booking for a TV chef for cooking demos. Now, we're not talking celebrity chef royalty like Gordon Ramsay or Nigella Lawson here, but she's been on *Saturday Kitchen* a few times. I feel a bit of a fraud accepting Mel's praise; this isn't natural ability – in fact, it's using the skills I learned from Mel himself. But I can't tell him that without sounding utterly insane, so I simply smile and thank him for his feedback.

I'd forgotten how much I'd enjoyed organising events as it isn't something I've done since the move to California and I'm keen to take on more responsibility within the team. By the end of the week, I'm no longer dividing my time between the events office and the reception desk. I am now a fully-fledged events assistant, with my own desk, with its own drawer and stapler. I haven't stapled anything yet, but I'm itching to use that bad boy.

'I'm so proud of you.' Otis leans in to kiss me. We're in the pub, celebrating my promotion with Yvonne, Ed and Heather. Tomasz is here too and it takes every ounce of restraint not to

163

push Otis away, but I do turn my head so his lips land on my cheek. Even Mum and Dad have joined us with Gran and Laura, and it could only improve slightly if Gillian was here, but she's been swept up by meetings lately. She did congratulate me earlier as she passed on my new name badge, which I wore with pride, before she had to dash off.

'Does this mean you get a pay rise?'

Ed tuts and glares at Yvonne for asking the question. But then he turns to me, resting his forearms on the table as he leans in closer. 'Does it?'

It does. Not mega bucks, but enough so that I can add to my paltry America fund.

'You'll be able to pay for more proper driving lessons now and leave me out of it.' Dad tries to make it sound jokey but he fails. He still hasn't recovered from the motorbike incident.

Yvonne gasps. 'You'll be able to buy yourself a car instead of borrowing your dad's or Ed's.'

Ed snorts. 'Believe me, Elodie won't be getting in my car. I quite like it dent-free.'

'Shut up.' I nudge Ed with my foot under the table. 'I haven't dented a car.'

'Yet.' Dad mutters the word but everyone hears and the table erupts in laughter. Even I join in, but I know I'll pass my test, miraculously first time.

Otis leans in close once the laughter has died down and the conversation has moved on, lowering his voice to little more than a murmur. 'Maybe you could move in with me once you've passed your test. It'd make the commute easier having your own car.'

I should have seen this coming. Should have prepared. But it's happening earlier than it did the first time round, probably because the promotion has popped up weeks – months, even – earlier than before due to my 'natural ability' at event planning. It would be easy to go along with Otis's plan, to keep things as they are until my hand is forced once I pass my test and Otis revisits his suggestion that we live together. Because I didn't move in with Otis. As good a guy as Otis is, as much as I'd enjoyed spending time with him, Otis simply isn't the one for me. Not back then. Not now. So as easy as it would be to smile and nod in a vague acceptance, I have to be brave and face up to this now, because I can't play along with our relationship when all I really want is Tomasz. And Otis will be fine. He'll find someone who deserves him. Someone who will love him with all their heart. I know it.

So it happens that evening. We go for a walk after Dad has migrated over to the Farmer's and Mum and Laura have taken Gran home because she doesn't want to miss *EastEnders*. We leave Ed and the others in the pub to have a wander through the village because I can't do this in front of them. Yvonne's too pissed to walk in a straight line anyway and would probably end up taking a dip in the canal if she came with us. It's still light out but it's cooled down and I find myself shivering in my vest top. Otis offers his jacket but I shake my head. Returning it later will make things feel even more awkward.

'Otis.' We've reached the footbridge over the canal but I stop, my hand tugging Otis back as he starts to climb the steps. 'I need to talk to you. About us.'

I try to remember what I said the last time. How I can make this better. Easier, for Otis, because this will come out of the blue for him, just like it did the last time. Because nothing bad happened. There was no real catalyst – no big row, no cheating – just a slow realisation that I was falling in love with someone else and that I didn't feel that way about Otis. He didn't give me butterflies when I saw him. My stomach didn't perform a happy little flip when he smiled at me. My pulse didn't speed up when I knew he'd be there. Tomasz had been there for years but I had no idea that he was the one I was destined to be with. It was a trickle, a long-drawn move from friendship to love and it took a long time for me to appreciate him, to really *see* him, but once I did, once I understood, there was no going back.

It turns out there's no easy way to break up with someone who doesn't want to break up with you. It's brutal, no matter how hard you try to soften the blow with platitudes and assurances that they will be better off in the long run. Otis is devastated and it hurts me, because although I know this is absolutely the right thing, that I'm not in love with Otis and I can't force myself to feel the butterflies and the racing pulse, he's still a good man and I'm hurting him. I have to assure myself that he'll be loved in the way he deserves, that soon he will discover the person he's destined to be with. And she isn't far away. She's right there, waiting for him to fall head over heels. Otis will be happy, even if it doesn't look as though he can be fixed right now as he climbs into his car, his face drawn with hurt and confusion. His life has tilted, but only fleetingly.

I head back to the pub, where my friends have moved through to the pool room. Sacha has joined them, and he glowers at me as he leans down to take his shot. He swears when he misses. Swears again when Tomasz pats him on the back with a grin and a snarky comment before he takes his shot. Sacha continues to watch me as he sips his pint, his eyes narrowed, nostrils flared. He thumps his pint down on the table and swipes the back of his hand across his mouth.

'Hey, Elodie.' Yvonne beckons me over to the table where she's sitting with Ed and Heather. She's grinning like a loon and swaying slightly and I feel bad about the hangover she's going to have in the morning. 'Did you know Ed was still in contact with Christine's grandson?'

'Are you?' I sit down on a stool, ensuring my back is to Sacha. I can't deal with him right now.

'It turns out they've been emailing all this time and he never said a thing.' Yvonne pushes her arm into Ed's. 'Selfish prick. Dominic was *our* friend too, but you've kept him all to yourself.'

This is news to me. As far as I'm aware, Dominic spent that one summer in Little Heaton and we hung out, had a laugh, everyone got the tattoos apart from me, and then Dominic left. Went home to Canada and became nothing more than part of fond anecdotes ('Do you remember that summer when we cycled a million miles?' 'Do you remember that summer Yvonne chased Ed with that tiny fish we caught in the river?').

'I haven't kept him all to myself.' Ed rolls his eyes. 'We just message each other now and then.'

'*Without. Us.*' Yvonne jabs Ed in the arm with her finger with each word and though he opens his mouth to respond, his words are swallowed by the roar of triumph behind us. I twist in my seat to see Tomasz, cue held in the air, jiggling a victory dance in front of his brother. While my lips flick upwards at the display of victory, Sacha's scowling at the defeat, emitting even more broodiness than usual as Tomasz celebrates.

I turn away from the scene as my stomach performs a happy little somersault. I love him so much it aches, but I have to be patient. I'm changing enough by saving Ed and I really do need to be careful with the butterfly effect. But by saving Ed, I'll be saving us too. We will be together, but forever this time.

'God, he's *fit*.' I don't even have to follow Yvonne's gaze to know she's looking directly at Sacha. The happy somersault turns into a churning as I'm filled with a sense of foreboding. Yvonne's crush on Sacha isn't going away and that can never be a good thing.

Chapter 23

Is it classed as stalking if you keep refreshing the social media of your ex simply to check that they're doing okay after your break-up? Otis hasn't posted much over the past few days – he posted about the new Premier League and Mo Farah at the World Athletics Championships over the weekend, nothing really to give a clue about his mental state – and though I know he *will* be okay, I can't rid myself of the squirm of guilt. I'm so distracted by Otis and the niggling shame, I don't notice the buzz of apprehension about the office until the tapping of Mel's foot grows to such a crescendo that he's in danger of wearing a hole in the carpet.

'Sorry.' Mel runs his hands over his face, his foot now still after I've jokingly threatened to chuck him out of the window if he doesn't stop with the jiggling.

'Do you need a hand with anything?' There's a spreadsheet up on Mel's computer screen but I don't think he's made any changes to it and he's been staring at it for at least twenty minutes.

He shakes his head. It shakes far longer than necessary and I'm under the impression he isn't going to speak when he finally opens his mouth. 'No. Thanks. Everything's fine. Thank you.'

Mel doesn't look or sound fine, but I don't push it. 'Shall I put the kettle on?'

Mel smiles, but it's tight, fleeting. 'That'd be lovely. Thank you.' His foot's jiggling again before I've even stood up.

The staff kitchen is along the corridor. It's quite a small space, with basic features – a sink, kettle, microwave and a tiny under-counter fridge – and it's crammed with people right now: office staff, housekeeping, restaurant and kitchen staff, all huddled together with the hum of several conversations competing to be heard. There's no way I can edge my way through the small crowd to the kettle.

'What's going on?' There's a waitress closest to the door and it's her I aim my question at, but it's the head of housekeeping who answers, shuffling around in the tight space so she can face me.

'The castle's being sold.'

'No, it isn't.' There was a rumour recently about this, which explained the weird atmosphere on the day Gillian offered me the chance to work on the Christmas Food and Drink Festival. Heather told me about the gossip doing the rounds later that day but it wasn't true then and it isn't true now.

Linda tilts her chin in the air and observes me through narrowed eyes. 'How would *you* know better than any of us?' The head of housekeeping didn't like me when I was a chambermaid. She's liked me even less since I moved to more administerial roles. Obviously I can't tell her how I know – for a fact – that Durban Castle is not being sold and that none of our jobs are at risk.

'Gillian assured me.' It sounds weak. Naïve. And Linda chuckles accordingly, shaking her head in a pitying way.

'Of course she did. She doesn't want speculation or mass panic. But where is she? Where's she been this past week? Jetting off to meetings, that's where. She's barely been here. Though, obviously, she was here just long enough to *assure you* that the rumours are false.' She gives me a long look, her head tilted to one side and a small smile on her face, before she turns her back to me.

I try to battle my way through to the kettle but everyone is too tightly packed in and I give up, heading back to the office empty-handed. I explain the situation to Mel, whose nervy foot-tapping is now understandable. I tell him what I told Linda but he's as convinced as the head housekeeper and his foot continues to drum against the carpet for the rest of the day. Maybe it's the drumming sending me up the wall or maybe it's Linda's absolute certainty that I'm wrong, but by the time I leave the hotel that evening, I'm starting to doubt myself too. What if I've meddled too much in the past and the castle *is* being sold due to the ripples of the butterfly effect? It would mean everyone would lose their jobs and I'd miss my opportunity to fly off to a new life in LA.

I walk the long way home, heading across the footbridge and along the lane alongside the woods until I reach the cul-de-sac of new-builds that have popped up since last summer. A new horseshoe-shaped road has been built, with four- and five-bedroom houses lining the outer edge and smaller two- and three-bedroom houses opposite on the inner edge. All of the houses are detached, built from red bricks with pitch-roofed porches above the doors and garages attached to the side. Once they're finished, neat little squares of lawns will finish them off and trees will be planted along grass verges between the pavement and road. Four years ago – or two years from this point in time – Tomasz and I had been standing on the pavement, him looking wistfully at the house with the cherry-red door. It was one of the smaller houses on the inner side of the curved road, because even our fantasyland was hampered a little bit by reality. There was no way we could afford one of these places – the deposit alone would gobble up our savings.

'This would be the ideal place to bring up a family.'

'I thought we were going to America.' I'd rested my head on his shoulder, still looking across at the houses. They were uniform, with only the gardens marking them apart, showing off the personality of the occupier. The house with the cherry-red door had an overgrown lawn, which could have looked messy compared with the manicured lawn of the neighbouring gardens, but it was bursting with wild flowers, giving off a tousled, bohemian look. It was chaotic but natural and I liked it.

'We are. But you never know – you might miss Little Heaton so much you want to come home.'

I'd laughed. An unattractive spluttery snort because I couldn't ever imagine wanting to come back here. Even with this beautiful, wild flowered house, with this beautiful man and our beautiful children. It seems a bit silly now, but I really couldn't imagine escaping this dull little village and wanting to return.

'Not long now. Two weeks.' He'd kissed the top of my head and we'd started to wander back along the horseshoe-shaped path. Back to reality, where we rented a one-bedroom flat above the charity shop.

I stand on the pavement of the house with the cherry-red door now. There are no wild flowers in the garden yet and it makes me a bit sad. The two weeks between Tomasz's daydream and our move to America didn't feel like a very long time but a lot would happen in those couple of weeks. I'd lose Ed and when I did move to America it would be on my own.

Dad's tending to his salad crops out in the garden and Gran's watching *The One Show* when I get in. Mum, Gran tells me with a face so scrunched up in distaste it's in danger of turning itself inside out, is out 'getting squiffed on mother's ruin' with 'that friend of hers' (who should know better, being the daughter of a vicar, apparently). I leave Gran in the company of Matt Baker, Alex Jones and their guests, and head upstairs to shower. By the time I'm out, Heather is home and lounging on my bed, reading the postcard Ed sent me from France. She holds it up, her eyebrow quirking in question as I toe the bedroom door shut behind me.

'When are you two going to get it on?'

'Never.' Making sure the towel is tucked in securely, I pick up the postcard and prop it against the America jar, which is more of a symbol than an actual saving device by this point. There isn't

171

much in there – a few quid in loose change – but my savings account is starting to look quite healthy. Changing my mind, I pick up the postcard and slip it under my mattress. It feels safer there with Ed's words tucked away.

'But you're single now. Why dump Otis – who was *fine*, by the way – for nothing? And has Ed ever had a proper girlfriend?'

'No offence, Heather, but I'd quite like to get dressed, so can you bog off?'

Heather ignores my request and tucks her feet under her calves so she's sitting cross-legged on the bed. 'Have you heard?'

'Have I heard what?'

She gives me a withering look, like she can't believe I don't know what she's talking about. 'The hotel. The castle. It's being sold and turned into a casino.'

'I hadn't heard that one.' Though I've heard everything else that the castle is apparently being developed into today, including flats, a cinema and my favourite of all, an immersive 'haunted castle' theatre, which sounds amazing and I sort of wish the castle *was* being sold for that purpose.

'I think I'd make a good croupier.' Heather straightens her spine and adopts a serious expression. 'I just need to learn how to play poker and stuff. Do croupiers do poker?' Her serious expression slides, her brow furrowing.

'I have no idea but you'd be wasting your time learning to play either way.' I sit down on the bed, my hand holding my towel in place. I don't think either of us wants me to flash a boob. 'The castle isn't being sold.'

'That's not what Aggie said. She said Marv had told her that Gillian Quinn had told Gio that the castle *is* being sold but he has to keep it a secret.'

'Well, Gio's done a fantastic job with that.' I roll my eyes. 'Trust me, Heather. The castle isn't being sold.'

'We'll see.' Heather uses a sing-song tone. I don't tell her that I *have* seen, and that the castle isn't being sold and turned into a casino. It will still be a hotel six years from now. In fact, it'll be the venue for Heather's wedding. The voice inside my head is confident on this. I wish I felt as sure that I hadn't stuffed it all up with my time-hopping.

'What does it matter to you anyway? It's only a summer job. You'll be out of here at the first chance you get once you've qualified.'

Heather shrugs. She uncrosses her legs and pulls her knees up towards her chin. 'I don't think I'll go that far, actually.'

'Why wouldn't you?' I frown, confused by my sister's U-turn. I thought we were on the same page on this, at least back then, before Heather found the love of her life and decided to stay. I'd thought returning to Little Heaton had been a compromise, not a desire.

She shrugs again. 'I guess I just miss it when I'm away at uni, and once you've lived in a mouldy flat next door to a squat, being back in Little Heaton isn't so bad. It feels cleaner, for a start. And quieter.'

'You don't strike me as the kind of person who likes a quiet life.'

Heather gives me a hard stare. 'Our neighbours played happy house music at top volume, night and day. I'd take silence over that any day. And I'm not saying I'll stay right here in the village but I'd like to be close enough to Mum and Dad. And even Gran.' Heather grins at me. 'Nobody slags off the contestants of *Love Island* like Gran. She's pure comedy gold when she gets going.'

'What about me?'

She nods at the America fund jar. 'You're out of here. Off to live your best life in the States.'

'Yeah.' I try to push a smile on my face, ignoring the gnaw of loneliness that's still fresh in my mind, reminding myself it will be different this time. 'I am.'

Heather isn't the only one in the village convinced the castle is being sold. There's a buzz as I step into the pub that evening, and it isn't the usual beer-induced merriment. The air is thick

173

with tension and chatter, surging out from the group huddled around one of the larger tables at the back of the pub. The group is headed by Irene Nowak, who's standing up, facing the crowd with her fist lifted in the air as she gives a rousing speech.

'What's going on?'

Tomasz is behind the bar, one of only three people – myself included – not gathered in front of his grandmother. He's still wearing a plaster-flecked T-shirt so I'm assuming he's been roped in to help after work while the others are assembling around Irene.

'They're selling the castle. Knocking it down, apparently, and building more houses. Gran's not happy about it.'

We both turn towards the group, where Irene is red-faced as she delivers her passionate sermon. I hear the words 'legacy', 'immoral' and 'utter bastards'.

'She's organising a revolt, starting with a protest tomorrow.'

I remember the protest. Half the village set up camp outside the castle gates with placards and flasks of tea, and Irene chained herself to the iron rail. It made the front page of the local paper, something Irene was fiercely proud of even when it turned out there had never been any plans to sell the castle, never mind flatten it to the ground.

Tomasz pulls a face. 'Should I have told you that? What with you working at the hotel?' He waves the worry away. 'Never mind. You should be at the front of the protest with the biggest banner. It's you who'll be out of a job if it goes ahead.'

I'm about to assure him that it won't be going ahead, but keep my gob shut this time. Irene had been in her element during the protest and she'd revelled in rallying everyone's support. The photo from the newspaper had been used on the order of service at her funeral and I can't take that away from her.

'*You* could be in a job if it goes ahead.' I point at Tomasz's work shirt. 'New houses need plastering. Maybe it's *you* we need to keep out of the loop.' I narrow my eyes, trying to keep the rest of my face neutral as I tease him. 'The enemy within.'

'Damn it, my cover's blown.' Tomasz leans his elbows on the bar and presses his palms together. 'Please don't rat me out to Gran though. She'll have me strung upside down by my nuts from the castle's turret if she finds out I'm a traitor to the cause.'

'Your secret is safe with me.' I mime zipping up my lips.

'What secret's that then?'

I hadn't sensed Sacha's arrival but his hand appears on the bar beside me. He lounges against the bar, looking between his brother and me, a lazy smile on his face that could quickly turn into a sneer.

'A secret that is absolutely none of your business.' My tone is sharp and Sacha's eyebrows rise above the sunglasses he's wearing.

'Ooh, touchy.' He snorts and looks at Tomasz. 'Who put fifty pence in the bitch meter?'

'Don't be a dick.' Tomasz shakes his head at his brother. While a moment ago we were playing around and having a bit of fun, the corners of his mouth are turned down now and his brow is furrowed.

'It's all right. We can tell Sacha your secret.' I look Sacha in what I hope is the eye, but it's hard to tell with the shades. 'But he can go first. Do *you* have any secrets?'

Sacha's face remains passive, but he takes a step back. 'Whatever. I don't have time for this.' He turns to Tomasz as he continues to back away. 'Tell Mum I won't be back tonight.'

'Off to Nottingham?'

It could be an innocent question, but I see Sacha's jaw tighten, ever so slightly. He doesn't say anything, doesn't even answer the question, he simply raises his hand in farewell as he turns and saunters from the pub.

'What was that about?'

I sometimes wondered if Tomasz had been aware of Sacha and his jaunts to Nottingham, about Ronnie and everything, and I'd asked him outright after the accident. Despite his denial, there had always been the tiniest niggle that he'd kept Sacha's secret, but he looks utterly perplexed as the door swings shut behind his brother. I'm in no doubt that he knew nothing before everyone else, and it's a comfort.

'Dunno.' I shrug, acting none the wiser. 'I was just messing around, but it sounds like he's up to something in Nottingham. He got very touchy, didn't he? Maybe you should ask him about it?'

It would solve the conundrum of how to keep Yvonne and Sacha apart, if she could see him for what he is before it's too late, and it'd also prevent the accident. Because Sacha wouldn't be in any great rush to get away that day if his secret was unveiled beforehand, and he wouldn't take Ed with him. The accident wouldn't happen and Ed would be saved. Tomasz could be the answer to everything.

Chapter 24

The protest has already begun by the time I arrive at work the next morning, with Irene heading up the demonstration. She hasn't chained herself to the rail yet but she's thrusting the biggest banner and shouting the loudest. Gillian's trying to reason with the group, which is quite small at the moment with only a dozen or so pensioners, but they're having none of it. They woke up ready for a fight and they're not swallowing any 'corporate lies' and backing down. Especially as the bacon butties haven't arrived from the café yet.

Gillian rolls her eyes up to the sky as I pass, and she catches up to me as I'm making my way to the events office.

'I am going to throttle whoever started that bloody rumour.' Poor Gillian looks stressed. Her shoulders are hunched and her usually neat hair is askew on the right-hand side. 'I just need to find out who it was and hunt the bugger down. You don't happen to know who it was, do you?'

I shake my head. Past me had no idea and present me is just as clueless. 'Did you tell them it isn't true?' Silently, I add *can you tell me it isn't true?* Because I really need to have not caused a change in my getting-out-of-Little-Heaton timeline with my interfering in the past.

Gillian gives me an exasperated look. 'I've told them every way I can think of. There are no plans to sell and there never have been. Someone must have heard . . . something . . . and got the wrong end of the stick.'

'You could tell them what the right end of the stick is?'

Gillian's shoulders slump even further. 'I wish I could. I wish I could go out there and tell them all what's going on, but I can't. Not yet.' Gillian's eyes widen. 'Not that there's anything to tell.' We've reached Gillian's office and she darts inside before she blabs the whole proposed deal. But even though she hasn't leaked anything, I'm convinced enough by her mini slip-up that the castle – and therefore my ticket out of the village – is safe.

Mel's on the phone when I step into the events office, his body hunched over his desk as he speaks in hushed tones. I can't make out everything he's saying, but I manage to pick out odd words and phrases as I wait for my computer to load up.

'What more do you want? Tanks rolling over the old dears?' Mel, in a heated state of annoyance, has forgotten his need to be discreet. 'Great. Thanks a lot, Will.' He slams the phone down and throws himself back in his seat, his head lolling back so he'd be looking up at the ceiling if his hands weren't covering his eyes.

'You're taking a risk getting the papers involved.' My computer has loaded up so I open my email, which is mostly spam.

'What else am I meant to do?' Mel peels his hands away from his eyes, leaving his fingers resting on his cheeks. 'I can't go out there and join the protest. Not if I want to keep my job. But I *can* drum up a bit of support on the quiet.' He straightens in his seat and spins around to face me. 'You won't say anything, will you?'

I pull my fingers across my lips. 'I won't say a word, though I think you're getting worked up about nothing. You all are. The castle isn't being knocked down. It isn't being sold.'

'No offence, Elodie, but how would you know if it was or not? Because Gillian told you so? Don't be naïve.' He turns his seat to face his desk again and grabs his phone, jabbing a number in aggressively.

He doesn't bother with the hushed tones this time as he attempts to get the protest covered by another reporter.

By lunchtime, the protest has started to gather momentum; there are now at least fifty people gathered outside the gates – and no longer restricted to pensioners – and there's an amp blaring out Wamdue Projects' 'King of My Castle', which Irene is jutting her placard up and down to the beat of. There are teenagers sunbathing on towels, mums trying to get their toddlers to sit on picnic blankets and prodding sandwiches and carrots sticks at them, and more bacon sandwiches being passed around from the café. Even Gran's here, a finger stuck in one ear against the music while she chats with Reverend Carter.

I sneak past and head down to the café. I usually grab lunch from the restaurant at the hotel – perk of the job – but I have plans this afternoon. The café is empty due to the non-working population of the village having decamped to the hill, but the owner is happy as their bacon butty runs have filled the till more than a usual weekday morning. With a couple of bacon sandwiches and takeaway coffees, I head across the footbridge and along the lane until I reach the new housing development. I thought I might have to hang around for a while but I've timed it just right as I see Tomasz heading for his van as I follow the curve of the rubble that will one day become a pavement.

'Lunchbreak?' I hold up the paper bags. 'I thought I'd come and update you on the protest.'

'Is that a bacon butty?' Tomasz's face has lit up as he walks towards me, his cheeks rounding as he grins. The sun has brought out the freckles across them and lightened his strawberry blond hair.

'With red *and* brown sauce.' I pass over one of the paper bags. 'Which is disgusting, by the way.'

'Everyone says that until they've tried it.' I *have* tried it. And it's as repellent as I thought it would be. 'So how's the protest coming along?'

179

'Pretty active.' We've started to wander along the rubbly street, me being extra careful in my espadrilles. They look pretty with my belted wrap dress but I'm in danger of breaking an ankle on the loose stones. 'They're blasting music and everything now, but nobody's glued themselves to the wall yet.'

Tomasz gives me a sharp look. 'Don't give Gran any ideas like that. She's already talking about chaining herself to the gate.'

I press my lips together tightly. Irene won't be simply talking about it for much longer. Still, at least it'll attract the attention that Mel was after this morning.

'Gran's in her element though. I don't think I've ever seen her this zealous about anything.'

'The castle means a lot to her. It's where she met your grandad.' I'm tempted to ask Tomasz to tell me the tale of how Irene and Franciszek met again, because it really is a lovely story. Maybe they should have added it to the newspaper article, to share it with a wider audience.

'I guess if it wasn't for the castle, I wouldn't be here.' There's a frown on Tomasz's face as we reach the end of the rubble and start to cut across the grass. 'Maybe I should join them after work. Add my support.'

'I think your gran would like that.'

Without discussion, we've made our way to the canal, and we use the beam of the lock as a makeshift bench. A couple of ducks glide their way towards us and Tomasz pinches off two bits of muffin to chuck down into the water as they approach.

'How are you doing? After the Otis thing?'

The ducks are bobbing on the water, waiting for more bread, and Tomasz keeps his gaze on them as he asks the question.

'I'm okay. It was the right thing to do.' I perhaps should have done it earlier. Maybe not while we were camping, as that would have ruined the whole festival, but sooner than I did. Once a scaredy-cat, always a scaredy-cat it seems. 'I keep checking up on him, seeing what he's posted on social media. Is that weird?'

Tomasz lifts one shoulder and releases it. 'It's all out in the public domain, and it's coming from a good place. It isn't as though you're camped outside his place with a pair of binoculars.'

'There's no point. The bushes are too high to see anything through the window.' I catch Tomasz's eye and we both snigger. The freckles across his nose are really evident in the sunshine, and I want to reach out and trace a finger over them. I've missed this. Tomasz and me. The bacon sandwich clumps in my throat as I think of all the terrible things I said to him after the accident, and I have to gulp down my coffee to shift it.

'What?' Tomasz reaches up to touch his face, touching the tips of his fingers to his nose. 'Sauce?'

'No. Sorry.' I didn't realise I was staring at him and I look down at my lap. 'I was miles away. Thinking about . . .' The past. Us. Everything I gave up because I was hurt and angry and grieving. '. . . the, um, the protest. And the castle. My job. It's all in jeopardy, isn't it?'

'I thought you were absolutely, one million per cent sure the castle wasn't being sold.' Tomasz leans across so he can bump his arm against mine. There's a lump in my throat again, but this time it has nothing to do with my sandwich.

'I am.' My voice comes out croaky and my eyes are starting to burn with the threat of tears.

'Hey, it'll be okay.' Tomasz's hand is on my back, his palm warm through the fabric of my dress, and that just makes it worse. 'Gran's on the case, remember.'

I smile, despite everything, and I nod. 'Yeah, she is. And everything will be fine.' I'll make sure it is. I've been given this second chance and I won't mess it up this time.

Chapter 25

The protestors are back the next morning. Franciszek brings over trays of wuzetka to keep morale up (because nothing gives a boost quite like home-baked cake) and someone brings a guitar and gets a singalong going. Over the next few days, the guitar is joined by a violin, bugle, two recorders and a keyboard. Irene fashions homemade maracas from empty plastic bottles and rice so anyone – no matter their musical talent – can join in the motley band. By Friday afternoon, Irene is chained to the railing and a local reporter is chatting to protestors.

'This has to stop.' Gillian is pacing up and down her office, which isn't really big enough for pacing, but she's giving it a good go. 'It's the Summer Food and Drink Festival tomorrow. We can't have people turning up to *that*.' She waves a hand in the general direction of the gates, where the protestors are singing and dancing and shaking their maracas. It looks like they're having a really good time, actually, and the camaraderie is electric whenever I have to pass through. 'We're supposed to be setting up, not trying to sort out a riot.'

It's hardly a riot, but Gillian doesn't look like she's in the mood for contrary opinions so I don't say anything, instead watching as she turns and strides towards the window. She leans her palms on the windowsill, looking out across the vast lawn at the back of the castle where tomorrow's festival will be taking place. I didn't have much to do with its planning as the organisation started months ago, back when it was still winter, but it gave me an idea of what to expect at the Christmas version that I was helping to put together.

'It'll put people off, seeing that on the front page of the paper.' Gillian turns and wafts a hand in the general direction of the protest again.

'It's only the local paper, and readership is down. Plus, it might not even make the *front* page.' It will, but I'm trying to placate Gillian, to keep her from self-combusting with the stress of it all. Irene will be defiant in chains on the front page of the *Cheshire Post*, eyes blazing, lips set in an unwavering line. But the festival will be fine. The protestors will be gone by teatime.

'There's talk that *Granada Reports* are sending a crew over for tonight's edition.' Gillian looks like she might throw up. 'This is getting out of hand. I need to call head office.'

I back out of the office, leaving Gillian to her phone call, painting on a bright and breezy expression before I step into the events office. Mel is facedown at his desk, his forehead resting on his folded arms, but he peeks up as he hears me approach.

'Well?' His eyes are wide, pleading with me to deliver good news.

'It's all in hand. Gillian says there's nothing to worry about. The festival will be unaffected.'

'And the rumour about *Granada Reports*?'

I shake my head. 'Gillian hadn't even heard that one. She laughed when I told her about it.'

'So it isn't happening?'

'Absolutely not.' This bit is true, even if my nose should be growing like a politician's who's been caught in yet another scandal with the other stuff I've fibbed about. 'There won't be any camera crews out there.'

Mel sits up straight and gives his shoulders a wriggle before stretching his hands high above his head. 'Right then. Let's get this festival up and running.'

The announcement comes late afternoon. Gillian gathers most of the hotel staff currently on shift in the largest conference room and delivers the news everyone's been waiting for.

'Durban Castle – neither the hotel or the building itself – is *not up for sale*, and there are absolutely *no plans* for it to be sold in the future. In fact, quite the opposite.'

There's a murmur as people turn to their neighbours with hushed delight and then questions: *The hotel isn't for sale! Our jobs are safe! But wait, what is the opposite of the hotel being sold?*

'Devon Fox Hotels Group, who own Durban Castle, have hotels in the UK and Europe, and they're planning to expand into the US, with the acquisition of a small chain of hotels on the West Coast.'

The murmur turns into a buzz as the chatter increases at Gillian's announcement. *What does this mean for us?* Gillian holds up a hand, waiting until the babble has died down before continuing.

'The acquisition will not affect the day-to-day running of Durban Castle. It will not affect any jobs.'

A hand goes up, a voice calling out before Gillian even has the chance to acknowledge it. 'Can you guarantee that?'

'Yes.' Gillian's nod is decisive. But she is wrong. *My* job will be affected by the acquisition. I am on my way to California, baby. I wait for the fizz of excitement to bubble up in my belly but I feel quite flat. But then I suppose this isn't the new and exciting adventure it was the first time around and I am quite stressed about saving Ed and keeping hold of the relationship with Tomasz that hasn't even begun yet. Never mind buzzing with excitement, I'm surprised I'm not rocking in a corner and whimpering.

Gillian sends everyone back to work, though most hang around the conference room, faces lit up as they deliberate this new development. News travels down to the gate (at the insistence of Gillian, who is keen for the group to dissipate as quickly as possible) and Irene is unchained from the rail, though she will still appear on the front page of the next edition of the *Cheshire Post*. I text Tomasz on my way back to the office, to let him know the good news and to invite him out for a celebratory drink tonight.

I'm nervous as I get ready, and I have to take deep breaths to keep the butterflies under control. It feels like a first date even though it isn't a date at all – it's simply two mates having a drink in the pub – and I've been on many, *many* dates with Tomasz already. I choose my outfit with care. I want something casual, to befit the occasion – or lack of – but I also want to look hot enough to blow Tomasz's socks off. In the end, I opt for a pair of skinny jeans for the casual sense but dress them up with a black cami top with lace detail, gold strappy sandals and chunky earrings (which are actually Heather's, but I'm sure she won't mind too much, and I'd have asked to borrow them if she was home). The butterflies are fluttering again as I step into the living room and Laura tells me I look 'absolutely gorgeous'.

'Are you off out?' The corners of Mum's lips turn down. 'But you'll miss *Celebrity MasterChef*.'

'You can tell me all about it later.' I check I've got my purse and my keys in my little fringed handbag (also Heather's, but seriously, she'll be fine with it. She's very generous with her belongings). 'I shouldn't be too late – I've got an early start with the festival tomorrow.'

'We'll probably see you there.' Laura lifts her wine glass as a farewell gesture. She turns to Mum. 'Do you remember those strawberry tarts they had last year? I'm going back, just in case they have those again.'

'Sod the strawberry tarts.' Mum lifts her glass. 'I'm going for the wine.' Mum and Laura's heads press together as they giggle and I leave them to it. The butterflies are swarming in my stomach as

I walk the short distance to the high street. Taking the deepest breath my lungs can manage, I push open the door of the Royal Oak and step inside. I spot him over by the pool table and for a moment my heart soars. But then disappointment crashes down over me. Sacha's here too, his sunglasses perched on the top of his head as he takes his shot.

Great.

The door opens behind me, and I'm almost knocked over as Ed barrels into me. We both apologise as we right our footing, Ed's hand gripping my arm to keep me upright.

'Sorry, didn't see you there.'

'No, no, *I'm* sorry. It's my fault for standing around the doorway like a lemon.'

'Why are you standing around the doorway like a lemon?' Yvonne has squeezed past Ed to step into the pub.

'I just got here.' I try to catch Tomasz's attention but he doesn't spot me before he leans over the table to take his shot. 'I was just going to the bar. What are you having?'

So this really isn't a date. There's a full house, especially when Irene pops over to tell us all about the protest and the promise of an article in the paper.

'I'm slightly disappointed *Granada Reports* never turned up, but you can't have everything, can you? And it's good news about the castle not being bulldozed.'

'They wouldn't dare with you around.'

Irene beams at Yvonne's words, and her chin tilts upwards. 'Too right. You just give me a shout if you hear even a whisper of any deals going on and I'll have myself chained to that gate before you can say crazy old lady. I'll show 'em.' Irene puts her fists up and boxes the air until Sacha gives her a withering look. 'Right. I'm off for my evening walk. But remember.' She catches our eye in turn. 'A whisper of a deal and you come to me.' She walks away, boxing the air again, and she almost accidentally whacks Heather on the boob as my sister heads towards us.

'Sorry about Gran.' Tomasz steps aside so Sacha can take his shot at the pool table. 'She's buzzing about the castle.'

'No worries.' Heather sits next to me and her eyes narrow as she clocks my earlobes. 'Are those my earrings?'

I touch one of the chunky earrings while pretending to look at Heather but focusing on the picture on the wall to her left. 'Are they? I thought they were mine. Silly me.'

'They suit you.' Heather raises her eyebrows as I meet her gaze. 'But that doesn't mean you can keep them. And I want my handbag back later as well.'

'Got it.' I try to catch Yvonne's eye, to see if she's as shocked at Heather's lack of annoyance at my borrowing her stuff without asking, but Yvonne's eyes are firmly on Sacha as he leans across the table to take his shot.

'I need a piss.' Handing Tomasz his pool cue, Sacha saunters off. I look at Yvonne again, checking she's as repulsed as I am, but she's gazing adoringly at the space he's vacated. But then her face changes, her chin tucking back and her nose scrunching up, and I think it's a delayed reaction to Sacha's crudeness. But it's so much worse than Sacha's crudeness.

'All right, knobheads?' Craig Radcliffe swaggers towards us, dipping down every time he takes a step with his right foot, as though the leg is a couple of inches shorter than the left. I haven't seen Craig for ages, and I was hoping that he'd packed up and left in this version of the past. Unfortunately not. 'Not very chatty, are we?'

Yvonne sighs, her eyes rolling up to the ceiling as she folds her arms across her chest. 'What do you want?'

Craig takes a step back and spreads his arms wide. 'I'm just being friendly. Saying hello.'

'Now you've said it, why don't you go away?'

Craig snorts. 'Why don't you suck my dick? Oh no, wait. Been there, done that, haven't you?' Craig titters to himself. He doesn't see or hear Sacha's approach, but he feels it when Sacha clips him

187

on the back of his head. 'The fuck?' Craig turns around, his face scrunched up, eyes ablaze.

'I suggest you apologise to the lady.' Sacha is taller than Craig. Broader. He makes Craig look like a tiny Lego man as he towers above him. 'And then I suggest you leave, very, very quickly.'

Craig doesn't apologise. That would mean backing down. Losing face. Instead, he shrugs as he backs away, muttering about the 'state of the place' and that he was going anyway.

'Oh my God. Thank you.' Yvonne propels herself forward, throwing herself at Sacha and wrapping her arms around his waist. Sacha doesn't return the hug – he holds his arms out wide while looking at his brother with one side of his mouth pulled up as though there's an invisible hook tugging at it – but I feel uneasy anyway. This pairing cannot go ahead. Sacha will hurt Yvonne and she'll never really get over it, will never move on to find someone she deserves, and finding out who Sacha really is when she's in too deep will cause irreparable damage to all our lives.

Chapter 26

It had been a shock to the system the first time I worked on a festival. There was the alarmingly early start and then the sheer amount of work involved in running the event, but this time I'm prepared. I've organised bigger events than the Durban Castle Summer Food and Drink Festival so even the seemingly endless to-do list doesn't intimidate me. I crack on with the job, designating car park space for staff, exhibitors and the public, and helping to set up stalls and seating areas while Mel focuses on the health and safety checks. Everything runs as smoothly as can be expected (there are always hiccups along the way, but we manage to smooth them over) and the stalls start to fill up with bread and cakes, cheeses, street food, and lots and lots of booze.

It's already a gorgeous day, with the sun shining and a light breeze, and there's a steady stream of couples and families arriving to browse and eat and enjoy the live music. By lunchtime, the place is packed. The reporter who covered the protest yesterday is back, but this time his focus is on Gillian as she poses in front of a gourmet ice cream van with a chocolate-dipped waffle cone topped with a scoop of caramel clotted fudge ice cream. When the photographer asks her to lick the ice cream while looking into the camera, Gillian tells him she doesn't have the time or the crayons to explain why that won't be happening, but thanks him for coming before moving on to the next task on her giant to-do list.

Mum's here, lounging next to Laura, both of them sipping wine and giggling every time they attempt to climb out of their deck-chairs, and Dad seems to be buying a bit of every cheese available, like a mouse armed with a bag-for-life and an empty fridge waiting at home. I've seen Yvonne and Ed knocking about too, and Heather said she'd pop over, though she probably won't drag herself out of bed until mid-afternoon. Tomasz isn't here yet – he's working on the new-build houses again so he said he'd come over this evening, but it doesn't stop me searching for him in the crowds, looking out for the floppy strawberry blond hair and freckles. I can't wait until he gets here; I've decided that today is the day I will tell him how I feel because I cannot hold it in for a moment longer.

Originally it was Tomasz who made the first move, on Bonfire Night of this year, but although it's less than three months away, it's still far too long. That night was beautiful, with the stars and the fireworks, the heat and the crackle from the bonfire and the smell of smoke and roasting meat in the air. Tomasz's fingers found mine as the sky erupted with bursts of red and green glitter, his cheeks pink from the cold and from the bold move. And then the kiss. So perfect. Unexpected but coveted. The swell in my chest. The beat of my heart, much louder, it seemed, than the booming from the sky. But as beautiful as that night was, I cannot wait.

Closing my eyes, I listen to the bustle of the crowds, the hum of the band playing in the distance, the sizzle and clatter from the demo kitchen. The smell of frying onions and popcorn and sun cream fill the air and a breeze cools the back of my neck even as the midday sun bears down. Today feels like a good day to begin a love story.

'El-o-deeeeee.'

I open my eyes, turning to see Yvonne stumbling across the lawn in heels. She lifts a plastic cup filled with crushed ice and points at me with the other hand.

'You need one of these, Elodie.' She finds the straw clumsily with her mouth and slurps noisily from it. 'G&T slush. Amazeballs.'

I wave my clipboard at her. 'Working, I'm afraid. Maybe later.'

'Forget work.' Yvonne takes another stumbled step towards me. I'm beginning to suspect the wobbliness isn't due to the heels on soft grass. 'Come and play with me and Ed.'

'Where is Ed?' I crane my neck looking around the stalls but I can't see my friend.

Yvonne gives a dismissive wave while she purses her lips and tries to catch the straw with them again. She takes a massive slurp before wincing and massaging her forehead. 'He's over there somewhere.' She waves her hand again. 'Talking to a boy. Works with him or something. Fit as, but *so boring*.' She pulls a face before slurping at her drink again.

'How many of them have you had?' I nod at the slush while Yvonne stamps her feet in a futile bid to chase off the brain freeze. She stops the stamping to grin at me.

'A few. Definitely more than one.' She sniggers and captures the straw with her teeth. 'Where's Sacha?' At least, that's what I think she asks, because her words are distorted by the straw that's still clamped between her teeth. 'I'm gonna snog his face off.'

'No.' I shake my head. 'You don't want to do that.'

Yvonne releases the straw from her teeth and spreads her arms wide. 'Er, yeah I do. I want to snog his face *right off*. Today. I've waited two years.' She holds up three fingers. 'Enough is enough. It's kissy time.' She puckers up and makes smoochy sounds into the air.

Seriously, how many gin and tonic slushes has she had?

'We need to get you some food.' Soak up the alcohol. Distract her from Sacha. 'What do you fancy?'

Yvonne sniggers. 'Sacha Nowak.'

I fight the urge to roll my eyes right up to the sun and guide her towards the nearest stall. 'Vegetable kebab? Falafel burger with skinny carrot fries? Beetroot burger?'

191

Yvonne looks at me sharply, her expression a mix of anger and repulsion. She's either going to shout at me or throw up. Which is fair enough. *Beetroot burger*? Perhaps we'll swerve the vegan barbecue today.

'Mac and cheese then?' I steer her past the grill and point at the yellow bus up ahead. It's an old US school bus, converted into a mobile kitchen. 'Look, there's loads of toppings you can choose from. Bacon bits, smoked sausage, meatballs?'

Yvonne takes a long, noisy slurp of her drink. 'You know, Sacha saved my life last night.'

I nudge her into the queue at the bus's hatch. 'They've got cut-up hot dogs? Or barbecue chicken?'

'You know, with the Craig thing?'

'Pulled pork?'

'He's my hero.'

I sigh and drag my eyes away from the chalk menu boards. 'Sacha is not a hero. He didn't save your life. He told Craig to get lost, like we all have over the years.'

Yvonne isn't really listening to me. She has a wistful look on her face, her eyes all big and dreamy, the hint of a smile on her lips as she plays out whatever fantasy is in her head.

'We had a really good chat last night, actually. About work and how unhappy I've—'

'Jalapeños?'

'What?' Yvonne's dreamy look vanishes as she focuses on me, on the present – for her at least.

I point at the menu. 'Do you want jalapeños on your mac and cheese?'

'I don't want mac and cheese.' Yvonne jiggles her plastic cup. 'I want another one of these bad boys. This is just ice now.' She thrusts the cup at me before she wobbles her way across the grass.

* * *

192

I manage to get some food into Yvonne, plus a coffee, and leave her in the hands of Ed so I can get some actual work done. After checking the loos and making sure the next band is ready to set up, I cover the break of the ticket booth staff before I have a break myself. I've been craving mac and cheese topped with pulled pork, so I grab myself a portion and head for the deckchairs in front of the entertainment stage where I left Ed and Yvonne earlier. Ed's relaxing in one of the deckchairs, sunglasses on, pint in hand, as he listens to the band. There are no free deckchairs so I kneel on the ground, using Ed's discarded leather jacket as a makeshift blanket.

'Where's Yvonne?' Her shoes have been tossed underneath Ed's deckchair but there are no other signs of her.

'Talking to Gillian, last time I saw her.'

'What?' I sit up, scanning the crowds of people. 'My Gillian? My boss? Gillian Quinn?'

'Chill out. She's sobered up. Mostly. She had a little nap in the shade and she can pretty much speak in full sentences now.' Ed nudges his sunglasses down his nose so he can look at me unhindered as he smirks, but the grin slides away almost instantly. 'Oi. You better not be getting grass stains on my jacket.'

'Don't be so prissy.' I'm still on the lookout for Yvonne and Gillian, because I can't imagine Yvonne has sobered up *that* much in the last hour or so. Goodness knows what she's babbling about. 'Where did you last see them?'

Ed waves his hand in the general direction of the food stalls. 'Yvonne went to get us some biscuits – I wanted a fudge sundae biscuit, which I'm still waiting for – but she got distracted by Gillian. Or it could have been the other way round, actually, with Yvonne distracting Gillian.' Ed nods and slides his sunglasses back up his nose. 'Yep, that sounds more like it.'

'Yvonne said you were talking to someone before.' I settle back down on the jacket and load my fork up with the cheesy pasta and pulled pork. 'Someone you work with?'

'Neil. One of the other youth workers.' Ed rests his back against the deckchair and stifles a yawn with the back of his hand. 'He's here with his mum.'

'Do you like him?'

'He's all right. He can be a laugh, but don't get him started on football. He won't stop.'

I blow on my fork before putting it in my mouth and chewing slowly. 'Yvonne says he's fit.'

Ed snorts, turning his head so he can look down at me. 'Yvonne once went out with Craig Radcliffe. I wouldn't trust her judgement.'

I load up my fork again. The mac and cheese is pretty good. 'You're my best friend. You know that, don't you?'

Ed snorts again. 'Have you been on the G&T slushes as well?'

'I'm being serious. You're my best friend and I love you. I'll always be here for you, no matter what. There's nothing you could tell me that would shock me.'

'I bet there is.' Ed purses his lips and tilts his head to one side as he thinks of something. 'How about the fact it was me who broke your mum's teapot? You know the cat one that's missing an ear? That was me. I knocked it off the side but was too chickenshit to confess.' He pulls the corners of his lips down in a grimace. 'Sorry. I should have bought a new one. I *will* buy a new one.'

I shake my head. 'Don't worry about the teapot. Just remember, I'm here for you. Always. And you're the best human being in the world, no matter what anybody says.'

'Why?' Ed struggles to sit up in the deckchair and twists so he's facing me. 'Who says I'm not?'

'Nobody. But just remember, okay?'

'Yeah, yeah.' Ed settles back down. 'Can you shut up now? I love this song.'

I want to say more but I spot Gillian over by the stage. Yvonne is no longer with her but I feel I should check in. Practically throwing the tray of mac and cheese at Ed, who doesn't seem to mind and is already tucking in before I've managed to scrabble up onto my feet, I hurry across the lawn, sidestepping deckchairs and bags and small children. I'm three deckchairs away from Gillian when a hand reaches out, grabbing me by the waist and stopping me in my tracks.

'There you are.' Tomasz smiles at me, his freckled cheeks plumping up with the movement in the most adorable way. 'I finished work early. I've been looking for you.'

I forget about Gillian. It doesn't matter what Yvonne said, or how drunk she was when she said it. Tomasz is here and I'm determined that today is the day it all begins.

Chapter 27

I still have to work because as much as I want to drop everything and shout about how in love with Tomasz Nowak I am, losing my job will seriously hinder our new life in California. So it isn't until it's growing dark that I get to catch up with him properly. The grounds are lit up by now, from the path lights and the strings of fairy lights and from the castle itself, and it's giving off extremely romantic vibes as we wander past the stalls. We buy chocolate-dipped strawberries to share as we make our way towards the stage. The area is heaving so we're pretty far back, almost perching on a display of artisan bread from one of the stalls.

My break is over and I should be back on work mode but I stay by Tomasz's side, and when the first firework screeches up into the sky, I don't look up and follow its track like everybody else. My gaze is on Tomasz, making up for all those times I refused to see him. For the four years when I ignored the calls and messages and emails because I couldn't face up to what I had done. What I had walked away from. I want to explain to Tomasz. To tell him that I never stopped loving him. That I didn't mean all those things I said after the accident. That I never really blamed him for Ed's death and that I wish I had never gone to America, because dreams change, don't they? My dream was once to escape Little Heaton, to spread my wings somewhere new. Somewhere *alive*. But I didn't realise that I had everything I wanted already, right here under my nose. I had Tomasz. I had a job I loved. I had a future, stretching out ahead of me, waiting to be filled with happiness.

But I can't say any of this to Tomasz. It hasn't happened yet and I'm determined it won't happen again. So instead I reach out and take Tomasz's hand in mine, threading my fingers through his. His gaze dips, away from the display in the sky, and he looks surprised at first, his eyebrows pulling down, but they quickly lift back up and he smiles at me. I feel his fingers squeeze mine and that's when I move, leaning to the left as I reach up on tiptoe to kiss him because I really, *really* can't wait another second.

I think it's a particularly loud firework at first, but the noise is too aggressive. Too near. Roaring, right in my ear. I cling on to Tomasz, gripping his T-shirt in my fists as though if I can hold on tight enough I can stay here, right in this moment. Because I don't want to leave. I don't ever want to leave him again. But of course I can't hold on tight enough and I'm pulled back, my eyes squeezing shut, hands finally releasing Tomasz as they cover my ears until the blessed relief of near-silence. Then there's the rustle of plastic packaging, the odd cough and the light murmur of voices, but the roar has ceased.

'I am so clumsy.' Dolly's still trying to mop up the water she spilled on her tray with a wad of sodden serviettes. 'I didn't get you, did I?'

I'm back on the plane. I've barely touched my food and there's no way I can eat it now. *Tomasz*. Of all the times to tear me away, it had to be that moment. The most perfect moment there could ever be.

'Elodie?' Dolly waves the clump of serviettes. 'Did I get you?'

I shake my head. 'No. I'm fine.' At least, I think I am. I'm frustrated that I left mid-first kiss with Tomasz, but I'm also elated. *I kissed Tomasz.* We will get together and live happily ever after.

But wait. Shouldn't *this* be the happily ever after? Shouldn't I be with Tomasz right now? If I can change the past and we got together five years ago, why am I still alone? Where is Tomasz?

Something must have gone wrong. Something must have pulled us apart.

Ed. I haven't saved him. I had my chance, but what did I really do? I haven't stopped the accident – that didn't happen until the following year – but I should have done *something*. Something more than a silly little pep talk. I should have gone to see Reverend Carter and talked some sense into the man so the argument never happened. I should have made Ed talk to me. And I definitely should have done something about Sacha, because he's still ready and waiting to wreak havoc and there's nothing I can do about it now, stuck on a plane in the future, when it's already happened.

'They really don't give you enough room.' Dolly pushes her elbows out to demonstrate how little personal space there is for passengers. 'It's no wonder drinks get sent flying. Oh, hi there.' She turns to the cabin crew and explains the situation with the spilled water. I shuffle out into the aisle as Dolly and the cabin crew clear up the table. The snorer isn't pleased that he's had to move, and I can still hear him grumbling as I move along the aisle, taking careful steps and gripping onto the backs of the seats because I'm very aware that we're in the sky and I'm convinced any sudden move could send us lurching.

The toilet is thankfully vacant and I squeeze inside, locking the door before inching in front of the sink, my movements even more cautious because I feel increasingly vulnerable in this tiny room with little to hold on to for safety should the need arise. Clutching the sink, I twist so I can see my shoulder blade in the mirror. There it is, poking out from my vest top. The tattoo I shouldn't have. Proof that I have time-travelled. That I altered the timeline.

But Ed still died. I can see it in my mind, as clear as though it happened yesterday: the row between Ed and his grandfather,

Ronnie turning up, the screams and the shouts and the tears as Yvonne discovered who her boyfriend really is, the motorbike engine revving, the roar as it sped off. Two people left the village on that bike but only one returned.

I didn't save him. I didn't save Yvonne or my relationship with Tomasz. I failed, but there must be another chance. There *has* to be. This can't be it.

The meal has been cleared away. The drinks trolley has done another round. The snorer is snorting and snuffling away, his blanket thrown over his head. And yet I'm still sat on the plane, frustration and inadequacy burning in my chest. I need to get off this plane. I need to go back, to save Ed, to put everything right. *This can't be it.*

The plane dips and lurches. I close my eyes, squeezing them as tightly as I can as I ready myself for the transition, for the deafening roar, but nothing happens. The only noise is the background hum of the engines and the chatter of the passengers and when I open my eyes, I'm still sitting in the tight space between Dolly and the snorer.

'Darn it!'

It's Dolly who growls in frustration, but I share the sentiment. She jiggles her headphone wire at the port before settling back down to watch the film on her screen. But she's cursing within minutes, jiggling the headphone's wire again. She slips the headphones off her ears, resting them on the back of her neck.

'I give up.' She sighs and shakes her head. 'I'll be buying a set of my own for the flight back.' She shifts in her seat so she's facing me. 'How long will you be in England?'

'Eleven days.' I'd wanted it to be less – show up, attend the wedding, home again – but Heather insisted I go to the hen night, which was a week before the wedding. I tried to reason with her, insist she have the hen night the day before the wedding, but she was having none of it on the grounds that she didn't want to be hungover on her wedding day. Eleven days felt unreasonable. Now it doesn't feel like enough.

'Nice. I'm there for two weeks. Manchester first, to stay with my aunt, and then we're going to the Lake District?' Dolly turns the last bit into a question, tilting her head until I nod, signifying that yes, I know the place. 'There's a whole bunch of us going: me, my aunt and uncle, my cousins and their partners and kids. Fifteen of us all together. Can you believe it? It's going to be so much fun!' Dolly claps her hands together. 'I haven't seen my aunt or my cousins since I was little girl. I've never met their children – at least not face to face.' The joy on Dolly's face seeps away, her smile pensive rather than cheerful. 'So many years. *Too many* years. You don't realise how fast it's going, do you? How much you're missing out on.'

This is my life, my future, I realise. This is my first visit home in four years. I've already missed out on meeting Heather's fiancé, missed their first date, their engagement, sharing the excitement of planning the wedding. What will I miss over the next few years? Babies? I'll meet my nieces or nephews over FaceTime. Send them birthday and Christmas presents in the post. See their first days at school on Facebook, hear about nativity plays and certificates over the phone. And what about Yvonne? My best friend, who I haven't seen in four years while grieving for the best friend it wasn't possible to ever see again.

I've really, really messed up. I need one more chance to do things right.

Please.

'My aunt and uncle – Sydney and Philip, did I tell you that? – are then taking me up to Scotland, just the three of us. To Fort Augustus. My mom was born there. Lived there until she was thirteen and Aunt Syd was nine. That's when they moved . . .'

Dolly is still talking but I drift off. I can't concentrate on her history when my own is in jeopardy. How can I fix things if I can't get back? Does something trigger these time jumps or is it random?

'. . . That's when she met my father. Cute, right? But wait – it gets even cuter. They were married six weeks later. In Vegas. I got married in Vegas, the second time. It didn't last as long as Mom and Dad's marriage, though. They really were together until death us do part.' Dolly chuckles. 'Listen to me, going on and on. I'm like that. I have no off switch. I'll shut up now. Let you get back to your movie.' She points at the screen in front of me, which is still paused on the film I was watching earlier. I'm not interested in the film but I slip my headphones on anyway – any excuse to tune out Dolly's chatter.

'Darn it!'

I'm approximately thirty seconds into the film when Dolly's annoyance punctuates the dialogue. She's jiggling the wire again, trying to get the headphones to work. When it doesn't happen, she wrenches the jack out of the socket.

'This is ridiculous. I'm going to ask for a new pair.'

I hear the *bong!* of the assistance button as I tune back in to the film, but it isn't Tom Hanks's voice I hear. It's a whooshing sound. I drag the headphones down and open my mouth to tell Dolly that mine are dodgy too, but stop when I realise I can still hear the whooshing even without the headphones in place. And then I feel it. The rumble, gentle at first but quickly increasing until my seat is shaking side to side. The whooshing is now a roar and I squeeze my eyes shut in preparation of what is to come.

Chapter 28

It's the polish I smell first, shortly followed by a sickly-sweet perfume that makes my nose twitch. The room is bright, with sunlight streaming through the rows of tall windows, the light bouncing off the super-shiny wooden pews. I'm uncomfortable, both from the hard wood I'm sitting on that's making my bum numb, and the high collar of the top I'm wearing in the stifling heat. A hand squeezes mine. Tomasz. I smile when I see him, relief making me woozy. Or maybe it's the heat. It really is warm and I don't appear to be dressed for it. The collar feels as though it's strangling me. Tomasz isn't dressed with the heat in mind either. He's wearing black trousers with a matching jacket. A shirt, buttoned all the way to the top, and a tie. Why is he wearing a suit? Tomasz is a plasterer. He doesn't wear suits, unless . . .

We're in a church. I'm sitting in a pew and the windows that let the sunlight pour in depict religious figures and scenes. Have I jumped forward in time? Is this Heather's wedding? My eyes flick to the front, to where Reverend Carter is standing at the pulpit. This isn't Heather's wedding. Reverend Carter isn't officiating. He's no longer Little Heaton's vicar and hasn't lived in the village since he moved away shortly after the accident. My eyes flick to the coffin. I hadn't spotted it, right there beside the vicar. Or maybe

I had but refused to acknowledge it. Because to acknowledge it would be accepting the fact that I'm too late. I have jumped back in time, but not far enough to save Ed. The accident has happened and there is nothing I can do to stop it.

There's a noise. Something between a gasp and a keening. It's coming from me, I realise as Tomasz releases my hand so he can place his hand on my shoulder and pull me in close.

It's too late.

I'm too late. How can I save someone who's already dead?

On my other side, there's a hand on my knee, the fingers applying gentle pressure.

'You okay?' Yvonne mouths the words when I turn towards her, and I find myself nodding even though I am not okay. Far from it. She leans over to grab her handbag from by her feet and that's when I see him. Sacha. Sitting there in the pew next to Yvonne. *How dare he*? He shouldn't be here, mourning the loss of Ed's life when *he* is the one who was riding the motorbike. The one who sped him off towards his death.

Sacha disappears from view as Yvonne settles back into her seat, pressing a tissue into my hand and flicking one side of her mouth up into a smile of solidarity. But I still know he's there and it both angers and confuses me. Morals aside, Sacha really shouldn't be here. He wasn't originally because not only was he not welcome at Ed's funeral, he also wasn't physically able to be there. He'd been in hospital, recovering from the accident because although he'd been wearing the helmet that saved his life, he hadn't walked away unscathed. So why is he here now, and with Yvonne?

There's a bit of a commotion from the end of the pew. The pew creaks as bodies move, and there's the rustle of paper, audible in the otherwise stillness of the room. It isn't a commotion at all. It's simply a couple of people standing up. There's a fresh waft of the floral perfume as they edge out into the aisle. It's Micha and Franciszek Nowak, the latter hunched over, clutching a bundle of papers that tremble in his hand. Micha rubs her father-in-law's back before kissing him lightly on the cheek, smiling encouragement as he shuffles towards the pulpit. He pauses as he reaches the coffin. Dark wood, highly polished with gleaming gold fixtures. A spray of pale pink lilies and roses on top.

I sit up straight, twisting in my seat and catch Ed's eye. I gasp again and Tomasz's hand squeezes mine. Ed's sitting near the back of the church. His face is sombre, but he flicks the corners of his mouth up briefly. I try to return the gesture but my face feels numb and I simply stare at him as I feel a flurry of emotion inside: relief to see my best friend alive and well, hope that I can still save him, fear that I won't. I want to scramble out of my seat to be nearer him, to clutch hold of him, to convince myself that I can – I *will* – save him but I'm glued to the spot and Franciszek is starting to speak. It isn't Ed's funeral. It's Irene's.

'I first came to this country as a young man.' Franciszek's voice is hoarse. He clears his throat. Swallows hard. And when he continues, his speech is stronger. 'I was a pilot. Smart and capable in my uniform but terrified underneath. I was hurt. I didn't think I would make it. Didn't want to, to be truthfully honest, not after all the devastation I had witnessed. Had been part of. And then I was brought here, to this village, to rest and to get better, and I met an angel.'

The congregation is silent as Franciszek recounts the story I've heard so many times before, but never as beautifully, as poignantly as this moment.

Afterwards, we gather out in the churchyard, where Irene's coffin is lowered into the plot neighbouring her parents and sister. I hold on to Tomasz's hand as tightly as I can without snapping the bones of his fingers, wanting to tether myself to him for eternity. Ed is somewhere behind me. I can't see him but it's comforting to know he's there.

The wake is held at the Royal Oak, a private event for those wishing to celebrate the life of Irene Nowak. A daughter. A wife.

A mother and grandmother. A woman who chained herself to a rail to preserve a castle, with all its history and many more memories to come. Holidays. Weddings. Festivals with fireworks lighting up the sky.

'Irene was a wonderful lady.' I place my hand on Franciszek's arm. He's making his way around the room, proffering a tray of wuzetka, which became his wife's favourite, baked with love.

'She really was.' Franciszek drags his lips up into a smile, his cheeks creasing with the movement. I notice the pale freckles, just like his grandson's. 'I will miss her, very much, every day.' He nods down at the cakes and pushes the tray towards me. I take one, though I won't be able to eat it, not with the lump in my throat, and Franciszek moves on.

Tomasz is sitting with his mum, their heads together as they chat, her hand in his, so I wander around the pub in search of Ed. I haven't spoken to him since I arrived back here and I'm desperate to hear his voice. I spot Yvonne outside, but she's with Sacha, her hand on his back as they sit at one of the picnic tables, his head bowed. I know he's just lost his grandmother and he's grieving, but the sight of them makes my stomach clench and I have to back away.

I pull at my collar as I make my way through the pub. It's too high. Too tight. Too hot. I need some air but the beer garden is out of bounds with Sacha out there, so I head out of the main door and cross over to the war memorial, perching on the wall. If anything, it's even hotter out here, the sun glaring down without a cloud to be seen, and I can't seem to drag in a decent breath.

'You been to the funeral then?' Mrs Gacey's standing outside the minimarket, broom in hand, and she nods across the road towards the pub. 'They were a nice family, the Keyes. Irene had already left by the time I was born, but I remember her mum and dad, and her sister. They lived at the bottom of the hill, where the new-builds are now, above the post office. Back when we had one of those.' Mrs Gacey pulls a face and starts to sweep the path in front of the shop's doorway with aggressive strokes. 'My Dominic's coming to stay in a few days. You remember my Dominic, don't you?'

I nod. I remember Dominic Gacey, but I don't recall his second visit. I was probably too caught up in the grief after the accident to notice.

'We're thinking of emigrating.' Mrs Gacey stops her sweeping, straightening her back and swiping the back of her hand across her forehead. 'Selling up and joining the family in Canada. Family's important, isn't it? You realise on days like this.' She aims the handle of broom towards the pub. I follow her gaze and that's when I see Ronnie, standing outside the doors of the Royal Oak.

'Hey.' I don't think about what I'm doing, what I'm going to say as I scramble down off the wall and march across the road. 'It's Ronnie, isn't it?'

She turns, a frown lining her face because she doesn't know me. She's never met me, but I've met her and I can remember Yvonne's face on the night of the accident as though it happened four minutes ago rather than four years, the way her head had flinched back, the rapid blinking as she looked Ronnie up and down. The shaking of her head. The way she'd looked at Sacha with wide eyes, as though he could somehow fix this. Make it all go away. Make it untrue. And then the blast of emotion: the flush spreading from her neck, up to her cheeks, her nostrils flaring, the guttural roar that made me want to cover my ears with my hands.

'You shouldn't be here.' I move myself so I'm standing between Ronnie and the pub's door.

She pulls her chin back. 'You what?'

'You shouldn't be here.' And she shouldn't. The day she turned up at the pub and sent everybody's lives spiralling was not the day of Irene's funeral. What is she doing here? Is it the butterfly thing? Have I nudged the events of the timeline and brought Ronnie here earlier?

'There's a funeral.' Ronnie nods at the door of the pub. 'I was going to go in but when I opened the door I saw all those people. Grieving.' She shakes her head and looks down at the little girl at her side. 'We should go. This was a stupid idea.' She takes the girl's hand. Her daughter. Sacha's daughter. The secret he was keeping in Nottingham. She has his mop of dirty blonde curls and the same freckles across her nose and cheeks as Tomasz and his grandfather.

'Mummy?' The little girl tugs on Ronnie's hand. 'Can we feed the ducks now?'

Ronnie presses her lips into a thin line as she returns her gaze to the pub, as though she can't decide whether to stay or go. But then she bends, hoisting the girl up by her armpits and resting her on her hip.

'Come on then, but not here. We'll go to that big park we saw on the way here. Do you remember the playground with the helter-skelter slide?' The little girl's eyes light up and she nods her head vigorously. Ronnie's gaze lingers on the pub for a few more seconds before she walks away. I don't say thank you, but I think it, because by leaving now without causing the chaos of that terrible night, she's just inadvertently prevented a tragedy from occurring.

Chapter 29

I watch Ronnie and the little girl climb into a yellow mini parked across the road. I never did know the child's name as it all happened in a blur, and I'm not entirely sure formal introductions were made during the chaotic screaming and shouting. I take in a deep breath, as much as I can until it feels like I might pop, letting it out slowly as the car pulls away and disappears from view. Disaster averted.

I'm turning to head back into the pub when something catches my eye across the road. The salon. Or rather, the signage. It's no longer the monochrome 'Lady Dye' but neither is it the navy lettering of 'Little Hairton' on an aqua background that came with the latest owner's refurb. This is a sign I've never seen before, ever, and not just on these wild time-hops. The sign is now charcoal with 3D silver lettering. 'Berkely's Hair & Beauty'. The exterior has been updated to match the sign, with charcoal woodwork and silver fixtures on the door. It looks classy and modern and the kind of place Yvonne has dreamed about working in. The kind of place that serves more than the local pensioners for their once-a-week shampoo and set.

I cross the road so I can get a better look. It's bustling inside. There are new stations added to the backwashes and swivel chairs, and I can see clients having their eyebrows threaded and their nails buffed as well as having their hair coloured and styled. There's a reception desk and a chrome coffee machine and a seating area with tub chairs and fresh flowers. This is not the salon I remember. The salon I left behind when I flew off to California.

'Elodie?'

I drag my eyes away from the salon. Heather's on the opposite side of the road. She's wearing the waitress uniform I'm used to seeing her wearing now during these summers but her hair is different. It's been chopped into a shoulder-length bob and is straight and glossy. It looks grown up. Elegant. But I kind of miss the frizz.

'Everything all right?' She checks for traffic before she crosses the road. 'With the funeral and everything?' She places a hand on my arm as she reaches me, and I'm touched by the little act of care. It isn't only her hair that's become more grown up.

'Yeah. I was just . . .' I turn to look back at the salon. I was just what? Marvelling at the modernised salon I've never seen before? 'Thinking about making an appointment.' Mid-wake? That sounds sensible. But more rational than the truth, I guess. 'To get my nails done.' I splay out my fingers, releasing too late that they're already immaculate, painted a pearly rose with white tips. 'I want something a bit . . . less boring.'

Heather nods. She holds out her own hand, displaying fingernails painted in pastel shades of blue and purple, scattered with glinting silver specks. 'Mona did mine yesterday. She's amazing.'

'Are you even allowed nails like that while waitressing at the hotel?'

Heather lifts one shoulder up into a shrug. 'Who cares? I've only got twelve shifts until I'm finished there for good. If they sack me off, I'll just spend the next few weeks enjoying the summer until my PGCE starts.' She starts to move away from the salon, heading towards the hill. 'Save me one of those Polish chocolate cakes if there are any left.'

I cross back to the pub, heading straight to the beer garden where I last saw Yvonne so I can talk to her about the salon. But Ed's leaning against the bar as I pass, and he lifts his hand in greeting, a small smile pulling up the corners of his mouth, and I can't not stop. Not when his imminent death has been avoided by Ronnie's early arrival and her decision not to make a public scene. The chain of events that led to Ed getting on the bike has been disrupted and when I throw my arms around him and pull him in tight, a sob takes me by surprise as I remember earlier in the church, when I thought I was too late to save him.

'Life's too short, isn't it?' Ed strokes my back with slow, soft circles. 'But she was loved.' I nod, though I remain tucked into Ed's chest. 'He must be devastated.'

I move now, taking a juddering breath, and follow Ed's gaze. Franciszek is sitting in the corner, his head down as he studies the newspaper in front of him. But he isn't reading it. He isn't catching up on the news. The paper is a year old, and on the front of it is a photo of his wife, eyes blazing. Full of life. Of passion and determination. Somebody stops by the table, stoops to chat to Franciszek, but they don't stay long. He wants to be on his own for a while, with Irene and his memories.

'I want that.' Ed nods towards Franciszek. 'Not the sorrow, obviously. But the love. I want to be with my soulmate until the end.'

'Yeah, me too.'

Ed nudges me with his elbow. 'You've got Tomasz. You two are perfect for each other. Anybody can see it. You'll be together forever.'

'I hope so.' My gaze moves towards him. He's still sitting with his mum, his arm around her shoulders, and my chest feels full with love, and pride, and the ache of regret of the years I spent without him.

'You will. I know it.' Ed catches the attention of the bar staff and orders drinks for us both. We carry them to an empty table, one where I can still see Tomasz. His head is bent, his hair flopping

210

into his eyes, and I want to go over there, to tuck the hair back, to hold him and take away the pain he's feeling.

'Dominic's coming to stay in a few days.'

I tear my gaze from Tomasz and tune fully in to what Ed's saying.

'Yeah, I know. Mrs Gacey said earlier.' I take a sip of my wine, my gaze slipping back towards Tomasz and his mum. He's putting something in the inside pocket of his jacket.

'He isn't staying with his grandparents this time.'

Tomasz leans in towards his mum, lifting his cheek to meet her lips.

'He's staying with me. And Yvonne. At the flat.'

'Oh?' Micha pats her son on the back, but then my eyes snap back to Ed as his words register. '*Oh*.'

'What do you mean, oh? And why are your eyes all wide like that?'

I blink, trying to make my eyes normal-sized again. 'Nothing. I just meant oh. It's a word. A normal word with no really significant meaning. Like, if someone said it's raining, and you're like, oh, is it?'

Ed shakes his head. 'It isn't like that at all. It was an *oh*. A significant *oh*. And now you're babbling.' Ed's eyes narrow. 'Has Yvonne said anything to you?'

My jaw drops. In shock. In outrage. 'Yvonne knows?' Before *me*? His best friend? Now, I know Yvonne is his best friend too, but I knew him first, before we even started nursery, and that has to give me the edge, surely?

'Yvonne knows what?' Ed's eyes are nothing but slits now and his mouth is all scrunched up tight.

'Nothing. I don't know what I'm talking about.' I lift up my glass of wine. 'I'm tipsy.' I take a massive gulp, to drive the point home.

'Oh my God.' Ed's chin drops to his chest. 'You know.'

'I don't know anything. I'm clueless, about a lot of things. Most things.'

'Elodie.' Ed peeks up at me, and his eyes are full of trepidation. My stomach lurches. I shouldn't have said anything. I'm an idiot. A massive idiot with a big mouth. This is Ed's moment. He gets to decide what to say and when, but the words tumbled out before I could stop them. It was the shock. *Yvonne knew before me.*

'I didn't tell Yvonne. But we live together. In a pretty small flat. You can't really keep secrets.'

'Ed, it's okay. You don't have to say anything more.' I place my hand on his and give it a squeeze. My way of letting him know that when he does say anything more, I will be there. Always.

'But I want to.' Ed grimaces. 'I think.' He picks up his pint. Takes a sip. Takes another. He lowers his hand to place the glass back down on the table but changes his mind and takes a huge gulp, swallowing hard. He doesn't look at me when he speaks next. 'I'm gay.' He plonks the glass down on the table and looks me in the eye for the briefest of moments. I squeeze his hand, my chest filling up again, with pride and love. This is nicer than the last time I found out, when Reverend Carter spilled it out onto the street, roaring about sins and all sorts of disgusting things until Ed felt he had no choice but to get away, as fast as he could, even if it meant hitching a lift on the back of Sacha's bike without a helmet.

'But you already knew that.' Ed meets my eye, only for a second. 'How did you know?'

His grandfather told me. He told anyone in the village within earshot, violating his grandson's trust and spearing him with vile accusations. And then Ed had confirmed it, pulling me aside as his grandfather's charges continued to rain down.

I'm sorry if this changes anything, Elodie. But there was someone, in France. Nothing happened – I was too afraid – but I couldn't help the way I felt about him. The way I still feel. I've tried to push it away, but it's there. It's always been there, deep down, and it always will be. It's who I am and I'm sorry. Hey! Sacha!

And then he was gone, and I never saw him again.

I squeeze Ed's hand now, tighter than I intend to but I can't help the ferocity. 'I'm your best friend. I know you. Every bit of you. And I love you and I think you're amazing. Never ever forget how amazing, how loved you are, no matter what. Okay?'

Ed nods. His eyes are shining. Mine are streaming. I never got the chance to say any of that the last time around: Ed was eager to escape his grandfather and Sacha didn't want to stick around to face the fallout of Ronnie's appearance. But it's different now. Ed is safe and I hope that when he tells his grandfather and the reverend says all those awful things, he'll remember this conversation. Remember that he is loved and know there is nothing to run away from. I'm too late to save Yvonne a broken heart but I've managed to save Ed's life. Life isn't always perfect, but this is pretty good in my books.

Chapter 30

Yvonne and Sacha have been together – officially – for six months. They had a handful of one-night stands between the summer I just left and the day after Valentine's Day, when Sacha wooed Yvonne with a bunch of roses from the reduced bucket in the supermarket and a half-price mug with 'Boobalicious Babe' printed on the front. And that was that. They were an item. Boyfriend and girlfriend. Yvonne had only waited nearly three years for it happen.

I wish I'd been able to prevent it from happening, because it isn't going to last. It'll come out about Ronnie and everything one day and Yvonne will be crushed. It's hard to believe how much devastation there will be looking at them now as they sit out in the garden, Yvonne's fingers lightly stroking the stubble on his cheeks, Sacha bringing the fingers of her other hand to his lips. They don't look happy – that isn't a word I'd use today – but they look comfortable with one another, as though they fit, that underneath the grief they are content.

'Pint?' Ed holds up the glasses in his hand as we approach the picnic table. 'We can go back inside if you'd rather be on your own for a bit?'

Sacha shakes his head. His curls would usually bounce around his face but he's had them cut back, tamed, so they're still long on top but clipped at the sides. For once, he isn't wearing his shades.

'It's okay.' He nods at the bench opposite, and Ed and I sit down. He takes a sip of the pint Ed's placed in front of him. 'Is Tomasz all right? Mum and Dad? Grandad?'

I nod, deep lines furrowing along my forehead. I'm surprised by his concern for his family, but I shouldn't be. I guess I've built him up to be a narcissistic villain over the past few years after what happened with Ronnie and Ed, but he clearly cares about his family when it matters, and Yvonne believed he cared about her too, right up until the night Ronnie turned up at the pub.

'Tomasz is with your mum, and your dad's chatting to your grandad.' Franciszek had finally allowed someone to settle themselves next to him in the corner, and they'd sat looking at the defiant photo of Irene on the front cover of the newspaper in silence for a few minutes until a conversation started to flow, stuttering at first but now unstoppable. When we'd passed with the drinks, Franciszek had been clutching his stomach as he laughed about something his son had said.

'Are you okay?' Yvonne reaches across the table and takes Ed's hand in hers. 'You look . . . lost.'

'Nah, I'm good.' A smile flickers on Ed's face. 'Just thinking.'

Yvonne pulls a face, baring her teeth. 'So that explains the steam coming out of your ears. The old brain's working overtime. Careful, there.'

Ed sticks his tongue out at her. 'I was thinking about me and . . .' His eyes slide towards me. 'I've told Elodie about me. About me being gay.'

I'm shocked again. That he would say it, just like that, in front of Sacha. But Sacha doesn't seem fazed in the slightest. He doesn't react at all, unlike Yvonne who leaps out of her seat with a little shriek and somehow squeezes herself onto Ed's lap on the picnic bench. I watch Sacha as Yvonne smothers Ed's face and hair with kisses, telling him how proud she is of him. Nothing. No smirk. No jibes. No arsehole behaviour at all. No sense of *revelation* at all.

'You knew.' I turn to Ed and Yvonne, who stops pecking at Ed but keeps her lips puckered up as though the kiss has been frozen in time. '*He* knew before me.'

'I didn't exactly tell him.' Ed looks down at the table as Yvonne slides off his lap and returns to her seat beside her boyfriend. I glare at her until she puts her hands up, palms out. How could she tell him? How could she betray Ed like that?

'I didn't tell him either.'

This time there is a flicker of a smirk on Sacha's face. 'I walked in on him going at it on the sofa.'

Ed's mouth gapes open. 'We weren't *going at it.*'

Sacha snorts. 'You always have your trousers round your ankles then?'

Ed looks at me, his eyes rolling. 'He's exaggerating. But yes, we may have got carried away. But you were home early.' He aims this at Yvonne, his eyebrows arching. She holds her hands up again.

'But you never said anything.'

Sacha looks up and meets my eye. He shrugs. 'Not my place. Not my business.'

But he didn't say anything to anyone. No snidey remarks. No sly digs. No unsubtle hints. This is not the Sacha I've painted in my head for the past four years.

'Does Tomasz know?' Or Heather? My parents? Christine Gacey from the minimarket? Because everyone seemed to know but me.

'Nope, just these guys.' Ed indicates Yvonne and Sacha with his pint glass. 'And now you.'

Yvonne grins as Ed takes a sip of his drink. 'And Dominic.'

Ed keeps his eye on his pint as he sets it down on the table, but I can see him fighting a smile.

'Did something happen with you two that summer? Is that why you stayed in touch?'

Ed squirms in his seat, which tells me everything I need to know. 'Maybe a little something.'

Yvonne arches an eyebrow. 'If it was only a *little* something, why did you bother staying in touch?'

I lean my head on Ed's shoulder. 'Ignore her. I'm glad you kept in touch and I'm so happy he's coming to see you again. Who knows – maybe he's your soulmate.'

At which point, Sacha reverts to form and makes vomiting sounds as he leans over the lawn.

More people start to drift out into the beer garden as the intense heat starts to die down. It's still hot but not quite as breathtakingly fierce. Jackets are removed. Top buttons undone. An old friend of Irene's, who chose to wear black tights in mid-August, peels them off and pads around the garden in bare feet, the abandoned tights and court shoes tossed under a table. Tomasz and his mum wander outside and Tomasz asks me if I'd like to go for a walk. It must be such a difficult day for him, supporting his parents and grandfather while dealing with his own grief. We slip out of the pub and my eyes stray straight to the salon: Berkely's Hair & Beauty, looking strikingly sophisticated sandwiched between the café and the hardware shop that haven't seen an update – inside or out – for decades. But Yvonne's vision seems to be right – there is a market for a more youthful clientele in Little Heaton.

Tomasz takes my hand and we stroll along the high street, turning off to cross the footpath over the canal. We follow the lane until we reach a gap in the bushes, where a small dirt path leads to a cluster of buildings. There's a For Sale sign poking out of the bushes.

'What are we doing?' Tomasz is leading me along the track, which I know doesn't lead to anywhere beyond the buildings.

'Playing make-believe.' He leads me past the single-storey building and a couple of smaller outbuildings until we're standing in front of the main house. 'Just imagine living here.'

I splutter. 'We'd have to win the lottery first.' The house is huge – five or six bedrooms, easy.

Tomasz lets go of my hand so he can put his arm around my waist. 'It'd be nice though, wouldn't it?'

I look at the house. At the vastness of it. I think of my little loft room at Mum and Dad's. Of the tiny apartment in LA, where the 'utility room' is a cupboard with a washer and dryer stacked one on top of the other, which is a plus point in itself as most apartments in the area don't have their own laundry facilities. Would I prefer this massive house, with so many rooms I wouldn't know what to do with them? Hell, yes.

'I bet the utility room is huge. With a sink and enough room to set out your ironing board so you don't have to lug it about.'

'Absolutely.' Tomasz nods. 'And I bet they have a mud room.'

'And a library. With one of those ladders on wheels.'

'A home cinema. They have to have a home cinema.'

'Which is just a room with a stupidly big telly. I can think of better uses of a room.'

Tomasz tilts his head as he looks at me. 'What would you use it for instead?'

I pull my chin back. 'A *huge* walk-in wardrobe, obviously.'

'A whole room, just for clothes?'

I tut. 'Of course not. There'll be shelves and racks for my handbags and shoes as well.'

Tomasz shakes his head. 'What a waste of a room.' He takes my hand again and we make our way back to the lane. The sun's still beating down but there's a cool breeze that makes it much more bearable though my feet are throbbing after a day of heels in the heat.

'That big house would be amazing.' Tomasz stops and turns to look at another house. 'But I think this would be more my thing.'

We've reached the new horseshoe-shaped road. The houses are finished now, most of them already sold, and there are young trees planted along the new grass verges. Tomasz has stopped and is looking at one of the smaller houses on the inner side of the curved road. The door is cherry-red and there are wild flowers bursting from the overgrown lawn.

'This would be the ideal place to bring up a family.'

'I thought we were going to America.' I rest my head on his shoulder, still looking across at the cherry-red door, still caught up in make-believe despite my words.

'We are. But you never know – you might miss Little Heaton so much you want to come home.'

'Maybe.' I never thought it was possible, but I haven't hated being back and I've found it isn't as void of joy and interest as I'd thought it was. I think of the past few summers with Ed and Yvonne and Tomasz. And of the summer with Dominic where we explored and discovered and enjoyed all that Little Heaton and the surrounding area has to offer. It isn't a bad place, I realise now, and it doesn't deserve the hostility I've shown it all these years.

'Not long now.' Tomasz kisses the top of my head and we start to walk along the horseshoe-shaped path again.

'No, not long now.' The sale of the small chain of hotels in the US had gone through as smoothly as could be expected, and when Gillian had accepted a managerial role overlooking the running of the three hotels in California, she'd offered me a promotion to trainee assistant manager at one of them. And it had felt like a promotion in every possible sense – career-wise and an upgrade from Little Heaton to Los Angeles. Tomasz had agreed to come along with me, to stay for a little while and then, once his visa was sorted, on a more permanent basis.

'Two weeks.' Tomasz squeezes my hand. 'You excited?'

I nod. 'So excited.' But though I try to conjure the flutter of excitement I'd felt the first time round, I can't quite manage it.

Chapter 31

We loop back round to the canal, to the lock where we ate bacon sandwiches – over a year ago for Tomasz but just a few days ago for me – and my eyes travel along the towpath. There's a bloke with a fishing rod just ahead, the lad he's with having grown bored of the activity and now jabbing at ants with a twig.

'Shall we sit for a minute?' Tomasz taps the wooden beam of the lock, and I'm more than happy to take the weight off my hot, aching feet. I perch on the beam, wriggling back until my feet are lifted off the path, being careful not to snag my trousers. Tomasz sits next to me and we twist to look down at the canal, where the water is glistening in the sunshine. A pair of ducks glide by, slowing as they reach us but continuing their swim when they realise there's no food to be had. We sit in silence for a while, enjoying the cooling breeze rustling the leaves of the trees lining both sides of the canal. It's a beautiful spot. Tranquil, apart from the ant massacre further up the towpath, and sheltered from the rest of the village with the wall of trees.

Life in LA had been busy, busy, busy: learning the business of hotel management, flitting from work to restaurants to my apartment. I threw myself into my work, masking my need to forget about the life I'd left behind with enthusiasm for the job. Gillian had been impressed with my progress and I'd been promoted to hotel manager within a couple of years, and I've since moved to another hotel, slightly bigger with better facilities and more responsibilities. It's left little time to form friendships, and even if I did have time, I would have still held myself back because I'm aware of the cost of fully giving yourself to relationships. Four years on, my only real friend is Gillian and she's so busy with her own work, frequently travelling across the States, and now with a husband and a couple of kids in tow, her time really is limited.

I'm lonely in LA. I try not to acknowledge it, pushing the ache in my chest away whenever it nudges into my consciousness, busying myself with work, with anything that will distract me. But it's there, that stomach-sinking loneliness that I never felt in Little Heaton.

'What are you thinking?'

Tomasz's voice is low, as breezy as the gentle wafts of cooling air around us.

'California.'

Tomasz threads his fingers through mine. 'You sound nervous.'

'I guess I am.'

Tomasz squeezes my fingers. 'It's going to be amazing. You, me, the sunshine.' He glances up at the sky, squinting against the sun peeking through the canopy of leaves. 'Your brilliant new job. You're going to be amazing at it.'

I smile, squeezing Tomasz's fingers, a silent thank you for reminding me that I won't be on my own this time. I'll be with Tomasz, and I'll never be lonely when I'm with him.

Along the towpath, the fishing equipment is being packed away. The twig has been tossed aside, with the boy now kicking stones from the path into the water. I turn away from the path and look at Tomasz, at his open face with its freckles and long, pale lashes and that flop of strawberry blond hair constantly falling over his eye.

'We'll be together forever, won't we?'

Tomasz leans towards me so he can gently rest his forehead against mine, the flop of hair creating a curtain between us. 'We will.'

'Promise?' I'm asking Tomasz, but I should be demanding the vow from myself. Because it was me who ran away. Me who ended our relationship. Me who couldn't give my heart to Tomasz when it felt broken beyond repair.

'I promise. In fact . . .' Tomasz sits up straight and reaches into the inside pocket of his jacket, pulling out a faded maroon velvet box. 'I wasn't going to do this now, today.'

He wasn't going to do this today. He didn't. He proposed to me on the day I left for California, when he still thought he could talk me round, that we could still leave together. I thought he'd made a rash decision. Plucking a grand gesture out of the air to try to persuade me to change my mind. I had no idea he already had the ring, before I ended things. Before Ed died.

'Mum gave me the ring today, after the funeral. Gran wanted me to have it.'

'It was Irene's?' I'd had no idea. He hadn't told me that, but then I suppose he was too caught up in the desperation to save us.

'I know the day of a funeral isn't the ideal time for this. Or maybe it is.' Tomasz shrugs, a small smile flickering onto his face. 'I think Gran would approve, actually. She didn't believe in time-wasting. Not when it comes to love. Not after what happened with her and Grandad, all that lost time.'

'And nearly marrying that other guy.'

Tomasz huffs out a laugh. 'Yeah, that too. Imagine if Grandad hadn't come back to find her. If she *had* married that other guy. I wouldn't be here.'

'Life's full of choices. We just have to make sure we make the right ones. And if we don't, we have to learn from the mistakes we make.'

I think of Sacha and the mistake he made. Did he learn anything from it? Did the devastation he caused, both to Ed and to himself and those around them, teach him anything? Because Sacha may have survived the accident, but he wasn't unscathed. There were the injuries, most notably the break to his femur, which required surgery and physio and took months to recover from, but it must have affected him mentally. How could it not? His mistake resulted in death. It forced his family to pack up and leave their home and business because they felt judged. They all left, apart from Tomasz who refused to go, staying on in the flat above the charity shop, the flat we'd shared before I left to start my new life in California. Even Franciszek left behind his memories of Irene and the castle that brought them together, the place she'd yearned to return to, the place she'd put her everything into when she thought it was in danger.

All that had to have affected Sacha. As much as I've despised the man for the past four years, he isn't made of stone.

'You've gone all serious.' Tomasz flicks his hair out of his eyes. 'Do you think this would be a mistake?' He raises the velvet box, his eyes wide, his breathing shallow.

I shake my head. 'Absolutely not.' It would be a mistake to say no. To catch a flight to America and not return for four years. 'So what are you waiting for?'

Tomasz slides off the wooden beam. He lowers himself down on one knee and opens the velvet box. Inside, sitting on a cream, satin cushion, is a white-gold band set with a round-cut diamond flanked by two pairs of smaller, individually claw-set diamonds. The ring is further embellished by curves of tiny diamonds around the central arrangement. It is elegant and while it's a vintage piece of jewellery, it manages to still have a modern feel to it.

'Elodie Parker.' Tomasz takes a deep breath. He attempts a smile, but it's too shaky to be labelled as such. I reach out, my fingers cupping his chin. *You can do this.* 'I love you, more than I will ever be able to put into words. I will go wherever I need to if it means we'll be together, whether that's California or the moon.

I will never not love you. I will never not want the absolute best for you and will do whatever it takes to make you happy.'

A memory. Stabbing. Bitter. *What will make me happy is you if you turn around, leave, and I never have to see you again.*

I push it away, as hard as I can, and concentrate on this Tomasz, in this timeline.

'Will you marry me?'

Any residual sharpness from the memory vanishes as I smooth the wayward flop of hair away from Tomasz's eyes.

'Yes. I absolutely will marry you.' And nothing will come between us this time.

Chapter 32

Waking up next to Tomasz is heaven. I didn't think I would ever do this again and I have to pinch myself when my alarm chirps at me from the bedside table and I feel his arm sprawled across me.

I'm rooted to the spot, and not just because Tomasz's arm is heavy with sleep and pinning me down. I'm too scared to move in case I wake Tomasz and we have to get up. Which is ridiculous because my alarm is beeping and cheeping away and is far more likely to wake him.

'You have the most annoying alarm in the world.' Tomasz's words are slurred with drowsiness but there's more affection in them than annoyance. 'You do know that "for better, for worse" doesn't include irritating alarms, right?'

'I think you'll find that if it includes your terrible singing in the shower, it definitely includes my awful alarm.' I wriggle my arm free so I can snooze the alarm before snuggling right up to Tomasz.

'My what singing in the shower? Did you just say . . . terrible?' Tomasz's voice is laced with mock disbelief, because we both know he is no Sam Smith. There was a loose tile above the showerhead that I used to joke about, claiming it was working its way from the wall to make a bid for escape from the terrible noise that assaulted it every time Tomasz showered.

'Let's just say you should be thankful the ability to hold a tune isn't on my husband-to-be checklist.'

'Unlike breathtakingly handsome? Because if that's on there, you've hit the jackpot.'

'I'm not going to argue with that.' I snuggle in even closer to Tomasz and squeeze my eyes shut. I want to drift off back to sleep just so I can wake up next to him all over again.

'We need to get up.' Tomasz sounds as reluctant as I am to break this spell and when he attempts to sit up it doesn't take much for him to crumple back down under the covers again.

'Five more minutes. Ten, tops.'

'How about forever?'

I smile, my eyes still clamped shut. 'That sounds good to me.'

Unfortunately, my alarm barging back into our blissful cocoon with its incessant bleeps and chirps doesn't sound nearly as good, and this time Tomasz is adamant we need to drag ourselves from the covers.

'You can't get sacked now when you're so close to your promotion in LA.'

He has a point, but my emergence from the bed is lacklustre, my feet dragging as I move from our bedroom to the bathroom. We moved into the flat above the charity shop three months ago. It had been quite early on in our relationship the first-time round, when I'd waited for Tomasz to make the first move, but it had felt right. Most people had been pleased for us, and Heather had been super-pleased ('Does this mean we can take down the wall between our bedrooms so I get the whole space?') but Gran had been cynical about the move.

'Isn't it a bit soon? You're only young – there's no need to rush these things.'

I'd pointed out that she'd been married with three kids by the time she was my age – younger, in fact – and she'd said that times were different now, which just goes to show that you can't win with some people, no matter what you do.

The flat is small, but not California-apartment small. There's a tiny hallway that leads to the living areas, the bedroom, and the bathroom with the wonky tile. I shower quickly and head back to the bedroom to get dressed, leaving Tomasz to slaughter David Bowie's 'Heroes'. I change into a pair of trousers and a floral print pussy bow blouse before reaching into the bedside drawer and slipping out the vintage ring box. The ring doesn't quite fit. It's a little loose but Tomasz promises that we'll take it into town as soon as possible to get it resized and I slip it onto my finger now, tilting my hand so that the light catches the diamonds.

'You like it then?' Tomasz is in the doorway, leaning against the frame. 'Because you can choose your own if you want to. I won't mind.'

I shake my head, still watching the sparkle of the diamonds. 'I love it. It's beautiful and it means a lot to you and your family.' I drag my eyes from the hypnotic shimmer. 'And now to me.'

I hate to return the ring to the box and confine it to the drawer but I can't risk losing it and I really do have to go to work. My mind remains on the ring, however, and I'm imagining our wedding day when Mel drags me away from my fantasy Big Day.

'Dreaming about life in LA?' His voice is dripping with revulsion, and I think he's actually going to heave as he says 'LA'. 'Because you've still got work to do here until you go. Did you finish that report?' He looks pointedly at my blank screen. 'Or even start it?'

There's a couple of weeks to go until the life-changing move, but I'm still too fidgety with nerves to relax and enjoy the anticipation. There are no butterflies yet, just a feeling of dread about the life I chose the last time around, about the huge mistake I made.

'Do you mind if I take an early lunch?' I'm already rising out of my seat and grabbing my jacket from the back of the chair.

'But it isn't even eleven.'

'Thanks.' I shove my arms into the sleeves of my jacket as I scurry across the room, leaving Mel wide-eyed and slack-jawed.

I hear him muttering as I close the door behind me ('Gillian chose *her* to fast-track to management?') but I let it wash over me. I can feel the panic rising as I rush through the hotel, my pulse racing as I clatter down the stone steps and my breaths are shallow and unproductive as I scuttle down the hill. I head for the pub but I don't go inside. Instead, I find myself edging down the side to the drive, fear making my footsteps sluggish. There's a strange impulse to see the motorbike even though I know that events have changed and Ed is safe, but the garage is locked.

'Elodie? What are you up to?'

I snatch my hand away from the garage door, which I've been trying to yank up, and stand up straight. Yvonne's on the pavement at the end of the drive, a look of amusement on her face.

'Nothing.' I step away from the garage. 'I'm not doing anything. There was a squirrel.'

'In the garage?' Yvonne arches an eyebrow. 'The locked garage?'

I take another step away. 'It ran down here. It looked like it went inside and it was trapped. But clearly not.'

'Have you been drinking?'

'It isn't even eleven o' clock.' Yvonne shrugs so I try a different tack. 'Are you free to get some lunch?' Food is always a good distraction.

'Only if we can call it brunch. And I have a client due in twenty minutes so we'll have to be quick.'

I hurry to Yvonne's side, threading my arm through hers as we head across the road to the café.

'You bought the salon.' I look at the sign: Berkely's Hair & Beauty.

The amusement's back on Yvonne's face, because this isn't news. '*Have* you been drinking? Should I be staging an intervention?'

'I just think it's great. I'm proud of you.'

Yvonne beams. 'I'm proud of myself.'

'You always said there was potential for a wider client base.' We pass the window of the salon. It's busy inside, with clients sipping

228

from charcoal-grey mugs in the waiting area by the window. I don't recognise any of them, which is a bit weird in a place as small as Little Heaton. 'Where have they come from?'

Yvonne gives me an odd look. 'Seriously, Elodie, have you been hitting the voddie for breakfast? You're acting really weird.'

'I promise I haven't been drinking.' We stop in front of the café and Yvonne opens the door. We're hit by a wall of heat and the delicious smell of sizzling bacon as we step inside. We order sandwiches and tea before sitting by the window. I can see the pub from here and my eyes are drawn to the side, where the bike is kept.

'So. The salon. The clients.' I smile my thanks as a mug of tea is placed in front of me. 'You never said where they've come from.'

Yvonne takes her tea, setting it down in front of her. 'There is something seriously wrong with you. Either you need an AA meeting or you've hit your head.'

'I'm just showing an interest in my best friend's business.' I blow on my tea. Take a sip. It's too hot and scorches my tongue.

'Which is great, but you already know the answer.'

I pick up the laminated menu from behind the condiments. One corner of the plastic is curling away and I try to smooth it back down. 'Do you remember the story of how the Nowaks met? At the castle?'

'Yes.' It's a tiny word but Yvonne manages to stretch it out.

'And do you remember how many times we've heard it?'

Yvonne smiles. 'Too many to count.'

'Well, this is like that. I'm proud of you and I want to hear the story of how Yvonne Berkely became a successful businesswoman.'

Yvonne eyes me from across the table. I take another sip of my tea. It's still way too hot. I place my tea down, meet Yvonne's eye again. Raise my eyebrows to prompt the story. Yvonne sighs, but there's a hint of a smile on her face. Despite the hesitation, she'll enjoy telling the story.

'It started just over a year ago. Do you remember that night Craig Radcliffe was in the pub, being a dick? It was a couple of months before he was sent down for assaulting his girlfriend.' She winces. The image from the newspaper has probably flashed up in her mind. I know it has in mine. 'And Sacha told him to get lost?'

I nod. I remember. It was only a matter of days ago for me.

'We got talking that night and I was moaning about the salon and how management was holding it back. How much *more* it could be. And I told him how I'd do things differently. "Why don't you?" he asked. I didn't know what he meant at first, but he meant why didn't I run my own salon. Put my ideas into practice. I thought he was a loon. How could I run my own salon?'

'Because you're amazing?'

Yvonne nods. 'Fair point. But being amazing doesn't mean you can afford to buy and run a business.'

'So what happened next?'

Yvonne rolls her eyes, but she plays along. 'I saw your boss at the summer food festival thing last year, and I'd had a bit to drink and was feeling brave so I went up to her and put forward one of my – quite frankly – genius ideas, and she liked it. Said we could talk some more about it during the week. Which we did and she liked it even more because you helped me to put together a little presentation.'

'I did?' I clear my throat. 'Yes, I did. Because I, too, am amazing.' I lean forward across the table. 'So what was the idea?'

Yvonne tuts, but I can tell she's enjoying herself. 'The idea was to work with the hotel to offer guests hair and beauty packages, whether they were at the hotel for a break or for weddings and other events. There are no spa facilities at the hotel – though I think they sometimes hired beauty therapists for special occasions – but we could offer manicures and pedicures, massages and mud wraps, hair and make-up for weddings and parties, or just a bit of pampering. Once we'd taken on trained professionals, obviously.'

'That *is* a good idea.'

Yvonne stares at me for a moment. 'I know.' Then she sighs. 'But the stupid salon manager wouldn't go for it, even after I'd put so much work into the presentation and getting Gillian on board. He didn't even have to do much – just fix the place up a bit so it didn't look like a time-warp salon. Something a bit more than a lick of paint.'

'So then what happened?'

Yvonne doesn't fight the storytelling this time with an eyeroll or a tut. She's too into it, leaning towards me now, eager to continue. 'So the salon limped along with its pensioner specials until the stupid manager had had enough and put the place on the market.'

'So you made an offer?'

Now Yvonne does roll her eyes. 'As if. Where would I get the money?'

'A business loan?'

There's the eyeroll again. 'You say that like it's obvious, but I didn't think anyone would lend *me* any money. Sacha had to practically drag me to the bank.'

'Sacha did?'

Yvonne smiles, her lips stretching so wide it must hurt. 'He was amazing. I couldn't have done this without him. Or you. I never would have gone for it if I hadn't seen how much you were pushing yourself at work, reaching for all those goals and getting them. And now you're going to be an assistant manager at a hotel in *LA*.'

'Trainee assistant manager.'

'Which is *huge*.'

And it is. I know it is, and I'll keep climbing the career ladder, reaching even more goals. But for some reason, when my sandwich arrives, I'm not hungry anymore.

Chapter 33

Tomasz is working late, Ed has gone to the airport to pick Dominic up and Yvonne is in Manchester. It had been hard to mask my surprise that Sacha was taking her to see *Hairspray* at the theatre, even the second time round, because musicals are as far from the brooding Sacha Nowak as you can get, but it seems Sacha is willing to sacrifice his bad-boy image to please her, which I'll begrudgingly admit is a good thing.

So I'm at a loose end with everyone busy doing their own thing. The flat is quiet. Too quiet, and there's a hard knot in my stomach. An uneasiness. Almost a sense of foreboding. Rain has been threatening all day, the sky a slate grey with angry-looking clouds and I keep pacing to the window to look out across to the pub. I put the telly on but nothing is grabbing my attention, and though I flick through the magazine I find in the living room, I don't take in any of the articles. I feel unsettled but I can't put my finger on why. I'm prowling around the room, shuffling from sofa to window and back again when Ed texts to say he and Dominic are in the pub if I want to say a quick hello before Dominic collapses from exhaustion. I jump at the chance to get out of the flat, throwing on a coat and clattering down the stairs while tapping out my reply.

Ed and Dominic are sitting in a quiet corner of the pub, away from the bar and the pool table and the fruit machines. They already have drinks, so I order a glass of wine and join them. Micha tries to coax me into getting a cocktail – she's going to be hosting a cocktail night soon and wants to practise – but I'm not in the mood for anything more complicated than a chardonnay.

'What is that?' I sit opposite Ed and Dominic, who have both succumbed to the cocktails. Dominic has opted for a martini while the glass in front of Ed is filled with what looks like bright green mouthwash, garnished with a lime wheel.

'It's a shamrock sour.' Ed takes a sip. 'Tastes better than it looks.'

'Good, because it looks vile. I'm glad I stuck with the wine.' I take a sip. It's delicious and cool but it doesn't shift the unease. 'Have you been to see your grandparents?' It feels a bit weird sitting here with Dominic, because this definitely didn't happen the first time round. Although things are a bit jumbled in my mind, I know Dominic didn't visit a second time while I was still in the village.

'Yep.' Dominic scratches at the stubble under his chin. 'Gran was not happy that I'm not staying with them.'

'You're brave, going against her wishes. I used to work for her at the minimarket, before I started at the hotel. I was never brave enough to stand up to Mrs Gacey.'

Dominic shrugs. 'You only get one life. You have to do what makes you happy sometimes.' His gaze flickers to Ed and I see a smile tugging at his lips. 'And it isn't as though I'm miles away – I'm only on the other side of the war memorial.'

Ed and Yvonne are still living together in the flat above the salon. I wonder if the sale of the salon came with the flat, which would make Yvonne Ed's landlady. I'd ask Ed now but I don't think I'd get away with the 'tell me the story again' ploy this time.

'How long are you staying for?' I don't know if I already know this, but I ask it anyway and nobody gives me a strange look.

'Three weeks.'

'Which isn't long enough.' Ed tilts his head as he looks at Dominic. 'You should move to the UK.'

'*You* should move to Canada.'

'Nah.' Ed scrunches up his nose. 'Too cold.'

Dominic snorts as he picks up his drink. 'And the UK isn't? Don't you guys freak out if the thermometer sneaks past seventy degrees?' He places the glass to his lips, hiding a smile.

'We're not *that* bad.'

'It does rain a lot.'

My stomach lurches at the thought of rain, and I press a hand against it to try to settle it.

'That's true.' Ed takes a sip of his Hulk's piss drink before turning to me. 'I ran into an old friend of yours while I was waiting for Dom in arrivals. They were coming back from their holiday *with their girlfriend.*'

'Who was it?'

Ed pauses, for dramatic effect, I think, but it's just really annoying. I'm about to kick him on the shin under the table when he finally speaks. 'Otis. He didn't stay to chat long – he wasn't allowed to. His girlfriend wanted to get going. She was tired. Her feet were hurting. She was kind of annoying. Kept calling him *baby*. Ugh.'

Reena, his police officer housemate. I'm still Facebook friends with Otis in the present day, though we don't really chat or anything. I did like his posts when he and Reena got married and when their babies were born, and he liked my post a few months ago, when I moved over to the Heron Mill Hotel, which is much bigger than the hotel I'd transferred from. I'd liked Reena when Otis and I were together, and I didn't find her annoying, but anyone can be a bit grumpy after a long flight. Nobody wants to stick around the airport any longer than absolutely necessary. The thought of returning to the airport in just over a week is already filling me with dread.

The feeling of dread is still with me when I return to an empty flat. Tomasz is still working, pushing himself to finish the jobs he has lined up by the end of the week so he can have a few days off before we head out to California, so he can spend time with his family and sort out any last-minute issues. I know he's going to miss his parents and his grandad – even Sacha because he's Tomasz's brother, despite his faults – but he's willing to leave them behind, for me.

The flat is quiet and dark, and it's when I hear the hum of the fridge from the kitchen that I realise why it's making me so uneasy being here: it reminds me of the apartment in LA. The place I would spend hours on my own, lonely but unable to forge new friendships because I was afraid of letting anyone get too close again. I've been at Mum and Dad's place while I've been on my jaunts to the past until now, where there's usually someone else around, the TV blaring *Wimbledon* or the soaps or the latest crime drama. But here, in the flat on my own, I'm taken back to that apartment. To that life. And I feel afraid all over again. Afraid that I'll end up with an amazing career that I love but not much else.

But that isn't going to happen this time. I'm going over there with Tomasz. I won't be alone and broken-hearted. I will be loved. Supported. There will be someone to share my achievements, to share my life with. It won't be lonely. And yes, I'll miss my friends and my family, and part of me will miss Little Heaton now I've come to appreciate it, but I can't give up on my dream to live in America. I've wanted this for a long time and while the reality may not have lived up to the fantasy the first time round, surely it will be different now with Tomasz by my side.

I head into the bedroom and sit on the bed, sliding open the drawer of my bedside table. My Walkman is in there, the wire of the headphones wrapped around it, the tape still inside. I unwind the wire and place the headphones over my ears, hoping the batteries are still working as I push down the play button.

There's the rapid beat and synth sound and then Kim Wilde is looking down at the city through a window, and I'm wondering *why*. Why was this so important to me? Because I'm not feeling it right now. I dig deep to capture the need to fly away to another life but I can't seem to grasp hold of it and it's an ominous feeling I catch instead. A feeling of dread, as though my life is spiralling in a direction I no longer want to be heading in, as though I'm being swept away, silently kicking and screaming rather than soaring towards a bright and wonderful future.

It feels as though I had a choice to make and I made the wrong one.

I know I needed to save Ed and rescue my relationship with Tomasz, but would it be greedy to change one more thing? And am I brave enough to step off the path I know and throw myself into an unknown future?

Chapter 34

It must have been really late when Tomasz got back from work, because I'd eventually fallen asleep in an empty bed after midnight. I'd woken briefly to find him curled around my body, warm and comforting, but he's already gone again by the time my alarm wakes me. He really is pushing himself to make sure he's ready to leave in a few days' time, but the problem is, I'm no longer sure *I'm* ready. I want to talk to Tomasz about it, to air my worries and concerns so I can work out whether they're true doubts or simply my scaredy-cat tendencies surfacing and making me think I want to stay, pushing down my dreams and keeping me from going for what I really want.

My gaze automatically shifts to the right as I leave the flat, seeking out the pub, and the knot tightens in my stomach. I thought it had gone, but it's simply been hiding in the background, ready to pounce should I feel the slightest inkling of trepidation. I don't know why, but I half expect to see Sacha tearing out from the drive with Ed riding behind him. But all is quiet on the high street. The heavy curtains are drawn across the windows of the pub and the shutters are still down on most of the shops and businesses. Only the café and the minimarket are open as I make my way through the village to the path at the bottom of the hill.

A car passes as I near the hotel gates, its horn beeping twice, and I raise my hand as I recognise Gillian's car. She's making her way across the gravelled car park, laden down with bags and boxes as I reach the end of the tree-lined drive, and I hurry over to unburden her of some of the bags looped onto her wrists.

'A few nibbly bits.' She puffs away a stray bit of hair that's falling into her eye. 'And cake.' She shifts the weight of the two wide boxes she's carrying. I see an assortment of iced doughnuts and buttercream-topped muffins through the transparent plastic lid.

'It's your last day.'

Gillian's move to the US was slightly ahead of my own, and although it had only been a few days, she'd seemed completely at home by the time she met me at the airport in California. As she had at Durban Castle, she'd taken me under her wing, settling me into the apartment where she'd already stocked the fridge and the cupboards with a few basics, and she'd insisted on taking me out to eat that first night, which was lucky as I don't think I'd have eaten at all if she hadn't been so firm. She assumed my lethargy was due to jet lag but it was more of a stricken, hollowed-out feeling. *What have I done?*

Gillian puffs the stray hair away again now, more aggressively this time. 'In a matter of hours, I'll walk down these steps for the last time.' She ascends the first stone step carefully, making sure she doesn't drop the boxes of cake. 'And then I have to go home and finish off my packing. My cases for the flight are all sorted, but it's the rest of it that's the problem. How can one person own so much? I'm having to get rid of most of it – there's no way I can ship everything from my two-bed semi and expect it to fit in my new place.'

'Can't you keep some things in storage for when you move into a bigger place?' Like the yellow three-bed family home in Baltimore she lives in now? It's on the other side of the country to California, which is why we barely see each other these days and I've only been to the new house once, for the baby shower of her last pregnancy, but it was such a pretty house and so warm and so clearly full of love. Family photos lined almost every wall in the place and it made me ache to see what I was missing out on.

'Nah.' Confident now that she isn't going to splat the cakes on the ground, Gillian skips up the rest of the steps. 'It's a fresh start, isn't it? No need to keep hold of the old life I'm leaving behind.'

I push a smile onto my face as the knot hardens in my stomach. 'I guess not.'

'It's mainly crap anyway.' Gillian nods her thanks as she steps through the door I've just opened for her. 'I'm taking the important stuff, obviously, but I don't need stacks of ancient CDs – who listens to CDs anymore? – or boxes stuffed with old school reports and certificates. And the shoes! I've got pairs I haven't worn since I was in my twenties and never will again. This is the perfect excuse for a declutter, and I'm going to be brutal.'

I think of the things I left behind, in the flat and in my loft bedroom back at Mum and Dad's. I'd viewed it as a fresh start too, and I'd been even more brutal in my culling than Gillian as I wanted to leave everything behind, including the memories of Ed and of Tomasz. I wanted to start again, pain-free, and I'd certainly done my best to leave it all behind in the past where it belonged. It didn't make me happy though.

'How are you getting on with your packing?' We're in the hotel lobby now, and Gillian nods in greeting as we pass members of staff.

'We're getting there.' Which translates as 'we haven't even started yet'. But then we aren't taking much with us; the flat above the charity shop is rented as furnished, so we don't have anything big that requires shipping. We're mostly taking clothes and a few sentimental bits and pieces. Everything else is staying up in my loft bedroom at Mum and Dad's (which Heather is not happy about. *What a waste of space. I could be using that room as a massive walk-in wardrobe*).

239

'Are you excited about the move?' Gillian's marching along the corridor, eyes focused ahead, so she doesn't clock the hesitancy on my face.

'Yeah. Course I am.' I try to inject springiness in my voice but my words limp out. Gillian stops and twists to face me.

'It's a bit scary, isn't it?' One corner of her mouth flicks up. 'A big change. But also a big adventure.' She sets off walking again. 'You'll be fine. You'll *flourish*, I'm sure of it. I have every faith in you, Elodie.'

Which is great, it really is, and I know that, once in California, I'd work my little socks off to live up to Gillian's expectations, to prove that she was right to have faith in my abilities. I know I can do it. The question is, do I *want* to?

Mel's in a huff again. I bring him a chocolate honeycomb muffin from one of the boxes in Gillian's office but even that isn't enough to lighten his mood. He shoots daggers from across the room, gives terse answers using as few words as possible (or simply grunts if he can get away with it) any time I ask him a question or attempt to chat. In the end I give up and leave him to his gloomy attitude and concentrate on my work. I'm trying to tie up as many loose ends as possible, to make my replacement's first few days as smooth as possible. I'd met the new girl briefly, on her way out after her interview, but it was four years ago and I'm struggling to picture her now. Struggling to picture her sitting at my desk, using my computer, sliding open my drawers and fixing papers together with my stapler.

I head over to the staffroom at lunchtime, where Gillian has set out the nibbly bits and the cakes that have survived the morning. Mel refuses to join us, claiming he has too much work to do (*because some of us aren't jetting off to California,* he adds with a pointed look) but Heather's there, even though she isn't on shift.

'I wanted to come and say goodbye to Gillian.' Heather leans in close, her eyes on the hotel manager across the room even though she's speaking to me. 'Plus, Marv texted me to say there was free food.' She takes a huge bite of a doughnut topped with caramel icing and fudge pieces. 'And it isn't as though there's anything else to do around here. I can't even work on my tan.' She stretches out a pale arm. 'Why is it raining so much? It's supposed to be summer.'

My gaze flicks to the window. There are dark clouds looming, giving off an ominous vibe, and the knot in my stomach constricts again.

'You're so lucky, moving to LA. You'll have a tan within a week while I'm stuck here, soaking wet and miserable. You'll be on the beach and I'll be listening to Dad going on and on about his cucumbers.' Heather lifts the doughnut to her mouth, but she hesitates before taking a bite. 'What? Why are you looking at me like that?'

'I thought you liked it here now. I thought you wanted a teaching position close by.'

Heather shrugs. 'Maybe I've changed my mind again. Maybe I'm sick of being stuck in this dump. Or maybe I've just got really bad PMT.'

Heather didn't change her mind again because four years on she's still in the village. And she isn't stuck here. She *chose* to stay, and she's happy. Can I do that too? Choose to stay and be happy?

It's still gloomy once I finish work for the day, the indigo sky peeking out from between the charcoal-coloured clouds. Gillian left an hour ago, slipping out without fuss as she told me she would because otherwise she'd be a gibbering wreck. She'd squeezed my hands the last time I saw her in her office, and she'd told me how proud she was of me, how she knew I'd flourish, and I'd felt like a fraud. Like I was letting her down.

I'm still thinking about Gillian and California when I step through the hotel gates, my mind full to the brim with decisions, of the future and what it holds, and I jump when someone pushes themselves off the gate's pillar, where they've been lurking.

'Tomasz.' My hand is on my chest, and I laugh with relief. 'What are you doing, loitering like that?'

Tomasz kisses my cheek. 'Waiting for you. I thought we could go for a walk.'

'In this?' I look up at the sky. It isn't raining, but the opportunity is there.

'Scared of a bit of rain?'

I am, actually. It was raining the night Ed died. Big fat sheets of it bearing down. Maybe the accident wouldn't have happened if the roads hadn't been so treacherous. My stomach is in knots again even though I know Ed is safe now that Ronnie has been and gone without incident.

'Why don't we go to the pub?'

Tomasz shakes his head. 'I've got something else in mind.' He takes my hand in his and leads me down the hill. Instead of turning right towards the high street and the flat, we head left, over the footbridge and onto the lane that runs along the edge of the woods.

'We're not going on the rope swing, are we?' I remember the first day I arrived back in Little Heaton, when I thought I was dead, especially when I saw Ed standing on the river bank. It was the day I found the Kim Wilde cassette up in the loft. The day the dream of escaping the village solidified and I discovered a destination to aim for. I fulfilled that dream but here I am, back in Little Heaton, and I don't want to say goodbye.

'We're not going into the woods.' Tomasz leads me along the lane until we turn onto the horseshoe-shaped cul-de-sac. Buttercup View, with its pretty gardens and grass verges. We pass the garden overrun with wild flowers and I notice the iron bench that's been added underneath the window. The perfect place to watch the wildlife enjoying the plants. There's a bee flitting among the forget-me-nots and a butterfly hovers for a moment before it flutters away.

We follow the curve of the pavement until we reach the dead end, but instead of turning around and heading back, we cut across the field to the canal, stopping at the lock. Tomasz indicates that I should hop up onto the wooden beam, and he lowers himself down onto one knee once I'm settled.

'I stopped off at the jeweller's after work.' He reaches into his pocket and pulls out the vintage ring box he produced after his grandmother's funeral. 'I know I've asked before, but I quite liked it when you said yes, so I'm asking again now the ring's been resized.' He opens the box, and there's the beautiful engagement ring, glittering despite the gloomy day. 'Elodie Parker, will you marry me?'

I want to answer immediately. To say yes and throw my arms around him. But I can't. Not yet.

I place my hand over the ring. 'Before I answer, I need to talk to you.' Tomasz's smile falters and his eyebrows pull down. There's a flash of panic in his eyes, and I realise he thinks I've changed my mind. Which I have, but not about him, about us. *Never* about us. 'Of course I want to marry you. I'd marry you tomorrow if I could. Right now, in fact. But I spoke to Gillian today. About the move to California.' I swallow hard and shift my gaze so I'm looking at the trees beyond the towpath rather than at Tomasz. 'I told her that I don't want to go after all. I want to stay here, in Little Heaton. And I know it's stupidly short notice, and I'm messing everyone around . . .' I'd been afraid to voice my concerns to Gillian, but she was unbelievably understanding, and she's promised to sort everything out. She was so lovely to me, even though I've added more stress and work at a time when she has those things in abundance, and when I suggested I was letting her down, she told me that I absolutely wasn't and that by going along with the move to please *her*, I'd be letting myself down.

'Elodie.' Tomasz shifts so I'm forced to meet his eye. 'I've told you I'd go wherever I needed to be to make you happy, whether that's California or the moon or right here. I love you and I want to marry you, and it doesn't matter to me where we are, as long as we're together.'

'So you don't mind that we'll have to un-organise everything?'

Tomasz shakes his head. 'Couldn't care less.'

I lift my hand, uncovering the ring. 'You'd better ask me again then.'

'You want me to ask for a third time?'

I shrug, a smile tugging at my lips. 'You did say you liked doing it.'

'I said I liked it when you said yes.'

I quirk an eyebrow. 'Then ask me.'

He does – for a third time – and I say yes. I wouldn't dream of saying anything else. Tomasz slips the ring onto my finger. It's the perfect fit. Sliding down from the wooden beam, I throw my arms around my fiancé. And then that's when I feel the first fat drop of rain.

Chapter 35

We run through the village, our shoes slapping on the wet ground. The rain escalated from a few drops to full-on, puddle-forming sheets of rain in a matter of seconds, as though someone has tipped a giant bucket of water down on Little Heaton. I'm drenched, my hair plastered to my head and my face, and I'm shaking uncontrollably, though it has nothing to do with the cold. I remember this bleak, relentless rain as though it had poured down on me yesterday.

Tomasz pulls me towards the flat when we reach the high street, but I resist, tugging him in the opposite direction, more insistent. He relents and we scurry towards the pub, crashing through the doors and dripping water onto the carpet.

She's here. Ronnie. Standing centre stage, the child resting on her hip as she faces Sacha. They're standing near the bar, the girl's face half-hidden as she tucks herself into the safety of her mother's neck. Yvonne's standing to the left of her boyfriend, a couple of paces back, while Micha leans across the bar, straining to hear what is being said. The bar is littered with empty glasses and bits of fruit and decorative paper straws. I can't see Micha's husband or father-in-law but everyone else in the pub is watching the scene in front of her, shamelessly twisting in their seats to gawk.

'What's going on?' Tomasz looks at his brother and his mum for an answer, but it's Ronnie who responds.

'Hello, Tom.' I flinch at the shortening of his name. Nobody calls him Tom, ever. 'Long time, eh? I thought it was time I introduced you all to Poppy.' She shifts the child on her hip, so she's sitting more upright. 'Your niece.'

Tomasz laughs. He frowns. Turns to his brother. 'She's joking, right?'

Sacha runs his hand through his curls, his face all scrunched up, somewhere between discomfort and pure agony. 'No.' He glances at Micha before fixing his gaze on Yvonne. 'I'm sorry, but she's not joking. Poppy's my daughter.'

'No.' Everyone turns to Micha, who's shaking her head, over and over again. 'No. This isn't happening.' She looks at Sacha, her eyes blazing. 'It's my cocktail night. You are not ruining my cocktail night. I was just making a Bellini. Here, Elodie. Taste this. It's gorgeous.' She thrusts a champagne flute topped with a slice of orange towards me and she has such a wide-eyed desperate look that I take a couple of steps forwards and take it gently from her hand. 'You do not have a daughter.' She's no longer looking at me. Her eyes are boring into her oldest son. 'Because you would have *told us*. And she's, what? Two? Three?'

'She was two in January.' Ronnie tilts her chin upwards. 'And Sacha always said he was going to tell you. Clearly he hasn't, because he's a coward. Always has been, despite the big-man act.' She looks Sacha up and down, lip curling. 'You're not a man at all, are you? You're a silly little boy who'll never grow up.'

Sacha looks at his mum, but Micha holds her hands up. 'I'm not going to disagree with that.' She lowers her hands and snaps her gaze back towards me. 'How's that cocktail, Elodie?' Her lip is trembling but she's refusing to give in. She will stay strong. In control. Even if it means pretending none of this is happening and it's just her planned cocktail night. I play along – and not just for Micha's sake – and gulp half of it down in one go.

246

'It's good. Delicious.'

Micha nods, her lips trembling again as she attempts to smile. 'Why didn't you say anything?' She's glaring at Sacha again, her arms folded across her chest. Sacha shrugs, dropping his head so he's looking down at his boots.

'I was going to, but it was hard. And the longer I left it, the harder it got. And then Poppy was born and I couldn't exactly go up to you and say, hey, guess what? You're a granny. And so I left it a bit longer and it got even more ridiculous. She started crawling, eating solid food. She turned one. Then she was walking and talking and I couldn't tell you then, could I? Not after so much time had passed.'

'So you said nothing at all?' Micha shakes her head. Her mouth is all squashed up and her nostrils are flaring as though flames are about to erupt from them. 'Where's your dad? I can't cope with this on my own.'

'He's gone out with Grandad.' Sacha peeks up at his mum. 'I'm sorry. I didn't mean for it to happen like this.' He turns, his hand reaching out for Yvonne's, but she doesn't take it. 'I should have told you.'

'Yes.' Yvonne jams her hands in the pockets of her dress. 'You should have.'

Ronnie steps to the side, so she can get a better look at Yvonne. 'And who are you?'

Yvonne opens her mouth to reply, but it's Sacha who gets in first. 'My girlfriend. Yvonne. I've mentioned her before, the last few times I've been down to see Poppy.'

Ronnie hitches her daughter further up her hip. 'I see. And I thought this was why you'd stopped . . . well, you know.' She places a hand on her stomach. 'Thought baby number two had scared you away.' She arches an eyebrow. 'See what I mean? Coward.'

'Baby number *two*?' Yvonne takes a step back, her hand reaching up to cover her mouth. She looks like she could throw up on the carpet. My shoes squelch as I stride towards her, putting a hand on her arm. I should have warned her about Sacha's double life with Ronnie and their daughter. Tried harder to stop her getting together with Sacha. I've failed as a friend because I was focusing so much on my relationship with Tomasz and trying to save Ed.

Oh, God. *Where's Ed?* He can't be with his grandad. He can't. *I stopped this.* I changed the timeline. Ronnie was here after Irene's funeral instead of today. Unless . . .

My knees feel as soft as dough and my grip loosens on the champagne flute. I've been an idiot! It wasn't the butterfly effect that made Ronnie arrive earlier than she originally did: she must have arrived on the day of Irene's funeral originally, thought twice about dropping her bombshell on such an emotional day and returned a few days later. She was always going to return today, while it's lashing it down outside and Ed is dropping a bombshell of his own. I haven't saved him at all.

'She's pregnant again?' Micha looks as though she's about to vault over the bar and throttle her eldest son.

'No. I mean, I don't know.' Sacha shakes his head, his finger pointing at Ronnie's stomach. 'But that's nothing to do with me, I swear.' He looks at Ronnie, meets her gaze, his jaw set. 'We haven't been together since Christmas. There's no way that baby is mine.' He turns to Yvonne, trying to catch her eye but she won't look at him. 'I swear, Yvonne. I promise you. That baby isn't mine.'

Ronnie snorts. 'A coward and a liar. What were you going to do, keep this one a secret as well, just like Poppy?'

'I can't believe this.' Yvonne covers her mouth to catch a sob. 'All this time, wasted. Everyone was right about you.' She swipes at her cheeks, taking one last look at Sacha before she storms out of the pub. Sacha tries to follow but Ronnie grabs his arm.

'You can't leave me here like this. What about Poppy?'

Sacha reaches out, stroking the curls on his daughter's head. He stoops to kiss her forehead and then he's striding towards the door.

'No you don't.' Micha's marching out from behind the bar,

her face thunderous. 'You're not going anywhere until you've explained properly what the hell is going on.'

I leave Sacha to battle with Ronnie and his mum, and rush outside in search of Yvonne. A car engine startles me. Hand on my chest, I turn my head, instinctively taking a step away from the kerb. The car is opposite the pub, outside the salon, its wipers waving manically against the sheets of rain. My attention is snatched away as the doors to the pub swing open so aggressively, they smash into the walls either side. Sacha strides out, followed by Micha and Ronnie, who are both yelling at him, none of their words decipherable as they collide. Tomasz plucks Poppy from Ronnie's hip and takes her back inside where it's dry, away from the shrieking. I'm not sure Ronnie even notices. I know I didn't the first time. I only knew Tomasz wasn't there, stopping it all from unfolding and I punished him for it afterwards. By the time he'd joined us again, it was all such a mess and I blamed him for not doing enough to keep my friend safe.

'Where's Yvonne?' Sacha zones out the words flying at him, focusing entirely on me. I turn and he follows my gaze, watching as Yvonne's car pulls away. He swears, stamping his foot down on the ground, splashing water up my calf. There's more yelling, masked by Ronnie and Micha at first, but growing louder and louder. I hear bits and pieces – *disgusting, disgrace, danger to those children* – but I'm watching Sacha, unease turning my stomach as he disappears around the side of the pub. I hear the roar and I think I'm being pulled away, pulled back onto the plane, and then I realise the sound isn't just for me. It's an actual sound that everyone else can hear. They all turn. I run.

No, not again. He can't. I won't let him.

My hands are held out in front of me as I approach the motorbike. Sacha is sitting astride, ramming his helmet down on his head.

'Sacha, you can't. The weather. It's too dangerous. You've been drinking.' My hand covers my mouth as I gasp. 'Yvonne's been drinking.'

'She hasn't.' Sacha yells over the noise of the engine but I still have to concentrate to pick out his words, muffled by the helmet. 'She's got a hen party booked in the salon in the morning. She didn't want to spoil it with a hangover.'

My hair is wet through and sticking to my face. I peel it away. 'Please, Sacha. Don't do this. She'd be devastated if anything happened to you.'

'I have to find her. Explain. Make her see.'

He wasn't running away from his responsibilities the night of the accident, like I always thought he was. He was running to Yvonne. To try to make things right.

'And you can. Later. Or tomorrow.' I take a step towards the motorbike, wincing at the noise. 'But only if you turn off the engine. You won't be able to do much explaining if you're stuck in hospital.'

Sacha snaps down the visor of his helmet. He isn't listening to me and he could easily swerve around me. Or plough into me. What do I do? How do I stop him?

'I'm not listening to another word.'

I turn, momentarily distracted by the voice behind me. The motorbike surges forward but I hold my hands up, stepping into its path. Sacha snaps the visor up and swears.

'Get out of my way, Elodie.'

I shake my head, strings of wet hair slapping me in the face. I once accused Tomasz of giving up too easily – I can't do the same. 'It's too dangerous.' Especially with Ed so close by. I can hear him more clearly now, arguing with his grandfather.

'I only told you because I thought you loved me enough to support me.'

'Support you? I *despise* what you are.'

The motorbike surges again. I move, hands held out in front of me. This can't happen again.

'And I despise what you are, *Reverend*.'

I know Ed's right behind me. I can feel him. Can feel my despair churning. *This can't happen again.*

'Where are you going?' Ed yells over the noise of the engine as he strides towards the motorbike. 'In fact, doesn't matter. Take me with you anyway. I need to get out of here.'

'Ed.' I reach out to him, but I can't move away from the bike as Sacha will use the opportunity to slip away. I can't let him go, even without Ed, can't let him put himself in danger. I couldn't live with myself if I knowingly sent Sacha on his way. 'Ed, wait. Let's talk.'

'Nah.' Ed clambers onto the back of the bike. 'I'm done talking.'

Sacha whips up his visor, turning to glare at his hijacker passenger. 'Get off. I don't have time for this.'

Ed loops his arms around Sacha waist. 'Then let's go.'

There's a moment of hesitation. I think Sacha is going to give up. Turn the engine off. Go back inside and wait for Yvonne to cool off. But the visor is snapped back down.

'Sacha, wait. He doesn't have a helmet.' I point at Ed. There are tears streaming down my face now the panic is setting in, but the rain is simply washing them away. Sacha's shoulders rise and fall. He doesn't care about Ed or the lack of helmet. He just wants to find Yvonne, to explain, to make her not hate him. Because I see now that he does care about her. He may be an idiot. A coward, like Ronnie said, but he needs to find Yvonne and he doesn't care about the consequences. But *I* care. I've seen what such recklessness can cause. I've lived through it and I never ever want to go there again.

'Elodie. What are you doing?' Tomasz is here. I feel him pulling on my arm but I shrug him off.

'I won't let you do this.' I step directly in front of the motor-bike, my feet just inches from the tyres, my fingers clutching the handlebars. If he wants to go that badly, he'll have to knock me down first. 'Think about Poppy. Your daughter. She's in the pub, wondering what the hell is going on. And you're out here, playing the big man. Proving Ronnie right. Have you ever done the decent thing in your life?'

251

I'm shouting the words over the engine roar, through the rain and the tears. Even if Sacha doesn't hear me, I need to know that I tried. That I did absolutely everything I could to save Ed. To save Sacha. To save everyone the heartache of what is about to happen.

Chapter 36

No time at all has passed really, but it feels like I've been standing out here forever, my hands clutching the handlebars of the rumbling motorbike. Sacha's visor is down but I know he's watching me, deciding what to do. He revs the engine, testing me. I stand my ground. I will do everything I can to stop this from happening again.

'Elodie, what are you *doing*?' Ed is leaning over so he can see past Sacha's broad shoulders. 'Get out of the way.'

I shake my head, wet hair whipping me in the face. The rain is pouring even harder now and I'm drenched. It's running into my eyes and making them sting but I will not move.

'You're going to get hurt.'

My grip tightens on the handlebars. 'And you're going to get killed.'

Ed laughs, his head tipping back, raindrops tapping on his face. 'Don't be so dramatic.'

'Don't *you* be so reckless. Look at you! You're about to ride off without a helmet, in poor conditions, with *Sacha Nowak*. He's hardly the most responsible rider at the best of times. You've seen him tearing around the village. He's an accident waiting to happen.' Ed doesn't look so amused now, but he still remains

253

seated behind Sacha. 'Think about it, Ed. Really think about what could happen. Yes, you're angry with your grandad – and rightly so, the man's a tosser – but is it worth losing your life for?'

Ed rolls his eyes but the movement is lacklustre, as though he can't be bothered putting the effort in. 'You're being dramatic again.'

'Think about it, Ed. Think about your mum. Jim. Me and Yvonne. And Dominic. He's come all this way to see you, which will be a complete waste if you end up dead because you threw a strop.'

'A strop?' Ed's mouth gapes as he points towards the street. 'Did you hear what he said? He thinks I'm a danger as a Scout leader and youth worker. *A danger to the kids*. As though I'm a pervert. As though I'd ever . . .' He shakes his head, and I'm pretty sure there are tears running alongside the raindrops on his cheeks.

'But you know that isn't true. *Everyone* knows that isn't true. Don't let one bigoted old tosser ruin your life.'

Ed curls his fingers into fists, roughly rubbing at his eyes.

'Please, Ed. I'm begging you to get off that bike.'

He locks his gaze on mine, his shoulders rising as he heaves in a breath. He puffs it out, shaking his head, and my stomach drops to the ground. No. He's saying no. He pats Sacha on the back: go.

But then he's climbing off the motorbike. One foot is on solid ground, then the other. I want to rush at him, to throw my arms around him and hold him tight. Hold him safe. But I can't move. Not until Sacha is safe too.

'I'm not going anywhere.' I stare at the visor, tightening my grip on the handlebars again. He revs the engine but I stand firm. Tomasz stands beside me. With me. He stoops to clutch the handlebars so we're a united front.

'*We* are not going anywhere.'

Sacha turns the engine off. We stay where we are, Sacha astride the motorbike, me standing in front of it, clutching it with all my might, Tomasz right there with me. I see Ed backing up against the wall of the pub, sliding down until he's crouching, his face in his hand. I want to go to him, to comfort him, and I will, as soon as I know everyone is out of danger. Now the engine has shut off I can hear the commotion at the front of the pub, with Micha and Ronnie still shouting, this time at each other.

Sacha's hand juts out and I flinch, but he's simply flipping up his visor. 'I need to find Yvonne. Explain. I swear, that baby isn't mine.' His eyes are fierce, boring into mine, and I'm shocked to find I believe him.

'We will find her, but not like this.'

Sacha continues to stare at me for a moment, but then his gaze drops and he removes his helmet. 'Have I messed everything up?'

'I honestly don't know.' The fallout from Ronnie and Ed was brutal. Nothing was the same afterwards. But what would have happened if Sacha had been given the chance to talk to Yvonne, to Ronnie, his family, without the tragedy and turmoil of the accident? I have no idea, but maybe he'll have the chance to find out.

'I love her.'

I find myself believing Sacha Nowak for the second time in a matter of minutes. I think he does love her, despite his flaws, and I know Yvonne loves him. I tell Sacha this and I think he's about to climb off the bike when I feel the rumble of the engine coursing through the handlebars and into my hands. It reverberates up my arms, into my shoulders and chest, and though I try to keep my grasp on the handlebars to stop him from taking off in pursuit of Yvonne, the noise is too intense and I let go, shoving my hands over my ears to block it out. I squeeze my eyes shut, grimacing against the powerful roar. Just when I think I've reached the point where I can't take any more, that something has to give – my eardrums, my brain – the noise recedes until there's nothing but a low hum and background chatter.

The rain has stopped. I'm somehow dry again, my hair no longer plastered against my skull, and it isn't my hands covering my ears, it's a pair of headphones.

I'm on the plane. Back in the present. Dolly isn't sitting in her seat next to me, though the snoring guy is still tucked under his blanket on my left. I feel disorientated, my brain fuzzy and my stomach swirling, the two sets of memories fighting each other: Sacha and Ed tearing off into the rain and Sacha, still on the bike but with his helmet off while Ed slouches against the wall.

The nausea increases and I reach for the paper bag, just in case. It eases off after a moment, not completely, but enough so that I don't think I'm about to hurl. Still, I shuffle across onto Dolly's seat and poke my head out into the aisle. The light indicating that the loo is engaged is on. I keep hold of the paper bag because the nausea doesn't seem to be lifting quite as quickly as previous jaunts back and forth in time.

I move back into my own seat and try to figure out what is happening. Did I manage to stop Sacha from riding off? And if I did, why am I still on the plane? Because if the accident didn't happen and I stayed in Little Heaton with Tomasz, I shouldn't be flying back to the UK for Heather's wedding. I should already be there, living happily ever after with him.

I concentrate on the night of the accident, trying to drag new memories out. Sacha was still on the bike but he'd turned the engine off. I thought he'd started it again but I'm pretty sure the roar was down to being hauled back to the present day.

But what if it wasn't?

What if he *had* started the engine? What if he'd torn off out of the village, lost control on the bend all over again? And what if Ed had pulled himself together enough to climb back onto the bike? Has it all been for nothing?

The nausea rises again. I open the bag. Shuffle along the seat to check if the loo is still engaged. The light is off but there's a woman inching down the aisle towards me so I remain seated. I hope she passes quickly because I really do feel like I'm going to be sick and I'd rather do that in the privacy of the little loo than here, in my seat, aiming into a paper bag.

The woman stops when she reaches me. 'Did you want to get out?'

I nod, not trusting myself to open my mouth to speak, and shuffle out of the seat. I move as quickly as I can along the aisle and lock myself in the loo. I take a few deep breaths and the nausea recedes, though it doesn't leave completely. Once I'm convinced I'm not about to be sick, I return to my seat. Dolly's back. I can see her elbow poking out as she rests her arm on the armrest. But as I reach the seat, I realise it isn't Dolly. It's the woman from the loo, who stopped to let me out into the aisle. I check the seats, to make sure I haven't gone too far along the aisle, but there's my bag tucked under the seat, my cardi bunched up in the pocket, the man under the blanket in the next seat.

The woman moves out into the aisle and I waddle along the small gap between the seats. Bizarrely, she sits down in Dolly's seat again.

'Still feeling off?' The woman nods at the paper bag I'm still clutching, and she tilts her head to one side as she pats my arm gently. 'Won't be too much longer now though. We're nearly halfway there.' She isn't American like Dolly. She's got a northern accent. Yorkshire, maybe. 'Try and have a little sleep. It makes it go quicker.'

Who is this woman? We've never met before, yet she's chatting as though we have. And why has she commandeered Dolly's seat?

Emily.

The name pops into my head. Emily, married mum of two. She was seated separately from her husband and kids. She's very happy about it.

We have met. Right here on this flight. It's a bit hazy but I remember it now. But what about Dolly? Did I make her up? A fear-induced hallucination? And if I dreamed Dolly up, maybe I made the rest up in my head too. The time-travelling. Revisiting summers of the past. Tomasz. Ed. Maybe I didn't save him at all. Maybe I've been sitting here this whole time, daydreaming a fantasy life. A life where my best friend wasn't killed in a road traffic accident. A life where I didn't try to outrun my grief, where I didn't push everyone away.

It didn't happen. Of course it didn't happen. People don't flit back in time. You can't change the past, no matter how much you wish you could.

It didn't happen.

Tomasz and I didn't live happily ever after.

Ed isn't living his best life. He's dead. I didn't save him. I didn't save any of us.

And now I really am going to throw up.

Chapter 37

I don't even wait for Emily to move out of the way. I make a dash for it, squeezing past her legs and the seat, scuttling along the aisle and praying nobody gets to the loo before I do. Throwing myself into the tiny cubicle, I slide the door shut and slam the lock across before turning and puking into the toilet bowl.

None of it was real. I didn't stop the accident. I didn't choose to stay in Little Heaton and be happy with Tomasz. I ran away and focused on my work so that I wouldn't have to think about the life I'd left behind. I didn't save Ed so he could live a long and happy life. I didn't inspire Yvonne to strive for her career goals, and I didn't get a tattoo of little wild flowers to remind myself of how brave I can be.

I wash my hands and face and stare back at the woman in the mirror. She isn't brave or inspiring. She's a coward who hides behind make-believe lands. I twist in the mirror and move my vest top aside, to prove to her that she's a fraud. A failure. See that blank space there? That's where you pretended to have a tattoo. And you believed it for a little while. What a fool! But wait. The tattoo *is* there. A sprig of wild flowers inked onto my shoulder blade. I reach round to rub it away but it remains on my skin as though it's real.

259

My return to my seat is slower as I try to get my head around what's going on. What's real and what isn't. But it's all jumbled up in my brain: Dolly and Emily, Little Heaton and California, the grief after the accident and the euphoria of stopping it. I boarded the plane and sat next to Dolly. But I also boarded the plane and sat next to Emily. They both offered sympathy and comfort. Before that there was the bar. Talking to Yvonne on the phone. Talking to . . . someone else. They're there, flashing up in my consciousness. I can see them sitting beside me in the bar, but only for a second, not long enough to grasp hold of the memory to see who it was.

'Feeling any better?' Emily moves out into the aisle so I can get to my seat, rubbing my back as I pass. 'You poor thing.'

'I think I will try and have a sleep.' I settle into my seat and close my eyes. I don't think I'll be able to drop off – there's far too much buzzing around my brain – but I need a moment to try to try to gather my thoughts and I'll be left alone if people think I'm dozing.

If I did time-travel – as the tattoo suggests I did – why am I still on this flight? And why has Dolly disappeared?

I must drop off because I dream about Tomasz. I can't see him, but I hear his voice, muffled but definitely him. And I dream about Ed, very much alive, his head thrown back in laughter. We're on a beach with a cliff or a hill covered in trees to the left, and Dominic is there with us. He's the one that has made Ed laugh and he's smiling, pleased with the reaction.

'Ugh. I feel rough.'

Neither Ed nor Dominic say these words. Puzzled, I turn to my right, and here's Tomasz. I can see him now and I take his hand and press his fingers to my lips. I'm so glad he's here, but where's Yvonne? She should be here too.

Ed sniggers. I think he's laughing at Tomasz for feeling unwell, which isn't very nice. But when I look at Tomasz again, he's pressing his lips together, his shoulders shaking, and then he erupts in laughter. He doesn't look unwell. He looks happy, which makes me feel happy. I feel laughter bubbling up inside me and I don't fight it. Out it spills, and it feels good.

My neck hurts and the corner of my mouth feels damp. It takes me a moment to figure out where I am: Little Heaton, California or Canada. Canada? Why would I be in Canada? I wipe a hand over my mouth and sit up, wincing as my neck twinges.

'Feeling any better?' Emily peers at me closely, smiling when I nod carefully. I'm still confused but the nausea has subsided. 'Good. He's popped to the loo, I think.' She nods at the seat beyond me, and when I turn – delicately, because of my neck – I find it's empty apart from the fleecy blanket.

'I've got the bag if I need it.' I rub at my neck with one hand while lifting the sick bag that's been resting on my lap while I've napped. 'How long have I been asleep?'

'Not long. Twenty minutes? Not quite an episode of this.' Emily points at the screen in front of her, which is paused on a sitcom.

'Your headphones are working?'

She frowns. 'They are. Aren't yours?' I shake my head, trying to clear the jumbled mess in there, but Emily assumes I'm answering her question and she tuts before leaning in close and lowering her voice. 'You should swap with your boyfriend. Quick, while he's in the loo. It isn't like he's using them – he's been asleep for most of the flight. Hangover, looks like to me. He's got the same haunted look my Graham has after a night out with the lads.'

'It was Ed's fault. He kept insisting on *one more drink, I won't see you for months.*'

My head whips round – jeez, my neck – and there's Tomasz, standing in the aisle, stooping to lift up the blanket from the seat.

'I knew it.' Emily places a hand on my arm. 'Is that why you're feeling poorly? I thought it was travel sickness.'

I don't answer her. I can't take my eyes off Tomasz. He lowers himself onto the seat, wincing.

261

'I'm never drinking again.'

Emily snorts. 'I've heard that before. Many times.'

Tomasz rests his head on the back of the seat and arranges his blanket before closing his eyes. Dolly's gone, replaced by Emily, and the snoring bloke's been switched for Tomasz.

'Ed made you drink?'

'Yep.' Tomasz doesn't open his eyes. He barely moves his lips.

'While we were in Canada.' It's starting to come back to me now. This isn't a flight from LA. I'm not going back for Heather's wedding, though she is getting married in a few days. We're going home. To Little Heaton.

The memories are starting to form now. I *did* stop the accident, and Ed is alive and travelling with Dominic. They're staying in Canada for the rest of the summer before moving on to Mexico, the Bahamas, Jamaica. Then they're going to make their way back through Europe before returning to the UK in time for Christmas.

The plane lurches suddenly, and I grab hold of Tomasz's arm, clinging on to him tight. I don't want to leave again. I want to be right here, with Tomasz, heading back to the life I love.

'It's okay.' Tomasz shifts so his head is resting against mine. 'It's just a bit of turbulence.'

I still don't let go.

Dad picks us up from the airport and I've never been so happy to listen to a mashup of politics and potatoes as he updates us on what we've missed over the past two weeks in government and his garden. He doesn't drop us off at the flat above the charity shop, carrying on instead to Buttercup View, to the house with the red door and the garden overflowing with wild flowers. Our home.

Tomasz and I aren't married yet. I look down at my hand as we make our way along the path to the front door. My finger is bare because one of the diamonds in my engagement ring is loose and it's at the jeweller's for repair. We will get round to planning the wedding, it's just we've been so busy with the new house and our careers. After their grandfather's death, Tomasz and Sacha inherited a chunk of money, which they invested in a rundown property to fix up. It sold for a healthy profit and they've been repeating the process ever since. I was lucky to keep my job at the hotel after I backed out of the promotion, because even though my position in events had already been filled, Gillian managed to keep me on in the department and I've been working my socks off to prove she was right to do so ever since. I may not be the manager of a hotel in sunny LA, but I am damn good at organising events in Little Heaton.

'Your mum's been over, to put a few bits in the fridge and the cupboard.' Dad hefts my suitcase over the threshold once I've unlocked the door. 'Bread, milk, that kind of thing. Laura wants you to phone her – Yvonne too – to let them know how Ed's getting on.' He rolls his eyes. 'The lad's only been out of the country for a few months – you'd think he'd fallen off the face of the earth.'

Sacha explained everything to Yvonne on the night the accident should have taken place. He waited outside her flat until she got home so he could apologise, and he grovelled (which Yvonne enjoyed quite a lot) until she forgave him. Yvonne believed Sacha when he said the new baby wasn't his, and she was right to, as Ronnie had to eventually admit she wasn't even pregnant again. Yvonne and Sacha live together in the flat above the salon now, where Poppy has a bedroom of her own when she visits. Yvonne has spent the past few years building her business, growing the brand, and expanding into the shop next door. She's successful and happy and I'm so proud of everything she's achieved. She's due to give birth in three weeks, which is why she didn't come to Canada with us.

'And your sister's in a flap. Says you're the worst maid of honour ever because you didn't get back to her about abseiling?' Dad raises his eyebrows, shaking his head when I confirm that yes, he does have that right. Heather is still in Little Heaton, and her wedding is just over a week away. She did move out of the village, briefly, before she applied for a teaching position at our old primary school. As an added bonus, she fell in love with the deputy head. The hen night is in a few days, and she wants to kick it all off with some indoor abseiling. I wasn't sure if I'd be up for it so I've been avoiding her calls and messages.

'Anyway, I'd better get going. My next taxi fare is waiting.' Dad rolls his eyes again. 'Your gran reckons she can't walk over to the church hall anymore for her knit and jabber group. Wants me to ferry her over.' He tuts, but he dashes out of the house after checking the time and realising he's running late.

'Shall we get the kettle on?' Tomasz nudges one of the suitcases with his foot. 'Sort this out later?'

'Good plan.' I should have been relaxing on the plane, watching films and napping. I've been running around the village for weeks on end. I'm knackered and I'm still feeling a bit queasy after the flight. Forget unpacking, I could sleep for a week.

I fill the kettle while Tomasz grabs the milk from the fridge.

'You can tell your mum's been round.' I'm reaching into the cupboard for a couple of mugs but turn to see Tomasz brandishing a bottle of wine with a metallic red bow stuck to it.

'Ooh, forget the tea. Let's crack that open.'

Tomasz slides the wine back into the fridge door and grabs the milk instead. When he nudges the door shut, I spot Ed's postcard from France. Mum found it when she was stripping the bed after I'd moved out and she'd kept hold of it for me, keeping it safe until it was discovered again during a massive clear-out Dad insisted on. It's been on the fridge ever since. A reminder of everything I could have lost.

Tomasz places the milk on the worktop. 'Aren't you forgetting something?'

Probably. It's been a tough flight and a lot has changed. I'm sure there are bits I haven't caught up with yet, but I can't explain this to Tomasz.

'There's a reason I'm hungover and you're not.'

I'm not hungover? I certainly feel as though I had a few the night before.

'The test?'

I snatch my hand away from the cupboard, where I've reached for the mugs again. *The test.* I took one before we set off for Canada even though it was a bit early. It was negative but I didn't drink anyway, just in case. My period was due while we were away, which means I'm now officially late.

'The test.' I close the cupboard. I no longer want tea. I no longer want to sleep for a week. 'I'll go and do it now.'

There are two pregnancy tests in the bathroom cabinet. We've been trying for nearly a year so I don't have to bother with the instructions. I give Laura a quick call while we wait for the required two minutes, letting her know that Ed is fine. Brilliant, in fact. I've never seen him so happy and I can't wait until Christmas when he'll be back in the village and everyone I love the most in the world will be in one place. I don't have time to call Yvonne so I send her a quick text, letting her know that Ed's doing great and I'll phone her later. Hopefully I'll have some amazing news to share with her.

I put my phone down and pick up the test. Tomasz takes my hand in his and gives it a squeeze. I turn it over and hold it between us, so we can read the result at the same time.

I don't know how and I don't know why, but I was given the opportunity to go back and alter my life, and I'll be forever grateful because as I stand here, one hand squeezing my boyfriend's hand so hard I think his bones will be crushed to dust and the other holding a plastic stick with two blue lines, I've ended up with the most perfect life I could ever have wished for.

A Letter from Jennifer Joyce

Thank you so much for choosing to read *Our Last Summer*. I hope you enjoyed it! If you did and would like to be the first to know about my new releases, you can subscribe to my newsletter or follow me on social media.

I'm a massive fan of time-travel fiction and although I've already written a Christmas-themed time-travel rom com, I wanted to set one during the summer. I immediately thought about someone on a plane, being transported every time the assistance button bonged and Elodie's story started to emerge: where was she going? Why might she not want to go back there? And what major events could she change in the past to make her life better in the present? We all have *what if . . .?* moments and this is Elodie's, only she gets to find out the answer.

I hope you loved *Our Last Summer* and if you did I would be so grateful if you would leave a review. I always love to hear what readers thought, and it helps new readers discover my books too.

Thanks,

Jennifer

Newsletter: https://mailchi.mp/310b4ee4365f/jenniferjoycenewsletter
Blog: www.jenniferjoycewrites.co.uk
Twitter & Instagram: @writer_jenn
Facebook: www.facebook.com/jenniferjoycewrites

The Accidental Life Swap

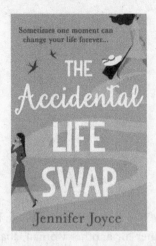

Sometimes one moment can change your life forever . . .

Rebecca Riley has always been a bit of a pushover. When her glamorous boss, Vanessa, asks her to jump, she doesn't just ask how high . . . she asks if her boss would like her to grab a coffee on the way back down!

So whilst overseeing the renovation of Vanessa's beautiful countryside home, the last thing Rebecca ever expected was to be mistaken for her boss – or that she would even consider going along with it! Far away from the bustling city and her boss's demanding ways, could she pretend to be Vanessa and swap lives, just for a little while?

The Single Mums' Picnic Club

Katie thought she had the perfect family life by the sea – until her husband left her for another woman, abandoning her and their two children! She knows it's finally time to move on but she's unsure where to begin . . .

Frankie is shocked when gorgeous dog-walker Alex asks her on a date! As a single mum with her own business she struggles to put herself first, but maybe she's ready to follow her heart?

George is used to raising her son on her own – but now he's at nursery, her life feels empty. So when she meets Katie and Frankie at the beach, she realises that her talent for rustling up delicious picnics could be the perfect distraction!

But of course, life isn't always a beach and as secrets begin to surface the three women's lives are about to be turned upside down . . .

A cosy and charming romance set at the English seaside, perfect for fans of Trisha Ashley and Caroline Roberts.

The Wedding that Changed Everything

Love happens when you least expect it . . .

Emily Atkinson stopped believing in fairy tales a long time ago! She's fed up of dating frogs in order to find her very own Prince Charming and is giving up on men entirely . . .

But then she's invited to the wedding of the year at the enchanting Durban Castle and realises that perhaps bumping into a real-life knight in shining armour isn't quite as far away as she thought!

Will Emily survive the wedding and walk away an unscathed singleton – or finally find her own happily-ever-after?

A cosy and charming romance, perfect for fans of Trisha Ashley and Caroline Roberts.

Acknowledgements

A massive thank you to my editor, Abi Fenton, and the team at HQ for bringing my summer time-travel rom com to life, with extra big thanks for the title, because this book wouldn't have one if it was left down to me.

As always, thank you to my friends and family for all your support. It really does mean a lot. Extra special thanks to the Joyces – Rianne, Isobel and Luna. You girls are the best.

And thank you to you, the reader, for choosing *Our Last Summer*. I hope you enjoy Elodie's story.

Dear Reader,

We hope you enjoyed reading this book. If you did, we'd be so appreciative if you left a review. It really helps us and the author to bring more books like this to you.

Here at HQ Digital we are dedicated to publishing fiction that will keep you turning the pages into the early hours. Don't want to miss a thing? To find out more about our books, promotions, discover exclusive content and enter competitions you can keep in touch in the following ways:

JOIN OUR COMMUNITY:

Sign up to our new email newsletter: http://smarturl.it/SignUpHQ

Read our new blog www.hqstories.co.uk

🐦 https://twitter.com/HQStories

📘 www.facebook.com/HQStories

BUDDING WRITER?

We're also looking for authors to join the HQ Digital family!

Find out more here:

https://www.hqstories.co.uk/want-to-write-for-us/

Thanks for reading, from the HQ Digital team